A glowing shape appeared beside the statue of the Unknown Waterman in the hallway.

A ghost. The ghost of my former husband, Sam Wescott.

"What was that all about?" he asked.

The old courthouse may be filled with revenants, but Sam Wescott is my own personal ghost. He's what remains of my devil-may-care ex-husband. Ever since he died under mysterious circumstances, he's been haunting me. Mostly it works out pretty well, much better than things did when he was alive.

"Knocked me down," I replied. "Some jerk went flying out of here in a hurry."

"Well, let's get going then. This place is creepy at night."

This from a ghost, mind you. . . .

By Helen Chappell
Published by Fawcett Books:

SLOW DANCING WITH THE ANGEL OF DEATH
DEAD DUCK

Books published by The Ballantine Publishing Group
are available at quantity discounts on bulk purchases
for premium, educational, fund-raising, and special
sales use. For details, please call 1-800-733-3000.

DEAD DUCK

Helen Chappell

FAWCETT GOLD MEDAL • NEW YORK

Sale of this book without a front cover may be unauthorized. If this book is coverless, it may have been reported to the publisher as "unsold or destroyed" and neither the author nor the publisher may have received payment for it.

A Fawcett Gold Medal Book
Published by Ballantine Books
Copyright © 1997 by Helen Chappell

All rights reserved under International and Pan-American Copyright Conventions. Published in the United States by Ballantine Books, a division of Random House, Inc., New York, and simultaneously in Canada by Random House of Canada Limited, Toronto.

Library of Congress Catalog Card Number: 96-91013

ISBN 0-449-15001-1

Manufactured in the United States of America

First Edition: August 1997

10 9 8 7 6 5 4 3 2

Let judgment run down as waters,
And righteousness like a mighty stream.
—Amos 5:24

decoy: *n.* 1. a. A living or artificial bird or other animal used to entice game into a trap or within shooting range. b. An enclosed place, such as a pond, into which waterfowl are lured for capture. 2. A means used to mislead or lead into danger . . . To lure or entrap by or as if by a decoy . . .
—*American Heritage Dictionary,* 1977 ed.

Acknowledgments

Many Thanks to One and All . . .

The author gratefully acknowledges that *Dead Duck* came to be only with a lot of help from her friends. Chief Wade Roche of St. Michaels (Maryland) Police Department, formerly with the Maryland State Police, was generous with fact checking, recollections, material and law-enforcement experience. Rosemary and Eddie Dean kindly shared hospitality, memories and a hunter-collector-carver's knowledge of decoys. Hal Roth's wonderful histories of the Eastern Shore offered many inspirations. The Anonymous Decoy Expert provided history, facts and an insider's view of the strange world of bird collectors. Arline Chase and Karen Basile read and critiqued the manuscript in progress and helped wrestle Sam and the plot into submission. All mistakes are, of course, entirely my own. No writer has ever been more fortunate with her friends.

Comments, praise or howls of outrage may be directed to:

Oysterback Productions
P.O. Box 201
Easton, MD 21601

For a reply, please include a SASE.

All events, people and places in this book, except the names of real decoy carvers used in passing reference, are completely fictitious products of the writer's imagination.

Prologue

DEVANAU COUNTY JUDGE GIVES CONVICTED WIFE MURDERER 6 MONTHS SENTENCE

"Sorry I Have to Give You Any Jail Time at All," Judge Findlay S. Fish Tells Harmon Sneed

By Hollis Ball
Gazette Staff

BETHEL — Onlookers gasped and a relative of the victim screamed when a Devanau County Circuit Court judge sentenced convicted wife murderer Harmon F. Sneed to six months in jail. "I understand how things can get out of hand," Findlay S. Fish said from the bench as he pronounced sentence, "so I'm going to go light on you. Your wife provoked you with those divorce papers and you just lost it. It's one of those mistakes a guy can make. I'm sorry that I have to give you any jail time at all," Fish added.

The judge then ordered Sneed to serve six months in the Devanau County Detention Center under a work-release program. Under work release, the convicted killer could continue to work at his job at the Chinaberry Poultry plant. As the judge pronounced sentence, an audible gasp could be heard in the courtroom.

The victim's mother, Wanda Repton Wells, began to scream and Assistant State's Attorney Melissa Hovarth, who had prosecuted the case, rose to her feet. Devanau County Victim Witness Program Coordinator Patricia Rodrick and Barbara Hooper of A Safe Place Women's Shelter both exclaimed out loud, as did several others present. Even Devanau County Public Defender Wallston Pitt expressed astonishment at the light sentence.

The convicted murderer was seen to smile at the victim's mother as he heard his sentence pronounced.

Sneed, 32, was convicted last April of the murder of his wife, Lucinda Wells Sneed, 28. The couple had been separated for over a year, according to trial testimony, when Sneed, who has admitted to drug and alcohol problems, broke into the house Mrs. Sneed shared with her mother and shot her in the back three times as she tried to run from him. Sneed then fled the scene in Mrs. Sneed's truck, taking with him a Bethel-area female juvenile, then sixteen. State police later identified the murder weapon as a .44 Magnum belonging to the girl's father. The couple was apprehended in an Ocean City motel two days later, and the girl was returned to her parents. Because of her age, her name is being withheld.

It was not Sneed's first brush with the law. Records show that Bethel police had answered seventeen domestic-incident calls at the Sneed residence in Patamoke over the past six years. According to trial testimony, Mrs. Sneed sought help from the women's shelter after Sneed had broken her arm and her nose, and ruptured a kidney. On the day before Sneed shot her, Mrs. Sneed had initiated divorce proceedings and asked for a restraining order against Sneed. . . .

—*Watertown Gazette*, July 9, 1994; On the Associated Press A.M. wire, July 10, 1994

DEMONSTRATORS PROTEST JUDGE'S "SLAP ON THE WRIST" SENTENCE FOR WIFE MURDERER SNEED

By Hollis Ball
Gazette Staff

BETHEL — Attention was centered outside Devanau County Courthouse yesterday, as anti–domestic violence groups protested, television cameras panned, police sought to maintain

order, and reporters clamored for a statement. Devanau County Circuit Court Judge Findlay S. Fish refused to defend his six-month sentence for convicted wife murderer Harmon Sneed. "I don't owe anyone any explanations," Fish called over the jeers of demonstrators, before being hustled away in a yellow Mercedes-Benz. . . .
—*Watertown Gazette*, July 25, 1994

IN MARYLAND, MEN CAN GET AWAY WITH MURDER, SAY ANTI–DOMESTIC VIOLENCE GROUPS
—*Washington Post* headline, July 26, 1994

EASTERN SHORE JUDGE'S SENTENCE RAISES SAME QUESTIONS MENCKEN PONDERED
—*Baltimore Sun* editorial headline, July 26, 1994

SHORE JUDGES HOLD KANGAROO COURT?

By Hollis Ball
Gazette Staff

WATERTOWN — One by one, they emerged from the private dining room at the Chesapeake Bay Country Club. It was enough to make one knowledgeable bystander wisecrack, "Hey, Judges! Who's minding the store?"

Acting on a tip from a highly placed source, a Gazette reporter watched as circuit court judges from all nine Eastern Shore counties emerged from a closed meeting room. Among those spotted was controversial judge Findlay S. Fish, whose recent six-month sentencing of convicted wife murderer Harmon Sneed has drawn nationwide criticism, including calls for his resignation and a judicial review of his record while on the bench. Although none of the judges looked happy, Fish's expression was particularly grim. . . .

"No comment" was the word of the day as the judges fled

the reporter, speeding toward their cars, but a source has told the Gazette that the Shore judges had convened a secret ad hoc meeting in order to pressure Fish into stepping down from the bench. . . .

—*Watertown Gazette*, August 14, 1994

STATE JUDICIAL DISABILITIES COMMISSION REFUSES TO CENSOR FISH: THREE WOMEN, TWO MINORITY JUDGES OPENLY VOICE DISSENT

"The Good Old Boy Network Is Alive and Well," Says Judge Mary Bruce Hopkins

—*Watertown Gazette* headline, November 3, 1995

BEATEN TO DEATH: CONVICTED WIFE KILLER HARMON SNEED CHARGED IN MURDER OF GIRLFRIEND TIFFANY CRYSTAL TUTWEILER, 18

Sheriff Briscoe: "Never Seen So Much Blood"

—*Watertown Gazette* headline, January 30, 1996

JUDGE'S DECOY COLLECTION ONE OF FINEST IN U.S. SAYS DECOY JAMBOREE COMMITTEE PRESIDENT, MAYOR MYRTLE P. GOODYEAR

By Hon. Myrtle P. Goodyear, Mayor of Watertown; President, Decoy Jamboree Committee
Special to the Gazette's Decoy Jamboree Supplement

WATERTOWN — As excitement over the annual Decoy Jamboree weekend continues to mount, a prominent Eastern Shore judge, decoy collector, and socialite prepares to judge an entirely different event that annually creates lots of excitement among downtown merchants, and waterfowl decoy lovers everywhere who come to Watertown just for this annual excitement. The Decoy Jamboree Weekend Special Supplement caught up with Judge Findlay S. Fish at his palatial and tasteful waterfront gracious home in order to interview him about his part in Decoy Jamboree weekend this coming month in Watertown.

Even though the Honorable Fish lives near Bethel in Devanau County and not Watertown in Santimoke County, he has graciously agreed to serve once again on the Jamboree Committee that has many prominent socialite Eastern Shore decoy collectors on it including him. He has the most prominent collection of all the collectors and is looked up to as a collector's collector of decoy waterfowl birds.

His Honor Judge Fish says he has more than one thousand prominent decoys carved by famous decoy carvers in his house and he has a whole room full of carved waterfowl birds around his swimming pool numbering more than five thousand more which is closed in all year round with glass shelves full of birds on the walls and is very unusual. He very graciously hosted a tour of the house which is palatially decorated in the Martha Stewart style and his collection is in the pool room except for the ones in the study and the living room.

The judge says that he has many famous carvers like the Ward brothers who were in the Smithsonian Museum where their decoys cost six figures. Other decoys include Ira Hudson, Currier and Ives, Shang Wheeler, Umbrella Watson, Cigar Daisy and many other Chesapeake famous old makers. His Honor says it is the great ambition of his collection to own a Scratch Wallace as Scratch Wallace decoys are very, very rare and almost no one has them. The decoys are also prized as antiques and folk art which is why many people collect them, but old-time hunters like he is really like to collect them because they used to hunt over the decoys when he was a boy. Mr. Fish thinks the carved and painted ducks and geese are very beautiful and says a true collector will do almost anything to own one of the really rare ones like a Scratch Wallace which is very old and rare. . . .

ONE

•

Once Upon a Midnight Dreary

I'd be willing to bet the farm that Brenda Starr doesn't know how to play tonk. On the two-dimensional, four-panel planet Brenda inhabits, the Girl Reporter never has to sit around an overheated, deserted courtroom till midnight waiting for the jury to come back on a two-bit felony.

Tonk's a jailhouse card game, in case you're wondering, and frankly, I'm not that good a player. You have to keep too many numbers straight in your head. But tonk's just one of the many skills a crime reporter learns in the course of her job for the *Watertown Gazette*. (Motto: Thou shalt not offend the advertisers.) My name is Hollis Ball; this is my life, as in I need one.

While playing tonk with Oder Bowley during a jailhouse interview, I got the whole story on how his criminal clan were running a tractor chop shop. Oder was stealing John Deere harvesters and Allis Chalmers hay balers, farm equipment roughly the size of your average McDonald's, then breaking it down into parts for resale to unsuspecting farmers over in West Virginia.

In my line of work, the ability to play tonk is a social asset.

As the current defendant, Smollet Bowley, brother of Oder, slapped his winning hand down on the table, his shackles jingled cheerfully. Smollet, the scrawniest of the scrawny Bowley clan, was not a prepossessing sight. Greasy blond hair hung in clotted tendrils to his shoulders, and a stubble of sparse down dotted his upper lip and chin. Tattoos featuring skulls, naked women and his undying devotion to heavy metal bands adorned his toothpick-sized arms. A golden earring, its verdigris matching that of his teeth, hung from his left lobe.

If you pressed me, I'd have to say he was somewhere between thirty and death, but I wouldn't be willing to go much further. And speaking of going much further, did I mention his habit of picking his teeth with long, black-rimmed fingernails?

"Will you quit doin' that, Smollet?" Barry Maxwell, the Santimoke County public defender, asked irritably. "It makes me lose my concentration." Barry had lost more than his concentration. Sourly, he pushed a couple of quarters across the table at Smollet.

"The jury will disregard the shackles on the defendant," I intoned, in my best imitation of Judge Findlay S. Fish. Did I mention Judge Wrist Slap was presiding over Smollet's trial?

"Why don't you leave that man alone?" Barry asked irritably.

"Because," I replied, discarding, "he is a scum-sucking pig and a disgrace to the bench and the law."

"Boy, you don't hate him or nothin', do you?" Smollet grinned.

"Don't get her started," Barry warned him. "You want a feminist tirade?"

"A what?" Smollet asked blankly. Current events were not his thing. He called, spreading his cards on the table.

"Barry, we agreed, no religion or politics," I said, throwing down my losing hand and giving up my few remaining coins. I was down five bucks and feeling rather dyspeptic myself. Five hours of the hateful Fish, an agonizingly dull trial and an eternity waiting for the jury to come in will do that to me.

"You know they never do disregard, no matter what the judge tells 'em. They see me come in, wearin' these shackles, they *know* I'm guilty of some damn thing. I says to Bailiff Bob, I says, 'I got me a urge to surge, so's you'd better get out the chains,' and he did," Smollet remarked cheerfully. He shuffled the deck, grinning as he used his little fingernail to pick the remains of *poulet frites en besoin de l'huile à la Santimoke County Detention Center* out of his greening teeth.

The remains of the meal, which had been sent over courtesy of the Santimoke County taxpayers, lay strewn on the other end of the defense table. A fly poked hopefully among the chicken bones and limp fries.

"You may not be going to the detention center, Smollet," Bailiff Bob Winters remarked, glancing at his watch. Bailiff Bob is a retired cop and my father's Uncle Dab's step-nephew, making him one of the cast of thousands around here that I'm related to. "That jury's been in there for over five an' a half hours now."

Smollet looked genuinely distressed. "They cain't do that to me! I wanna be nice and safe in jail before that goddamn duck carnival starts up!"

"If only it were that easy," I grumbled. "Three hots and a cot, cable TV and all the books I could read while everyone else on the *Gazette* staff has to go and chase down yet more glowing, tourist-friendly puff pieces about socially prominent duck collectors for the Decoy Jamboree. Whom do I have to kill to go to jail for the weekend, Barry?"

"Damn that jury, if they don't come back soon." He sighed, looking out the window at the wintry night. "I'll tell you why they're taking so long. They're all waiting for the salt trucks to come through so they don't have to drive home on the ice."

There was truth in what he said; an early winter storm had laid a thin, slick coat of snow and freezing rain across the Shore.

"What if they decide not to convict?" Smollet asked, fear suddenly clouding his dappled complexion. He glanced anxiously at the closed door of the jury room.

"Smollet, you were the one who went for a jury trial," Bob pointed out. "If they acquit, it's your own damn fault."

"Man, I don't wanna be home all winter. My wife's mother's comin' to stay with us." He looked genuinely distressed.

"For those of you who came in late, Barry, Smollet's mama-in-law is Miz Bertha Denton," I pointed out, picking up my hand and squinting at my lousy cards.

"Whoa!" Barry said, his Young Republican disdain forgotten. He peered at Smollet with a new respect. "Really?"

Smollet nodded disconsolately. Mrs. Denton, having had enough, after twenty-six years, of the violent and alcoholic Leathal Denton's abuse, had waited until he was sleeping it off, then doused him with lighter fluid and tossed a lit match. As he ran, literally a flaming asshole, from the house, Leathal was struck down dead, not by a Just and Vengeful Deity but by a passing Glack's Good Gas and Propane truck.

But Bertha still got fifteen years at the Women's Correctional Institute from the Honorable Fin Fish, of which she served eleven before making parole. It was an interesting contrast to Fish's six-month, work-release sentence on Harmon Sneed, I thought sourly.

Since Smollet's own domestic problems revolved around being henpecked rather than abused, I could see why he feared the return of Mrs. Denton from her stay in Jessup. It is said that some women achieve personal fulfillment in widowhood. Miss Bertha certainly did; she emerged with a hairdresser's license and a very interesting outlook on life.

Anyway, armed with this information, the rest of us could see why Smollet preferred six to eight months' penance for stealing seventeen bushels of oysters from Busbee Clinton's Seafood truck to going home to face his mama-in-law.

"You know, the detention center used to be a pretty nice place, for a jail, until you all started boarding them federal prisoners over there," Smollet remarked, discarding. "Used to be a man'd go to jail and he'd see people he knew. Now it's all foreigners."

"You mean the Colombian cocaine smugglers?" Bob asked. "They're all waiting for *federal* trials and the county just boards 'em. . . ."

"Yeah." Smollet sighed. "You're getting a bad class a defendants over there and now they're not even just from away, they're from damn all South America, *foreigner* foreigners—"

"What is going on here?" The icy tones of Ms. Athena

Hardcastle froze us in our seats. "Card playing in a court of law?"

Our new state's attorney for Santimoke County had been on the job for a week before we courthouse barnacles all started calling her Hardass Hardcastle.

After six months of Ms. Hardass, my mild annoyance with her drill sergeant, by-the-book attitude had turned into an intense dislike. And the feeling was mutual.

A woman who is a perfect size 10, all legs and expensive, well-suited elegance, skin the color of polished pine, accessorized with a law degree from Princeton, shouldn't feel threatened. It seemed to me that a tired, underpaid and sometimes bedraggled white reporter with a degree from the local college wasn't much of a threat. The "we're both women in a world of men" approach didn't work, either. She was impervious to my overtures of friendship, holding me at arm's length.

At first I'd put it down to reverse discrimination. I've had some experience with that myself. "Oh, well, Hollis Ball is out of that Ball clan from Beddoe's Island, White Trash Capital of Devanau County, where the gene pool meets the ce-ment pond, so she must spend her off hours in a sheet burning crosses."

Which is not true. Given time and exposure to my lovely self, Athena would soon discover that I am no bigot and despise everyone equally regardless of race, sex, creed, national origin or lifestyle.

Or for that matter, deathstyle, if you count Sam, my ghostly ex-husband, whose hobby, since his unfortunate demise, is haunting me. But that's another story. Now, I know what you're thinking about ghosts and all that. I didn't think much about them either, not until Sam's shade turned up on my front porch demanding that I track down a murderer—his. Not that playing detective was all that bad; I'd enjoyed it, once I'd survived getting to the truth.

Anyway, Sam aside, this stereotyping crap could have given us something in common, tools to build a professional understanding. But noooo. And I was detecting some other folks' tension about Athena Hardass, Santimoke County's Top Cop. My African American friends in law enforcement were especially pissed off at her, although I didn't know exactly what their beef was.

Worst thing for me? She didn't laugh at my jokes.

Ultimately, I had just given up. My attitude toward her these days was a cool politeness that said *Watch me, I'm carrying a concealed weapon.* Anyway, her secretary was a much better source of inside skinny, in return for which I filled Kenisha in on gossip from other areas of my beat. Little-known facts about well-known people are always welcome to those of us who are underpaid and overworked and definitely unappreciated.

"Mr. Winters, why isn't the defendant in the holding cell?" Madam Hardass demanded, looking for all the world like an outraged high school principal who had just caught us smoking in the boy's bathroom.

"Because we thought the jury would be back by now," Barry replied for him. Give it to our noble PD; after defending some of the scummier bottom feeders of the Eastern Shore, no one intimidated him, not even Madam Hardass.

"Yew wanna be cut into the game?" Smollet asked, giving her his best green grin. He rattled his shackles and shuffled the deck.

Hardass gave him the same glare she might use for something on the sole of her shoe. "Ms. Ball, Judge Fish would like to see you in chambers," she said to me in saccharine tones.

"What about?"

Hardass walked to the prosecution table and picked up some papers. "I don't know," she said, not bothering to look at me. "But he means now, not five minutes ago."

"Uh-oh." Barry snickered in a better-you-than-me tone of voice.

I threw my cards down on the table. It had been a bad hand anyway. "Hail, Caesar, those of us who are about to die salute you." I sighed. "Off with my head!" I tossed back over my shoulder as I trudged away.

Walking down the long, dark corridor that separates the judge's chambers from the courtroom, I mentally reviewed the way I'd covered the Harmon Sneed fracas, literally jamming the whole ugly thing onto the wire services for all the world to pick up. It was largely due to a remark I'd made over a couple of beers that people had started calling him Wrist Slap Fish, at least behind his back. That alone should have aroused the wrath of a proud and arrogant man, but I had to admit the rest of what I'd written hadn't been too complimentary. Sure, it had been over a year since the Sneed flap, but I hadn't forgotten, and I was willing to bet a macho idiot like Fish hadn't either.

Since he sat in Devanau County, our friendly neighbor across the river, where I rarely cover the show, Fish hadn't had an opportunity to get at me until now. It was his bad luck to preside over Smollet's latest trial only because Judge Franklin Carroll, who usually does the show in Santimoke County, was hearing some long, dull civil trial on the Western Shore, and Fish's docket happened to be free this week, allowing him to visit us. Just my luck.

Brave little soldier that I was, I tapped timidly on the open chamber door.

Judge Fish, pushing at a window sash, beckoned me in. The courthouse is kept stiflingly hot in winter. The ancient cast-iron radiators were hissing and steaming, keeping the room at a toasty eighty-five. I noticed he had removed his robes and his jacket and rolled up his shirtsleeves. He was dressed in baked-potato tones: tan slacks and a white dress shirt with a canvasback duck embroidered on the pocket. A line of needle-point geese flew around his belt and a flock of mallards were taking flight on his tie. He was somewhere between sixty-five and seventy-five, I guessed, but his hair was suspiciously dark and his eyebrows were suspiciously white.

A pompous old white guy with that attitude of entitlement one sees in old Republican white guys.

Up close, I could see the gin blossoms, the little broken capillaries in his cheeks that betrayed the hard drinker. A broad white band of untanned skin on the third finger, left hand, told me he was newly single. What had happened to Mrs. Fish, God help her? Imagine, I thought, being married to a man who can justify murdering his wife because she had the nerve to file for divorce after he beat the crap out of her once too often.

"Ah, Ms. Ball," he was saying briskly, "thanks for stepping back. By the way, how close do you think the jury is?" He grunted as the window finally gave way and opened a few inches.

I made some noncommittal remark. Since we were forbidden by law to discuss the case while the jury was still out, I wasn't falling in that trap.

A pile of case folders were spread across the desk. He beckoned me toward the sitting area, where a couch and a couple of chairs fronted a low coffee table featuring a dusty arrangement of dried flowers and some prehistoric magazines.

"I wish Judge Carroll wouldn't put his bird station right up next to the window," Fish grumbled, jerking open another sash. "There's some damn blackbird that's been rapping on the glass all night."

We both looked at the large crow perched on the edge of the feeder, who stared balefully back at us through the open window.

"That's Edgar Allan Crow. Frank—Judge Carroll—feeds him the french fries from his jailhouse dinners," I explained. "He lives in the big ivy trellis outside the window. Edgar, I mean, not Frank."

Fish snorted. "Typical. Frank always was a bleeding heart liberal." There were the remains of a sandwich on his desk. Fish picked it up and leaned out the window, dropping it on the feeder tray. "Eat that, Edgar!" he commanded.

"Nev!" Edgar croaked as he settled down to his ration of bread and tuna fish. He eyed us nastily as he shook the snowflakes from his back, swallowing a bread crust. "Maw!"

The old steam radiators hissed, belching out yet more heat.

Judge Fish glared out the window at the snow and the dimly lit windows of the Horny Mallard, the watering hole across the street where faint music could be heard whenever the doors were opened and closed by happy Decoy Jamboree revelers gearing up for the big weekend.

I supposed Fish was comparing a Bass ale, a thick steak and cottage fries to the greasy fried chicken provided by the county.

Edgar pecked at a half-eaten slice of pickle disdainfully. He shot the visiting judge a dirty look as he kicked it away from the feeder. *Pickles!* his beady glare proclaimed. *We don't need no stinkin' pickles!*

Fish turned. When he looked directly at me, I realized with a start that he had colorless eyes. There was no depth to them at all, only an opaque gray iris that was almost white. His gaze was unsettling, to say the least. The most unromantic of reporters, I felt as if by peering into those depthless ash-colored eyes, I was looking into something evil. I instinctively took a step back.

Fish blinked. Then he got right to the point. "Look, Miss Ball, I know we've had our differences—"

Differences? I'd done everything I could get past my cowardly editor, short of outright libel, to expose his sexist attitudes to the world.

"But," he continued, oblivious, "your father is Perk Ball, and I wondered if you have any influence with him."

This was about the last thing I was expecting. "My father?" I repeated stupidly.

"I've been trying for years to get him to sell me that pair of Eddie Dean old-squaws, but he's always saying he's not interested. And, of course, Eddie doesn't carve that much. Do you think you could ask him—"

I found myself speechless. I was expecting the full blast of wrath I usually get from important people who don't appreciate my coverage of their foolishness, and here the man was asking me to intercede with my father over a pair of decoys! Hel-lo?

I was looking for a tactful way to tell Fish I'd beg Dad to eat them with ketchup before I'd advise him to sell his prized Eddie Deans to a Neanderthal swine who was a public disgrace to justice. Fortunately for me, the door opened.

"Judge Fish?" Athena suddenly appeared. "I found this lady downstairs. The courthouse doors are all locked after five, you know, so she couldn't get in."

She stepped back to allow a blond woman, a Grace Kelly clone, to enter the room in a cloud of ozone and L.L. Bean. I wanted to think *bimbo*, but there was a sharp intelligence in those blue eyes that wouldn't let me pigeonhole her that easily.

"Did you get lost, Lenore?" the judge asked a tad waspishly.

"I've come a long way," the woman replied as she stepped into the room. Snowflakes clung to her scraped-back blond hair and the shoulders of her expensive down parka. Her feet were encased in sturdy rubber moccasins. "The roads are murder out there."

Without ceremony, she sat down on the couch and produced a heavily taped and bubble-wrapped package, which she placed in the center of the table.

That must have been Edgar's cue. With a loud caw, he flapped through the open window and circled around Athena's head. The state's attorney shrieked, throwing her arms up to defend herself. "Get that thing away from me!" she screamed. "Birds indoors are death omens!"

Deeply offended, Edgar dropped what my mother calls a birdie calling card on the floor and hopped up onto a bookcase, his tail feathers twitching indignantly.

"He doesn't mean any harm," I said, while Athena frantically brushed imaginary Edgar cooties from her hair. "He just misses Frank, that's all. Frank lets him in and feeds him—"

"I hate those blackbirds! They're like bats!" Athena cried, shaking. "I have a horror of them! Get him out of here!"

Edgar dropped another calling card on a leather-bound volume of *Maryland Tort Law Vol. 10 Addendum 1941–42* and turned his head around to look at Athena quizzically. "Naw! Maw!" he said.

"Oh, for heaven's sake," Lenore murmured softly. Slowly, she rose from the couch and crossed the room until she was standing right below Edgar's bookcase. Making a little clucking noise in the back of her throat, she gradually raised her gloved hand until it was parallel with his crooked claws. "C'mon, Edgar," she crooned.

As we all watched, the devil bird hopped from the bookcase to her fist, where he perched as if he'd been doing this shtick all his life. "Good boy, Edgar," Lenore hummed, stroking his silky feathers with her other hand as she walked him slowly across the room toward the window. Edgar preened, delighted with this stupid human trick.

Athena Hardcastle cringed, the color draining from her face.

"*Out* you go." Lenore lowered her arm and eased Edgar outside. He rose up on his bandy legs, glared at us with his nasty little eyes and flew away into the night.

Athena gave a long sigh and slid onto the couch. She looked as if she were about to faint.

" 'Quoth the raven, "Nevermore!" ' " Judge Fish pronounced solemnly.

Lenore shot him a look as she moved toward Athena. "Are you all right?" she asked, peering at the ashen-faced state's attorney with concern.

In response, Athena bent, placed her head between her knees and started taking deep breaths.

"Fin, can you get this lady a glass of water?" Lenore asked briskly. "I think she's going to faint."

"No, I'll be all right. I just have a horror of birds in the house," Athena muttered weakly. She continued breathing deeply.

"It's all right," Lenore soothed her, rubbing her back with the palm of her hand. "Mmm, *love* your Donna Karan suit. I just adore her clothes, don't you?"

"Mmmm," Athena muttered. She allowed Lenore to help her to lean back against the couch again, where she collapsed into the cushions with her eyes closed, still concentrating on her breathing.

Judge Fish looked utterly helpless, which was only to be expected. I procured a paper cup full of tap water from the judicial john.

When I came out, Athena was still deep breathing, her eyes

still closed. I handed her the cup of water and she opened up for a reality check, swallowing a little of it before she sat up straight, pulling at her skirt, all Hardass again. "I'll be fine in a minute," she informed Lenore and me through clenched teeth. "It's just one of those things."

"I know how you feel," I said. "I can't stand to be in a closed space. It makes me panicky."

Athena Hardcastle nodded glumly. "Just give me a minute and I'll be fine," she said, dismissing me with a wave of her hand.

"Lenore, open it up. I've got to see it!" Judge Fish exclaimed impatiently, pointing at the package. He was excited, bouncing up and down like a little kid on Christmas morning, watching sharply as Lenore began to undo the tape. Beneath her fingers, yards of bubble plastic were unwound from a long, ovoid shape.

"You didn't have any problem?" he was asking. "They've always been very good about financial arrangements."

"No, no problem at all. I didn't expect any. The Japanese are always so *polite*. . . . Ahhhhh!"

As she carefully unwound a sheet of padded cotton flannel, both of them sort of gasped in reverence at the object that was revealed.

It was a snow goose decoy. The body was hewn out of a block of wood. The long neck turned gracefully back over the body, as if the bird were asleep. It was made from a root that had been transformed, by dexterous hand carving, into the goose's neck and head, and that made all the difference. Even I could see that it had goose personality, that the carver had captured the spirit, the primitive essence of a snow goose. Paint had been dabbed on it at some point in its career, but the color had long ago weathered to a memory. It looked like a very old decoy.

There was a moment's reverent silence. Even Athena Hardcastle opened an eye in order to study it.

Old decoys, you must understand, are sacred objects on Chesapeake Bay, once one of the greatest waterfowl gunning areas in the country. Gunning is still an important part of the economy on the Shore, although nowhere what it used to be a hundred years ago. Or even last year; ducks were scarce, and goose season was almost closed down this year, due to a lack of migratory birds. Hunters used to carve, paint and put a string of fake wooden birds—decoys—out to attract the real thing within gunning range. As the waterfowl populations have diminished, old-time decoys have become recognized as genuine folk art, much sought after and passionately collected. The works of really good carvers like Lem and Steve Ward, Ira Hudson and Scratch Wallace have been elevated to the status of museum treasures, with prices to match. This information will be on the final exam, so remember it.

I know a tiny little about decoys because my father collects them, although apparently not on the same level of intensity or finance as Findlay Fish.

"A Scratch Wallace sleeping goose," Fish breathed reverently. "Genius!" With trembling hands, he reached out and took up the decoy by the body, turning it this way and that, as if he had found the Holy Grail.

"It looks a little beat up," I said dubiously, "but it's kinda cute."

Fish and Lenore looked at me pityingly.

"And your father is Perk Ball," Judge Fish said reprovingly. "You tell Perk you saw a Scratch Wallace, and he'll tell you what a great carver Scratch was. . . . Look!" He turned the bird over so that I could examine the flat, lead-weighted underside. "S.W., sixty-nine," the judge read, in case I was suddenly struck by illiteracy. "That's *eighteen* sixty-nine."

"Eighteen sixty-nine?" I asked incredulously. "Nobody has decoys that go back that far. They're all long gone."

"He was one of the earliest documented carvers," Lenore explained to me. "Some of his account books turned up recently, along with a dozen birds. They were found under the floor of an old shed over in Oysterback when the owner was tearing it down. I was asked to broker the sale. A Japanese decoy collector bought seven of them for . . . for a great deal of money. Two were knocked down at Sotheby's and went to a private collector in New York. Two went to the Smithsonian. I was fortunate enough to be able to negotiate this one from the owner's estate when Mr. Hiromata was disgraced in that big Japanese banking scandal. Seppuku is so messy," she sighed, then immediately brightened again. "This goose will go on display at the Decoy Jamboree this weekend. Judge Fish just bought it from the estate." She smiled at me, holding out her hand. "I'm sorry, I'm forgetting my manners! I'm Lenore Currier."

Enlightenment, always slow to awaken in my overworked brain, finally dawned. *Lenore Currier!* I should have recognized the name at once, I thought. In the land of the certifiable duck nut, Lenore Currier was a goddess. A few years back, her graduate thesis in folk art had enabled her to research and uncover evidence that collecting decoys was a direct mandate from God or something. Whatever it was, it had caused some enormous stir in the collecting world, and she had stepped instantly into the role of bird expert and duck dealer to the stars. The fact that she was a young, attractive woman in a field inhabited mostly by old, boring geezers made it all mediaworthy. She was very photogenic, I had thought cynically, since I didn't know enough about decoys to pass on her expertise. But ducks are always big news around here.

So this was the famous Lenore Currier, huh?

Interesting.

I told her my name was Hollis Ball, and she nodded. "You're Perk Ball's daughter? I know your father! I met him at the Slattery estate auction, now *there* was a decoy collection! He's a good collector, Perk. Anytime he wants to sell those Eddie Dean oldsquaws, I'd be thrilled to broker the deal—several collectors are always interested. Now, I know he doesn't want to sell that Lem Ward canvasback, but even with the wear and tear, it's still worth a lot more than he paid for it—"

"As you can see, the lines are quite primitive and the finish is an old oil-based paint. Notice the hatchet marks where Scratch hacked the body out of an old mast . . . ," the judge was happily informing Athena, who looked as if she appreciated decoys even less than I did. "Scratch Wallace is listed on the Devanau County census records from 1845 to 1904, and we know he was a Civil War deserter, and one of the earliest documented Chesapeake Bay carvers. . . . The only earlier known lures are some Indian feather decoys, like stuffers, they discovered in a cave in—"

"Native American," Athena corrected weakly, but Fish was on a roll and didn't even hear her.

". . . will be the crown of my collection. Note the exquisite grace of the . . ."

If I had been her, I would have fainted, but Hardcastle bravely and respectfully stuck it out as he pointed out the age of the wood, no doubt salvaged from some old boat washed ashore, and the unique shape of the neck, how an X ray had shown the use of hand-forged nails, the scrap-lead weight that ballasted the bird in the water, the age of the paint and the barely discernible traces of comb-painted detailing. . . .

And it was his, all his. I saw the fire in his eyes, the animation in his face, and knew that obsessive-compulsive-acquisitive look. It was the glow of the collector in breeding plumage. A collector. Of course. I should have known. A breed apart, collectors. And I should know; my father is crazy on one subject: collecting old waterfowl decoys. They ought to have their own listing in DSM IV.

It was a relief when Bob Winters thrust his head into the doorway. "Jury's ready, Yer Honor," he said shortly, disappearing again.

Judge Fish, Athena and I all rose and ran toward the courtroom like a trio of bats out of hell.

"What's happening?" Lenore asked, panting along the corridor behind me.

"Jury's come back with a verdict. The salt trucks must have come through." I didn't bother to try to explain that one to her.

She followed me as I took up my seat in the gallery, and I gestured her to sit down. "This won't take too long. Then we can all go home."

Except for Smollet, I thought. He grinned and rattled his shackles at me, waving a fistful of dollar bills, the result of his skill at tonk. Barry, on the other hand, looked like he'd been sat upon.

Athena and Judge Fish took their places and the jury filed in.

"Madam Foreperson, do you have a verdict?" Judge Fish asked, still hooking his robe.

"We do, Your Honor. We find the defendant, Smollet Lomar Bowley, guilty of—" and proceeded to roll off about five or six of his known transgressions.

"Yes!" Smollet cried, standing up, his shackles jingling. It sounded like Santa's sleigh had come to court.

Being a jerk isn't against the law . . . yet.

"Sit down, Mr. Bowley!" Fish reproved him impatiently. "You're scaring the jury! Don't frighten the civilians! It's hard enough to get jurors as it is!"

I scribbled some notes in my trusty reporter notebook and rose, grabbing my coat. "That's my cue to exit," I told Lenore Currier. "Got to file my story."

"I don't rightly know how to thank you all," Smollet was telling the jury as Bob Winters prepared to haul him back to the detention center pending sentencing. Smollet couldn't have raised bond if his life depended on it. The Bowleys were criminals, yes, but no one ever said they were good at it.

"Damn it, Mr. Bowley, will you calm down?" Fish roared, losing patience. He pounded his gavel sharply.

At that moment, all the lights in the courtroom went off, plunging us into utter darkness.

One of the jurors screamed, and I heard some scuffling around. Fish banged the gavel, demanding order, but I could have found my way out of there in my sleep. After twelve straight hours of Courtroom Capers, I was anxious to get moving. I had my story; *State of Maryland* v. *S. L. Bowley* was all over as far as I was concerned.

Besides, I wanted to get as far away from Fish as possible.

Under cover of darkness and confusion, I made my way through the heavy central door and out into the hallway. At this hour of the night the courthouse was still, and almost eerily silent.

I felt my way down the stairs in the darkness, holding on to the rail with one hand and my coat and notebook with the other. It was even darker in the hallway, and my eyes were slow in adjusting to it. I almost fell on the last step.

The county offices had long since shut down, their closed and locked doors strung along the marble hallway on the first floor.

In spite of the uproar from the courtroom, I could hear my footsteps echoing on the cold marble floor as I made my way to the door that led into the street, using my fingertips to feel my way along the walls toward freedom, nicotine, deadlines and sleep.

I never heard the other person.

Someone moved past me in the darkness, shouldering me out of the way with such force that I slammed into the wall. My pocketbook fell open, scattering loose coins, junk and pens everywhere. I heard them broadcast across the marble floor in the darkness.

"Hey!" I called, thinking it was a juror even more anxious to escape than I was. The side door swung open, allowing some faint glow from the streetlights to fall across the shadow of a human being.

Before I could register anything else, he, she or it was gone, the door banging loudly back into the frame on a gust of cold air.

TWO

•

The Only Difference Between Men and Boys Is the Price of Their 'Coys

As I wearily stooped to gather my stuff back together, a glowing shape appeared beside the statue of the Unknown Waterman in the hallway.

A ghost. The ghost of my former husband, Sam Wescott, making it a lot less interesting than you might think, even though he's an extremely good-looking ghost who hasn't lost any of his old careless charm.

"What was *that* all about?" he asked.

The old courthouse may be filled with revenants, but Sam Wescott is my own personal ghost. He's what remains of my devil-may-care ex-husband. Ever since he died under mysterious circumstances, he's been haunting me. Mostly it works out pretty well, much better than things did when he was alive. But still, if his mission is to look after me, he frequently falls down on the job. More often than not, he gets me into trouble.

"Knocked me down," I replied, stuffing the last of my things back into my pocketbook. "Some jerk went flying out of here in a hurry."

"Well, let's get going, then. This place is creepy at night."

This from a ghost, mind you.

"You didn't have anything to do with the lights going out, did you?" I asked suspiciously. With Sam, it always helps to be suspicious.

"Don't look at me," he replied airily. "I've got better things to do. Like get you to go down to Toby's with me."

"Uh-uh. I'm going across the street to the Horny Mallard for dinner, then straight home to finish up this story and fax it into the paper. Then right to bed. If I don't answer the phone or the door, I can have a nice quiet weekend."

I headed out the door, looking up and down the street for the rude person, fully intending to give him a good piece of what was left of my mind. But whoever or whatever it had been, it was lost in the crowds that were parading around the courthouse square, undaunted by slush.

"What's going on out here?" Sam asked.

"I'd forgotten the Decoy Jamboree, but apparently about fifteen hundred other folks haven't." I sighed, looking at all the people. Carved bird lovers were already jamming into Watertown, getting ready for the big weekend.

"Amazing as it is to some people, and I am one of them," I explained to Sam, "Decoy Jamboree is a big event that attracts a lot of people from everywhere. It's basically like a sci-fi con, except that instead of obsessed people wearing *Star Trek* outfits, trading Romulan flash cards, drinking a lot and partying down, it's full of obsessed people in camouflage outfits, buying and trading decoys, drinking a lot and partying down, and otherwise acting like they wouldn't at home."

We stood on the steps and watched a camouflage-clad couple exchanging much more than a smooch, oblivious to the jostling throng around them.

"Hey, you," Sam called, laughing, "get a room!"

Of course they didn't hear him. No one, save the select few who can see ghosts, can see him, unless Sam really wants them to.

"They would if they could. Every hotel, motel and bed-and-breakfast in the three-county area is booked solid," I explained. "For the next three days, we'll be crammed with suspiciously Aryan-looking types from somewhere else driving around in four-wheel-drive vehicles that have never been off a four-lane highway. They'll spend their time looking at displays of carved wooden birds, people who carve wooden birds and wooden birds carved by people who have long since gone to that big duck blind in the sky." I took a breath and lit my first cigarette in twelve hours, heedless of my mother's injunction never, ever to smoke in the street, lest I be thought a complete slut. "Saturday night, after a full day of this stuff, they give out cash prizes to the best living, or at least coma-tose, carvers, which is the only reason most of them tolerate the collectors. If that's not enough, it all culminates in the big decoy auction on Sunday, in which the oldest and rarest carved birds are knocked down for legendary prices. And if you ask me, the whole thing's a real annoyance."

"Uh-huh," Sam said absently. He was still watching the amorous couple in the middle of the sidewalk.

"Of course, to even think snide thoughts about Decoy Jam-boree is tantamount to saying you hate God in Santimoke County," I huffed sourly. "Not only do you get the notoriously humorless NRA gonzo bonzos ready to book you on suspicion of being antihunting, which I'm not, as long as you eat what you kill, but the local merchants and real estate agents who sponsor this circus want your head on a pike. So, when you work for the paper whose motto is 'Thou shalt not offend the advertisers,' and your father is a hunting guide and a decoy collector of the first water, you keep your mouth shut and stay out of the line of fire."

"Think of it as Protestant Mardi Gras with costumes by Orvis," Sam suggested. "It looks like fun. Something you could stand to have a little more of, Holl. Then, maybe you wouldn't resent other people having some."

"Go haunt a house or something, Sam," I snarled, digging for my car keys in the bottomless mess that is my pocketbook.

"On to Toby's Bar and Grill, right Holl?" He grinned. "I can smell those Tobyburgers all the way up here on the mainland."

"What do you care? You can't even eat anything. You're a ghost." I sighed, feeling tired and thwarted.

A couple of people turned to stare at the crazy lady talking to herself.

He just grinned. He loves it when that happens.

I should be used to this by now, but I'm not. Sullenly cursing under my breath I slid-and-slipped my way down the street past the happy revelers and found my Honda. It was coated with ice and parking tickets. I scraped off the former and stuffed the latter into the glove compartment with their brothers and sisters.

"Toby's?" Sam suggested.

"Toby's is way out of my way. Besides, there's a little matter of getting this story faxed in so it's in the morning folder. And after spending a whole day looking at that knuckle-dragging, redneck asshole Fish, I'm sort of soured on all men, living or dead—"

"How can you even think about a stupid story when there's Toby's Bar and Grill, where fat, juicy burgers are broiled on the flame grill with just a hint of rosemary? And Toby makes the best fries in the county. No one else keeps Diet Pepsi on ice just for you. And besides, he's your cousin. Your first cousin, and the only person, except for you, who knows I'm about and around," Sam whispered seductively in my ear.

The idea that Toby might find a way to keep Sam occupied and out of my hair while I finished the Smollet Bowley story *was* enticing, even though Toby's was all the way at the other end of the county. And of course, one of Toby's famous Toby-burgers, a cheeseburger by which all other cheeseburgers are judged and found wanting, was hard to resist.

"It'll be crammed to the gills with tourists," I sulked.

"And if we don't hurry, it'll be last call and the Big T will be all out of beef," Sam reminded me. "Say, isn't that Rig Riggle, your editor, stumbling into the Horny Mallard across the street with the advertising manager? The advertising manager who wants *everyone* in the newsroom to do three stories on the Decoy Jamboree merchants and real estate agents who sponsor this weekend? Aren't they the very people you've been trying to avoid all week?"

Horrors!

We fled Watertown right behind the salt truck, traveling at the lightning speed of thirty miles an hour. "This is not a great night to be driving all the way down to Beddoe's Island," I grumped at Sam, who was fidgeting about in the passenger seat like a little kid.

"Snow!" he exclaimed, delighted. "It's been years since I saw snow! Forgive me, dear Holl, but since I spent the decade before my untimely departure exiled to the Caribbean climes of Big Pig Quay, snow is a treat for me."

"Good, *you* can drive in it," I grumbled, wiping the fogged windshield with my glove and making it worse.

"You know, I bet I could," Sam said cheerfully. "Driving's one of those things you never lose your knack for. I bet if I really concentrated I could—"

"Oh, no you don't! The dead are expressly forbidden to drive my car. It's on my insurance policy. Besides, you'd have trouble materializing enough to do it. Driving a car requires a solid physical body and you don't have one."

"I've been practicing that, Holl, and I'm really getting quite good at getting solid for short periods of time. Why, I'll bet that—"

"I don't want to know what you'd bet on," I said sourly. "No driving."

"You just don't trust me." Sam sulked. "Why, I was a good driver. I used to race cars."

"Yeah, up and down county roads. You had more points on your license than anyone I've ever met."

"I won prizes for my driving."

"On planet Zardoc," I replied nastily. We turned into the parking lot at Toby's.

Making a rude sound, Sam disappeared, which suited me just fine.

The interesting thing about Cousin Toby Russell's establishment is that no matter what it's like outside, once you walk into the place, it's always 4 A.M. in some dark night of the soul. The dank, smoky air is penetrated only by the neon beer signs, and the clack of breaking balls on the pool table competes with the rhythm-and-blues and country rock that Toby keeps on the jukebox. Stuffed waterfowl and fake wood paneling are the only decorator accents, and the sign over the bar says WE DO NOT SERVE UNPLEASANT PEOPLE. You'd better believe Toby means it. Of course, when you're six-six, weigh two-sixty, most of it muscle, and have entertained offers from professional wrestling promoters, a lot of unpleasant people think it's their duty to mess with you. No one, to my knowledge, has tried to mess with Toby twice, but he keeps a .28 Handy Gun under the bar just in case.

In honor of the holiday season, Toby had cut his hair and trimmed his beard, revealing rugged features and the scar on his cheek. A lot of bad stuff happened to Toby in Vietnam that he doesn't talk about. He is, however, a genius in the kitchen and has won the hearts of a number of women with his haiku poetry and chocolate desserts. Toby's also my best friend. Since we're both family black sheep, we have to stick together.

And, best of all, he can see and talk to Sam.

Down at Toby's Bar and Grill, they serve the living and the dead, but not unpleasant people.

Toby says our ability to communicate with ghosts is inherited from our grandmother Russell, who had Santimoke Indian blood. I hope that's all we inherited from Mum-Mum Russell; toward the end of her life, she thought the Army of the Potomac was camped out in her tomatoes. Who knows? Maybe they were. Since Sam had started to haunt me, I was willing to consider anything possible.

The sound of Reba singing "Does He Love You?" washed over me as I walked in the door. The place was fuller than I'd expected, and as I stomped the ice off my frozen feet, I heard the unmistakable tones of a familiar voice telling a familiar tale.

". . . oh, my, honey, was that old marsh frozen? You neepert be that cold. Them muskrats was froze solid into the traps, and I couldn't feel my feet. My hair was froze down to my head. The snow was blowin' in so hard I couldn't see my hand in front of my face, and I'd looked up and realized if it weren't for my traplines, I'd be lost out there for good and sure. Then I lost my trapline; couldn't see a damn pole nowhere." There was a pause and a throat clearing. "Talkin's thirsty work," the voice remarked cagily.

"Bartender, give the man another drink, and put it on my tab, please," someone said, just as we all knew they would.

Harry Truman, the old waterman, not the dead president, took the shot glass Toby handed him, dropped the whiskey neatly down his throat, grinned at the throng of strangers surrounding him and resumed his tale. "Well, sir, there I was, lost and damn near froze to death, and couldn't even see the lights of Oysterback out across the marsh to guide me in. It might have been the dead of night, 'stead of high noon, it was so dark out there, with alla that snow and ice blowin' up a nor'easter." He glared around at his audience with dim eyes the color of a winter river. "I'm pret' near screwed, I thought. I'm gonna die out here on this marsh and they won't find me till spring."

Now even Toby was listening, both big hands propping his arms against the bar, dark eyes fixed on Harry Truman's face. Gently, Harry tapped his empty shot glass on the bar. A stranger in factory-fresh camo gestured Toby to hit it again. As soon as he'd had another shot of (I noted) Wild Turkey, Harry started up again. "What could I do? I was lost, and the marsh was freezin' over fast. I started to walk with my back to the wind, prayin' I didn't hit a hole and go in up to my waist. Oh, yeah, honey, there's soft spots out there that can swallow up a man like that there quicksand you see in the movies, you best believe it. I figured I was walkin' sorta southwest, which would put me out to Little Duck Island, at least. Then I tripped and fell over something and went down ker-splat." The sound of the flat of his hard old hand hitting the bar top was loud in the sudden silence.

Even the boys at the pool table had stopped to hear one of Harry Truman's epics.

"I picked myself up and what did I fall over but a rig of about five, six 'coys, all laying there tangled up on the grass, where they musta drifted away from someone's blind down the creek. And you know how I did?" He peered around.

"No," someone said, right on cue.

Toby filled the shot glass again. It disappeared fast. Harry licked his lips. "Followed the line on them 'coys down to the shore. I knew the tide musta washed 'em on up there, so the water had to be close to hand. Once I found water, I knew 'bout where I was, and how to get back, as long as I hugged close to the river. So, I gathered them 'coys up and slung 'em over my shoulder and walked down the shore till I come to the road. Then I knew I was all right, 'cause my truck was parked up there, not twenty feet away."

"How could you see it if the snow was that thick?" someone asked.

The world's oldest waterman blinked. "I couldn't! But I could hear my old dog howlin' inside the cab!"

"Aw, Harry," someone said, but he shook his head.

"Anyways, that's how I come up on this old 'coy." Dramatically, he reached into the game pocket of his jacket and withdrew a battered wooden black duck, which he placed on the counter in front of him. "It's right old. Heart pine and original paint, it looks like to me. It's been shot over, you can see that for yourself. Got some initials scratched into the bottom, but I can't make 'em out. I've got the mind to take it up to the decoy auction, get one of them experts to tell me how much it's worth."

"I say, old man, I know a bit about decoys," drawled a chubby young dude in a baseball cap decorated with a giant pair of flapping duck wings, with a bill that was a duck's bill, ha ha, get it? "Can I see that bird?"

"Help yourself, fella," Harry said indifferently. "Toby, where's 'at bottle, boy?"

The dude in the idiot's hat was turning the decoy over, peering at the bottom. Toby put the Wild Turkey on the counter and turned to the other end of the bar, where they were calling for more beers. The boys at the pool table racked 'em up again, and I tried not to wink at Harry Truman, who merely stared back at me with the innocent expression of a newborn baby.

Wing Hat Dude licked his lips. From his shirt pocket, he withdrew a jeweler's loupe, which he used to examine the underside of the bird. Although he tried to keep his expression neutral, I could see the shine of collector's lust in his eyes when he glanced at his pals with a little smile. The tip of his tongue flicked over his lips as he passed the duck to a freshly flanneled guy. I could almost see the thought bubble forming over his head as he strained for a casual note in his voice.

"I say, old man, I'd give you fifty bucks for that bird, not that it's worth it," he said, with a wink at his friend.

"There's a whole damn museum of them ole 'coys over to Salisbury, look just like that one," Harry Truman said. "I think I can do better than that at the auction. Likely get at least three hundred for 'im."

"One fifty," Wing Hat Dude said thickly. A thin line of sweat dappled his upper lip. Collector's lust; I'd know it anywhere.

"Two seventy-five," Harry Truman replied. "I weren't born yesttidy, ya know."

"Two fifty," the chubby boy said. "And that's my last offer." But you knew it wasn't. When collector's lust seizes someone, there's no telling what will happen.

Harry sighed. "Well, okay. But in cash. No checks, I don't fool with no banks."

The duck hat kid took out an enormous wad of bills and peeled several off, handing them to Harry Truman with the tips of his fingers as if touch with an old waterman would contaminate him. Actually, Harry's personal hygiene did leave a lot to be desired. You wouldn't want to stand downwind of him. He was an old bachelor waterman who lived in a trailer at the edge of the Narrows with a Portosan for plumbing.

Harry took the money and stuffed it into his shirt pocket. The bristles on his chin were shining with drops of whiskey, and his smile revealed black gaps. "She's yours now, bunk." He sighed.

Wing Hat Dude snatched up the decoy from his friend's hands. "Come on, Stan," he said breathlessly. "Let's go."

Stan tossed some bills on the bar and the two of them beat a hasty retreat, as if they'd committed a crime. No doubt they were worried that Harry would change his mind.

I watched them head out the door.

"Harry," I asked, "what did you carve on the bottom of that bird?"

Harry looked hurt. "I didn't carve nothin' into that bird. If it just happened to say 'I. H.' it ain't my fault, is it?"

"Ira Hudson." An old-time carver, much imitated and often duplicated, from down around Chincoteague. I shook my head. "Harry, you ought to be ashamed of yourself, carving those birds and antiquing 'em up and sellin' 'em to the tourists like that. Especially since everybody and their mother forges Ira Hudsons!"

"Shhh!" Harry said. But it was too late. Toby swooped down like an avenging hawk and plucked a bill from the old man's pocket.

"This oughta cover your tab," he said. "Finish the bottle, Harry. It's almost last call. And that decoy crawled out of the chemical toilet you use as an aging vat in back of your house just last week, didn't it?"

Harry looked indignant. "I ain't givin' away none a' my trade secrets!" he exclaimed. "When I go, I'm takin' 'em with me!"

He was mean enough to do just that, was old Harry Truman.

Which was why I didn't start telling him that he could probably make a lot more money if he was honest about his decoy carving. Lots of other old guys who'd been carving all their lives were gods to the duck nuts, had their stuff in the Smithsonian, had people making documentaries about their birds and all kinds of celebrity stuff that could have made Harry Truman's old age very comfortable indeed. But Harry didn't want to hear that. He got a bigger charge out of conning people.

Toby placed a Diet Pepsi in front of me. "Courtesy of Orm Friendly," he said.

I looked down the bar. My worst fear was almost ready to come true. Detective Sergeant Ormand Friendly of the Maryland State Police lifted his beer in salute and beckoned me toward his table with a devilish grin.

"Whatever next?" I asked.

"Well, Orm and I went gunnin' today." Toby grinned evilly.

I sighed. "I hope you all had a good time, you and The Man. Can I get a cheeseburger? I'm starving."

"Dumb question," he replied. "I'd say your chances of escape are slim to zero tonight." Toby leaned over and looked at me. "At least give the man a chance, Hollis. He's all right, even if he is a cop."

"That's just the point," I grumbled. "He's a cop. Beddoe's Islanders don't date cops. They elude them."

"He's a pretty okay kinda guy," Toby said. "We shot our limit. Had a good time out in the blind."

"I don't wanna know about your male bonding experiences!"

However, given a choice between sitting next to the truly noisome Harry Truman or a good-looking-in-a-Harrison-Ford-ridden-hard-and-put-away-wet sort of guy, what would you do?

"I'll bring your cheeseburger," Toby promised. "Just go say hi to him, Holl. Give 'im a half chance."

I found Detective Sergeant Ormand Friendly hunched over his chair, nursing a beer and contemplating a canvasback decoy sitting on the table before him. There was a suspiciously dreamy expression on his face as he regarded the bird. It was the look of a man who has found the next big toy in his life. Had Ormand Friendly been infected by decoy madness?

Worse, had the native Baltimoron been suckered by the world's oldest waterman?

"Friendly! Did you just buy that from Harry Truman?" I asked as I dropped into the other chair. "Did he tell you it was an Ira Hudson?"

He tore his eyes away from the bird reluctantly. "Yeah," he admitted a little sheepishly.

"Well, it's a fake. Harry makes those decoys himself and palms them off on tourists as antiques. Let me get him to give your money back to you." I reached out to pick up the bird, but Friendly snatched it away from my grasp, cradling it against his chest like a newborn baby.

"I know it's not an antique! Or a real Ira Hudson, whoever he was. But it was worth the price of admission just for the tale he told about it." Friendly looked deeply hurt. "That old feller is quite a storyteller. Besides, I kinda like this little guy. He's got personality. Look at that face, hon." Carefully, he placed the decoy on the table between us and resumed his contemplation. "I've always wanted to collect something. This might be the thing. And Harry gave me the law enforcement discount."

"Decoys?" My eyebrows must have shot clear up to my hairline. "Are you planning to bust poor old Harry Truman for duck fraud or something?"

He smiled thinly and shook his head. "Caveat emptor, as far as I'm concerned. I've got better things to do than harass poor old watermen in bars. I'm just interested, that's all. What with this Duck Jamboree thing this weekend and comin' to live on the Eastern Shore, it seems like a natural interest for a man to pursue."

I was distracted by the arrival of Toby and my cheeseburger. Mostly, my cheeseburger. Toby's huge, oozing bloody-rare cheeseburgers are bliss for the omnivore. Presented with my minimum daily requirement from the four major food groups—ketchup, fat, cholesterol and carbs—I was ready to chow down.

"Decoys seem like the hot thing," Friendly continued. "Looks like the guys that want them will do almost anything to get them."

"You can say that again," Toby agreed, wiping his hands on his apron. "I could tell you some tales about some of these big-time collectors comin' in here this weekend. Do anything. Absolutely anything—lie, cheat, steal, anything—to get a 'coy they want. Some of these old birds go for hundreds of thousands of dollars. But you'll see that at the Jamboree."

"No thanks," I said. "I plan to be as far away from Watertown this weekend as it is possible to get. My house is where you'll find me, with some videos, a stack of books and all the accoutrements for a long quiet weekend to myself." I sank my teeth into my burger and devoted half an ear to listening to Toby and Friendly talk about their successful day's shooting.

If Toby had decided that he and Friendly were going to do male bonding stuff together, that should have been all right with me. Friendly and I had recently spent four long days locked together in a small witness room, waiting to testify in a murder case. Close proximity to a member of law enforcement had done very little to advance our bonding. As far as I could see, we differed on every fundamental principle from politics to religion to music and movies. None of this seemed to bother Friendly as much as it bothered me. He was just as relentlessly glad to see me as ever.

I studied him as I ate. As usual, his clothes looked as if he'd pulled them off the piles at one of my mother's rummage sales. His heavy shirt was coming out at the elbows, which gave me a nice view of his faded gray thermals. His chino pants were frayed at the knees. It was a wonder his feet weren't frostbitten in those ancient boots; the man was a ragbag.

Ormand Friendly was never going to be a poster boy for *GQ*, I thought critically.

"Hello, Toby, hello Ormy." Peaches Brennan, the island's favorite serial divorcee, stopped by the table, leaning over to brush the shaggy hair on the back of Friendly's neck with long cerise fingernails. "Call me again, sometime, Ormy," she breathed in his ear before she sauntered away. I wondered how she could get her convex ass to strain at her skintight jeans that way.

"Ormy?" I repeated. *"Ormy?"*

"It's not polite to talk with your mouth full," Friendly said matter-of-factly, as soon as he and Toby could tear their eyes away from Peaches's well-formed butt undulating toward the pool table.

"Orm's been makin' some friends around here," Toby pointed out. "Peaches thinks he's cute."

"Peaches thinks anything with a penis is cute." I sighed.

If Toby and Friendly exchanged an amused look, I pretended not to see.

"Well, if you won't go out with me, I can find someone who will," Friendly said.

"I didn't say I wouldn't go out with you, I just thought that after what we went through with the Jason Hemlock murder—"

Happily, before I had to finish this sentence, a beeper went off. All three of us checked; it was Friendly's. He heaved himself up from the table. "Keep an eye on my decoy," he said. "Don't let anyone make off with it."

As soon as he was safely on the pay phone on the other side of the room and out of earshot, Toby glowered at me. "Holl, what's your problem?"

"I don't have a problem. It's just that—"

"That's he's not one of the usual Lifetime Achievement Award Losers you get involved with? Is that the problem?"

I threw up my hands. "I will be the first to admit that my taste in men has been terrible, but damn it, Toby, I—" A diversionary thought struck me. "Toby, have you seen Sam tonight? He insisted we come on down here, then he disappeared in the parking lot."

Toby shrugged. "He usually doesn't show up when there's a lot of people around, you know that. And Sam's another problem, Holl. Dead or alive, someone's got to pay his bar tab."

Enlightenment, however slowly, began to dawn on me. "You know, Sam was talking about driving a car. He thinks he can do it, ghost or no. You don't suppose he took my car, do you?"

Toby looked at me. I looked at Toby. We both made for the door.

In the dark, cold parking lot, there were quite a few cars, but the space where my red Honda had been parked was now empty. Wherever it was, there were my trial notes and the paper's laptop computer.

"Oh, shit," I said. "If he weren't already dead, I'd kill him. He's taken my car! That dead moron is somewhere driving around in my car!"

Toby's deep, booming laugh was the last thing I wanted to hear at that moment. I turned on him. "I don't think this is one bit funny, Toby! And neither would you if Sam had taken your truck."

"He knows better than that. Oh, Lord, what I would give to

see people's faces when a car with no driver goes rolling past them."

"Where could he have gone? He can't get that far; he doesn't have the strength to handle real-world stuff!"

While I was working myself into a snit over this latest development, Friendly came out of the bar, pulling on his coat and cradling his decoy under his arm. "Hollis," he said a little thickly, "did you tell me you had just come from the courthouse? The Bowley trial?"

"Yeah, but my car's—" I stopped. How can you tell someone that the ghost of your ex-husband stole your car? Toby, all interest, watched me wrestling with this problem.

But Friendly hadn't even heard me. "Maybe you'd better come back into Watertown with me, hon," he said grimly. "There's hot happenings at the courthouse. Smollet Bowley's escaped from custody and someone's killed Judge Findlay S. Fish. And it seems that your name was mentioned."

"What?" I gasped. I don't know whether it was the news that Fish had been murdered or the fact that my name had come up that shocked me more. "How?"

Toby winked. "I'll keep an eye out for your car," he promised. "You two just run on along."

"We'll soon find out," Friendly said. "On both counts." He dragged me toward his vehicle.

I was interested to note that Friendly was driving his own personal transportation rather than a cruiser. The Friendly-mobile was a 1976 cherry red Ford Ranchero, of all known vehicles. It was sort of neat in a Friendly sort of way, and that big V-8 engine sure did fly up the road.

Reality is frequently a matter of chance or choice, so I wasn't really surprised when Friendly made me go over my version of current events several times between leaving Toby's and arriving in Watertown. I had to refresh his memory about the whole Sneed thing, and then he wanted me to go back over it and pick it apart for him, point by ugly point.

"Jesus Christ!" he growled. "We work ourselves out, put

our asses on the line and then these damn judges turn these sons of bitches right out on the street again!"

I didn't think he was quite getting what I wanted him to get, but I wasn't in the mood to argue about it. And Friendly had other things on his mind. He started questioning me closely about my long, long day in court. "You're supposed to be a trained observer," he kept saying. "Now tell me what you saw. Even if you think it wasn't important, it might be."

He was particularly interested in the shadowy runner who had knocked me down in the courthouse hallway. But try as I might, I couldn't recollect anything more than being slammed against the wall. The lights had been out, after all, and it was pitch black.

"You must remember something, anything," Friendly growled.

"I remember being slammed up against the wall, and all my stuff scattering all over the place. But it was dark."

"Do you suppose it could have been Smollet Bowley making his escape?"

"He was shackled. Unless he got the key between the time the lights went off and the time I got downstairs, there's no way. Besides, he was talkin' on and on about how he wanted to go to jail to avoid a protracted visit from his mother-in-law, Miz Bertha Denton."

Then I had to explain to him all about the Bowley clan and Miz Bertha, Friendly not being from these parts but from Baltimore.

As generous as I was with my information, he wasn't being a whole big help to me with what he knew. The thing of it was, he was so good at dancing around the subject that we were pulling up in front of the courthouse before I realized that I knew as little about what was going on as I had when we'd peeled out of Toby's parking lot.

THREE

•

Concurrent Jurisdiction or a Pissing Contest? You Be the Judge

"Whatever happens, we don't want this mess to get out and scare the tourists," Herroner Mrs. Myrtle Goodyear, mayor of Watertown, said as she wrung her hands and got in the way.

Apparently, Herroner and Doc Westmore, who is what passes for the Santimoke County medical examiner, had been at the pre–Decoy Jamboree cocktail party at the Santimoke Inn. Neither of them looked to be feeling too much pain, but then rumor has it that these two geriatric lovebirds start the day with Stoly-spiked Bloody Marys and end it with a half gallon of J&B.

Herroner was shredding a tiny cocktail napkin as she paced the crime scene in her duck carnival costume, a crisp khaki skirt and jacket tastefully hand painted with a canvasbacks-in-flight motif. "God, if this gets out, the Decoy Jamboree will be ruined," she moaned, straining against the yellow plastic crime scene tape that was draped around the room like a party streamer. "People will be afraid to come; they'll think it's not safe!"

"They've got a better chance of getting ripped off by the quaint little bed-and-breakfast places around here than getting murdered," I muttered. Herroner's my mother's cousin once removed, but still, there are limits. "It won't come out till the Monday edition, and they'll all be gone by then. The duck people I mean, not the murderer." I didn't have the heart to tell

her that the murder of a scandalous circuit court judge was
going to be monster news. I just stood on tiptoe to take a look
around her shoulder at the corpse.

It was not a pretty sight.

Whoever had killed the Honorable Findlay S. Fish had been
pretty thorough about it. The judge, still in his black robes, lay
sprawled on the floor like a big, dead crow. Someone had
stove in the back of his head; his skull was smashed like a
rotten cantaloupe. I glanced at all the gore and glanced away
again, feeling sick. His blood and brains blended nicely into
the colors of the Tabriz.

You'd think I'd be more used to this. But you never get
used to it. At least I don't. Having just talked to the man about
two hours ago didn't make it any easier. Who? Why? If you'd
wanted to kill him, it seemed to me you'd have to take a
number and stand in line.

I dug into my bag and found an almost unused notebook,
ready to scribble furiously.

"Jesus H. Christ!"

Behind us, Friendly exploded yet again.

Ever since we'd gotten into Watertown, he'd been going
ballistic about every ten minutes. The courthouse was lit up, as
my father would say, like a holy roller church and crawling
with town and county law. It was a good thing I was there;
Friendly didn't have his shield, but they all knew me, so they
let us in.

That was the first explosion.

When we'd come into the building, there had been enough
uniforms milling around halls to hold tryouts for a Keystone
Kops movie. The Watertown Police Department, the Watertown Rescue Squad, the Watertown Volunteer Fire Company,
Santimoke County Advanced Life Support, and the County
Sheriff's Department had turned out en masse as soon as they
got the word from the central dispatcher. Violet knew just
where to call: the Dippy Doughnut out on Route 50. I swear,
most of them get their mail out there.

Anyway, that was the second explosion. When we walked
into judge's chambers, we found Bailiff Bob Winters, Water-

town Chief of Police Hooper N. "Wink" Ringgold and Sheriff Bryan "Bry" Ackermann all arguing about jurisdiction, trampling all over the evidence and spilling doughnut crumbs on the clues, at least according to Friendly, who pitched his second major fit about what he called "contaminating the evidence" and "a sideshow atmosphere," which looked very interesting in my notes.

Needless to say, this attitude did not win Friendly points with local law enforcement. But then again, we don't get too many murders in Santimoke County, so this was a big deal for our Finest. I still don't know who called Doc Westmore and Herroner, but they'd brought along Sheriff Wesley Briscoe from Devanau County, thus adding to the fun but causing only a minor eruption from Friendly.

I thought, wrongly, that by then he had resigned himself to our Eastern Shore ways, because he just muttered and growled instead of yelling and told everyone not essential to the investigation to get lost.

This thinned the herd quite a bit, but you could tell there was going to be trouble all the way. Nobody tells Wink and Bry when to leave, but Sheriff Briscoe, who hadn't held his job for twenty-eight years without learning to avoid unnecessary hassles, gracefully took himself back to the Jamboree cocktail party, muttering on his way out that he wouldn't have touched this mess with a ten-foot pole and was damn glad it hadn't happened on his turf. "And don't you even think about draggin' him over the county line either." He grinned at Wink. "This ain't some crack killing, even if he is our judge."

Fish, I assumed from that, would not be missed on the bench in Devanau County. I knew his folly had already created some rather unpleasant media scrutiny of law enforcement down there. For my part, I intended to stay until Friendly threw me out. But my trick, honed through years of practice, is to become invisible. I found myself a seat as far off in a corner as possible, stayed quiet and watched carefully.

Friendly was in consultation with Bailiff Winters, Chief Ringgold and Sheriff Ackermann, the four of them tensely huddled together in the opposite corner. From time to time, they all snarled at once. Apparently, when Bob called Violet she'd panicked and called everyone else in town before she'd thought to call the state police.

In the eternal pissing contest between different branches of law enforcement, this seemed to be a serious violation of protocol, but what do I know?

The usual internecine cop squabbles were in operation, and Friendly was still furious about the possibility that evidence had been contaminated by what he called sightseers. And who, he finally asked, was looking for Smollet Bowley, escaped convict, while everyone was milling around the crime scene?

Well, that sort of stopped them right there. It seemed that no one was putting out an APB on poor Smollet. In fact, he seemed to have been forgotten in the excitement.

"I took him down to the jail," Bob insisted. "I left him right there with your men, Bry, still in the shackles."

"Well, he's not there now," Bry Ackermann retorted. "And I don't know where he is, but we ain't got 'im down to the detention center."

They both looked at Wink as if it were somehow his fault. Wink shrugged and looked at Friendly.

"Jesus H. Christ in a handbasket!" Friendly thundered, throwing up his hands.

"Well, it's not like he's a serial killer or something," Bob said. "I mean, he's only Smollet Bowley, for pete's sake!"

"He'll turn up." Wink sighed. "He always does. Right after we got him, we got the call that the judge was dead."

Bry looked at the corpse on the floor, shaking his head. "He's not even our judge," he said. "He's Devanau County's judge. They've got two to our one. They'll never even miss him. Now, if somebody'd gotten Frank Carroll, we'd be in a whole world of shit. We only got one circuit court judge in Santimoke County."

"Well, thank God we didn't have this sumbitch. That asshole Sneed went out on work release and killed a girl. Sheee-yit."

Which I think summed it all up pretty well.

"Oh, Smollet'll turn up. He might have just gone to Wal-Mart to get a toothbrush and a change of underwear," Wink declared earnestly. "Smollet's a good ole boy."

Before Friendly could go ballistic again, the tinkle of minia-ture liquor bottles, followed by a genteelly suppressed belch, heralded the arrival of the county medical examiner. We all fell silent, respectfully watching the elderly man in the embroidered decoy-patterned jacket stagger into the room.

Doc Westmore, somewhere between eighty and death, teetered precariously as he peered at the corpse from the safe distance of ten feet away. I could smell the alcohol on his breath from where I sat.

Doc had long ago drunk himself out of practice on live patients. These days he was hauled out for events like this, then quickly thrust back into the care of Herroner again when his function had been served. It was all whiskey cake to him, but it made him feel useful and saved the county money.

"Oh, he's dead all right," Doc finally pronounced. From a pocket, he withdrew an airline-sized bottle of Jim Beam, from which he took a healthy slug before carefully screwing the top back on and returning it to his jacket.

One of the medical techs handed him something to sign.

He blinked at the bludgeoned corpse on the floor again. "You know," he added uncertainly, "I think somebody *killed* the poor son of a bitch."

Friendly looked completely lost, as well he might. Doc had been a local crime scene fixture for so long no one paid much attention to his antics, but I was suddenly aware how off it must look to a stranger. I could have explained it all to him, but not being born and raised around here, he'd never under-stand the way things work in Santimoke County. Instead, I waited for another explosion.

Friendly just sighed. "Well, where the hell is Smollet Bowley?" he asked in a cut-and-dried voice. "Did Bowley do this?"

Wink, Bry and I had all gone to high school with Smollet Bowley. We knew all about his petty criminal career and his utter harmlessness. Friendly would never get it in a thousand years: Smollet was about as capable of killing someone in cold blood as I was of being crowned Miss Decoy Jamboree.

"I wouldn't have been surprised to hear that Smollet was sleeping in Bry's office, waiting to be processed," Wink said comfortably. "We don't need to worry about Smollet. He wouldn't hurt a fly."

"What the hell is this, *Mayberry*?" Friendly yelped, outraged.

"You're going to get Bry and Wink all feathered up to no good end, Sergeant. We take our law enforcement seriously around here, in spite of what you think. There's people around here so evil they oughta be shot on sight. We just know the difference between them and Smollet," Bob soothed him. "When you've been around here for a while, you'll figure it all out. Aw, he can't help it," he told Bry and Wink. "He's a foreigner." Bob looked at the three younger men sternly. "Man and boy, I've got more years in service on me than all three of ya put together and . . ."

At that moment, the techs closed the zipper on Fish's body bag. The sound was loud in the sudden silence.

"Come along, dear," Herroner said, taking Doc Westmore's arm. "We've got people waiting at the Santimoke Inn." She looked at Friendly, Ringgold and Ackermann, and it was a glare that could peel paint. "This is the most important weekend on the county calendar," she hissed. "We take in more than two million dollars during Decoy Jamboree. Very important people are coming tomorrow. Not just the collectors, but the governor, the state's attorney general, maybe even the vice president! All of them big decoy collectors! And, the governor will want to see that this mess," she turned that Medusa look toward the judge's corpse, "has been cleared up quickly, quietly and efficiently. We've got a controversial visiting judge, who is also a prominent bird-carving connoisseur, dead on our hands, and a thousand collectors in town all ready to spend, spend, spend! How fast do you think they'll clear out if it gets around that Fin Fish has been killed? I want someone in jail *yesterday* for this, even if it's Smollet Bowley! There's been quite enough controversy around Fin Fish lately. You were right, Westmore, we should have asked for his resignation! I want this done quietly! A breath of scandal, and I promise you, heads will roll! Am I clear on this?"

"Yes'm," Bry and Wink both said at once.

"Yes, Cousin Myrtle," I whispered.

Herroner nodded. God, she was small, but she could get right fierce. She drew herself up to her full five feet, grabbed Doc and sailed majestically out of the room.

"I need a drink," Westmore was saying as she hauled him away.

I think we all did.

There was a moment of thoughtful silence while the techs went to work on the crime scene dusting for prints and taking more pictures.

After that, the pissing contest was quietly and quickly resolved. Neither Bry nor Wink wanted any responsibility for this one, and who could blame them? They knew what it was like to be on the hot seat in a small town.

"We'll be right behind ya all the way," Bry promised.

"You can rely on us," Wink agreed.

And that was how Friendly caught the red ball. Anyway, the state police had all the best FBI toys, like trained techs, equipment and the resources to handle a homicide.

"God, this is all we need on Decoy Jamboree weekend." Wink sighed, running his hands through his few remaining hairs. "Fin Fish was on the board of directors! If he doesn't show up tomorrow for the grand opening, people will start to wonder!"

"I'm sure it will be all right," Bry replied, happy to have escaped with his career and life intact. "You know nothing's ever stopped Decoy Jamboree before, not even the winter we had the big blizzard."

"We've never had a murder before, though. You know that we depend on Decoy Jamboree to pump a lot of money into the town and the county, Sergeant, especially in winter, when things are dead," Bob pointed out.

In the winter, when things are dead. An unfortunate choice of words, I thought. Bob suddenly looked greenish and exhausted, showing every second of his seventy years. He slumped into the sofa, staring at the coroner's men with unseeing eyes as they picked up the last bag of Judge Findlay S. Fish, robes and all, and placed him on the gurney, while another tech was videotaping the crime scene.

Friendly walked slowly around the perimeter of the room, then paused, staring out the window, conferring in a low voice with a uniform.

Ormand Friendly had accused me of falling down on my job as a trained observer, so I thought about what chambers had looked like when last I'd seen it earlier this evening. To my mind, things looked unchanged. The aluminum foil and paper wrappings from Judge Fish's tuna sandwich were still on the desk, along with his files, which as best I could recall, were undisturbed. Edgar's white, dripping calling card still graced the bookcase. The windows were open, just as Fish had left them when we'd all run back to the courtroom. The bubble wrap from the Scratch Wallace decoy was still on the coffee table—

"Scratch Wallace!" I exclaimed. "Where's the decoy?"

FOUR

·

Smollet Bowley Clouds
the Issue

Everyone turned to look at me as if this were *Perry Mason* and I had suddenly confessed from the witness stand.

"Where's the decoy?" I looked around. "There was a decoy here, this expensive, rare antique goose Fish just bought!"

Now everyone who had just suspected before, *knew* I was nuts. "When we were here waiting for the jury, this duck dealer, Lenore Currier, brought in a Scratch Wallace decoy that the judge had bought. They were talking about how rare and expensive it was, then Bailiff Bob came in and said the jury was back, and we all ran back to the courtroom. But the decoy was left here. It was on the coffee table."

There was nothing on the coffee table now but a stack of last year's *People* magazines and that dusty flower arrangement.

Bailiff Bob nodded. "I saw it there. She's right."

"Was it there when you came around to lock up and found Fish?" Friendly asked. He pulled out a cigarette and Bob and I followed suit. We all lit up and inhaled deeply and illegally. Arrest us.

Bob shrugged. "Like I said, the lights came back up and Fish dismissed the jury. I escorted 'em all downstairs and counted 'em as they left the building. Twelve. After that incident last year when old Mrs. Bruckart had to spend the night sleeping in the clerk's office, we're always extra careful with 'em."

Friendly looked at me, but I studiously avoided his gaze.

"Then, Ms. Hardcastle, Barry Maxwell and the judge's lady

47

friend left, so I walked 'em downstairs, showed 'em out and locked the door behind 'em. Then I went back upstairs and the judge went back into chambers. I unshackled Smollet from the chair, and we walked down to the jail. I left him there." He gave the chief a look, but Friendly reined him in.

"Then what?" he asked.

"I came back to finish up the paperwork and clock out. When I let myself into the south door with my key, the lights went out again. I went down the hall to check the fuse box in the storeroom."

I nodded. I knew where he was talking about. The box was outside the county administration office, only about ten or fifteen feet away from the door I'd been trying to find when someone ran me down.

That seemed like it had happened a million years ago.

"Before I could find the box in the dark the lights came back up," Bob said, shaking his head. I suddenly realized that he was an old man, and very shaken up. For all his years on the force, this must be a hell night for him. "So, I went upstairs again, to tell Judge Fish what had happened and get his signatures on the paperwork."

Friendly's lips were set in a thin line. I could tell what he was thinking about us small-town types. He was probably right, but still.

Bob's skin was the color of wood ash. "That's when I found Judge Fish with his head stove in," he finished, shuddering. "So I called down to the jail for the chief. I used the phone in the clerk's office," he added righteously. "I didn't touch nothing. One look and I knew he was a dead duck."

"We completely forgot Smollet for a while," Wink added sheepishly. "Havin' a judge killed right in the courthouse threw us all the hell off. County owns the courthouse, so the sheriff's department should catch it, but it's in town, so Watertown's PD may have jurisdiction. I mean, he ain't even one of ours." Wink threw a resentful glance at the judge's mortal remains. "I ain't no fan a them women's libbers, but when he come down with six months' work release for that Sneed asshole, well, doo Jesus! It makes us all look common sorry poor."

Sage nods all around. We all did know.

"You'd think the least he could do was get killed in the Devanau County courthouse," Bry growled. "Let them boys down there sort it out."

"It's called concurrent jurisdiction and I'm not about to get back into that again," Friendly grunted, but he was acting almost human again.

"Well, it sure has thrown us for a loop."

"Well, who wouldn't be thrown?" I asked loyally.

"Maybe I'm getting too old for this job." Bob sighed, shaking his head. "Hell, I was a cop for forty years when I retired. Maybe Louisa is right, we oughta move to Homosassa Springs and get that condo—"

"Aw, Bob, what the hell," Bry mumbled, shuffling his feet. "It ain't all that bad. You done everything you was supposed to."

Wink comforted him with a pat on the shoulder. "We'll find who killed Fish. And I'm sure Smollet will turn up."

"He always does," I added nastily. "If ever there was a man to take the line of least resistance, it's Smollet Bowley."

"I still can't believe you lost a prisoner—" Friendly started in again on that.

I quickly stepped on his foot. "Smollet's not a hard case. He's . . . he's . . . well, he's *Smollet*." I waved my hands in the air, which is what people usually do when they're forced into trying to describe Smollet. "I mean, he's like, totally . . . Smollet."

Friendly gave me a look that should have peeled my paint.

I backed off fast. After all, this was my ride home.

"I can't understand how—" he started to say to Bry and Wink, but before he could finish, one of the techs stood up and peeled off his gloves. "We're finished, Sergeant."

The techs wheeled the gurney out of the room. We watched Judge Fish begin his last state-sponsored trip down the stairs.

Looking around the room, I didn't see anyone shed a tear. Least of all me.

"One thing's for sure, Sarge," a young trooper said as he stuck his head through the back door and grinned at Friendly. "If anyone was hiding out in here before, they're not here now. We've searched this place from top to bottom with the pooch, and there ain't a living soul to be found." He held the leash of a German shepherd, who gave us a nasty look, as if we were supper and he hadn't eaten since breakfast.

"Back, Sherwood," the uniform commanded, and the dog sat down. But his ears twitched and he looked around the room as if he could see something we couldn't. The young uniform must have been surfing my brain waves. He shook his head. "I'll tell ya though, Sarge, this place is spooky at night, even with all the lights blazing."

"It's true," Bob agreed, "this place *is* spooky at night. Old buildings like this make a lot of strange noises."

"No footprints in the slush either," the young cop said, consulting a notebook. "All the doors are fire code, meaning you can lock 'em from the outside, but they gotta open from inside. Windows are secure. If they got out by the doors, we'd never find 'em. The streets were full of people in town for the duck carnival."

"The lights went off twice," Friendly said. "Anybody check the fuse box for tampering?"

"There's a main that switches down everything but the emergency lights. They're on a battery-operated generator that kicks in when the power goes down."

"But they didn't come on in the downstairs hallway," I pointed out, and Bob nodded his agreement.

"Someone check out the emergency lights. See if they've been fooled with," Friendly commanded.

"You oughta get Tige Russell out of bed, then. He's the courthouse maintenance chief. He knows all this stuff," Bob suggested.

The uniform nodded and started to back out of the door. But Sherwood the dog wasn't ready to go. He laid back his ears and growled, his eyes focused on the window.

Edgar Allan Crow looked in at us with yellow eyes. He perched on the edge of his feeding tray and flapped his wings.

"Naw! Maw!" he croaked, eyeing Sherwood with distaste.

" 'Quoth the raven, "Nevermore!" ' " Friendly remarked absently.

Why did I know he was going to do that?

"Keep that damn bird out of this room!"

Athena Hardcastle appeared in the doorway. Even in jeans, no doubt hastily thrown on when she got the call, she was a knockout. But judging by her expression, Santimoke County's top cop was not a happy camper. Her dark, angry gaze swept the room and came to rest on Friendly.

Oh boy, here it comes, I thought. Now she's going to tear into Friendly for not calling her in. As the county's state's attorney, she had every right to expect to be called to the scene of a crime, especially one this important. This could be a battle of the Titans. I winced, waiting for the inevitable explosions.

"Ormy?" Hardass Hardcastle trilled, smiling.

Friendly turned, just about to look irritated. "Teeny?" he asked in a quavering voice. "Is that you?"

They met in the middle of the room in what I can only describe as an embrace, while I was thinking *What's wrong with this picture? Teeny? Ormy?* Huh?

"My God, Teeny, what are you doing here?" Friendly demanded, holding Hardass at arm's length, looking at her as if he could eat her up. With a spoon.

"I could ask you that, too!" she replied, fiddling with his collar. "Ormy, when are you going to get some decent clothes?"

"Hey, I was off duty when I got the call. But you look great, Teeny. Is that a new perfume?" He dipped his head to sniff at the collar of her jacket, a gorgeous Japanese kimono-style number that probably cost what I make in a week.

"Same as always—Joy," she cooed. "Oh, I can't believe it's really you, Ormy! What are you doing here?"

"I've been exiled, I mean, reassigned to the Eastern Shore," Friendly informed her whimsically.

Hardass Hardcastle laughed, a low, throaty sound. She actually laughed. "Who did you offend?" she asked.

Friendly just grinned. "You know me all too well, Teeny."

"Well, I ought to! How long were we married?"

If I'd been a secondary character in a Jane Austen novel, I would have fainted. I could have caught a softball with my teeth, my mouth was hanging open so wide. All my clever assumptions, of which I was so proud, had been crumbling like rotten concrete lately. But this was something else entirely.

"Too long, Teeny. Too damn long," he said, but he was laughing.

"Well, I'm now acting state's attorney over here, till the next election. But *you*—"

It was enough for me to quietly fold up my notebook and steal away into the night. I figured I'd find one of the cops downstairs who lived in my direction and would give me a ride home. Surely the excitement was wearing off by now.

Remembering my car had been stolen by a ghost didn't make me feel that this night was getting any less surreal. I trudged down the stairs to the central hallway and came right on top of a milling crowd of state, county and town cops who all seemed more intent on a big box of Dippy Doughnut's best than gathering evidence.

I picked out a lemon cream butter crunch and went outside to sulk. Upstairs, Friendly and Hardcastle no doubt relived old times.

Totally stunned? Who, me?

Well, of course I needed a cigarette. And a chance to ponder what cosmic twists and turns of fate brought that pair together. And I hate it, absolutely hate it above all else when my clever and cynical assumptions about other people turn out to be wrong, dead wrong.

For one thing, I'd pegged them both as bigots. For another, imagining the fastidious and soignée Athena *(Teeny?)* romantically involved with the slovenly and laid-back-to-the-point-of-being-mistaken-for-a-Quaalude-overdose Ormand Friendly *(Ormy?)* was too much for my overloaded circuits to deal with. The doughnut tasted like wood shavings.

Abandoned by the duck lovers, the streets around the court-house square were dark, cold and silent. The snow was melting into a thin slush. I sat down on the cold marble steps beneath the portico where it was dry at least. I put the dough-nut on a napkin on the step, inhaling the cold, sharp night. I fished for a cigarette in my battered old Coach bag and blankly contemplated fate.

"Well! I should have known!"

I looked up to see a large, tall man with one of those stick-on HI! MY NAME IS cards appended to his lapel. His said HI! MY NAME IS: JUDGE DECOY JAMBOREE. Obviously a stray from the pre-Jamboree cocktail party at the Santimoke Inn around the block, and just as obviously, feeling no pain as he twirled a plastic glass of amber liquid and teetered on his feet.

"What are *you* doing here?" demanded a voice from my other side, and I whipped my head around to see a short, thin man with an identical JUDGE DECOY JAMBOREE sticker on his lapel. Another stray, and just as obviously three sheets to the wind.

"Lenore told me that Fin had bought the Scratch Wallace." The tall man looked right over me, frowning at the short man.

"Lenore told *me* that Fin had bought the Scratch Wallace," the short man hissed.

They just stood and glared at each other for a long moment. They might have been frightening if they both didn't seem so silly.

"May I help you gentlemen?" Carl, one of the baby troopers assigned to guard the courthouse leaned out the door, his hand resting uneasily on his hip holster.

They just stood and glared at each other; they seemed barely aware of the trooper's challenge, so intent were they on each other. You could feel the hostility radiating from them, fueled by the serious drinking they'd evidently been doing at the cocktail party.

"We're judges from the Decoy Jamboree."

"We're looking for Fin Fish."

Lights flashing, no sirens, the meat wagon pulled away from the side street, carrying Findlay Fish away to Baltimore.

"That was him," the baby trooper said. "He just died. Is there anything I can help you with?"

Two prosperous-looking, middle-aged white guys sporting Decoy Jamboree tags don't get asked why they're hanging around; God knows they don't get questioned, especially by newly minted state troopers young enough to be their grandsons. Even I didn't question their presence, although I did halfway consider telling them that Fin Fish wouldn't be judging this year's duck pageant. But I had other things on my mind at that point.

After a moment, the unhappy pair seemed to sense that lurking about glaring at each other might not be a wise idea; without a word, they both turned and staggered away in the direction of the Santimoke Inn, giving each other a wide berth as they did so, disappearing into the downtown shadows.

"Just a couple of disgruntled duck nuts?" I ventured.

Carl shrugged, retreating into the courthouse again and closing the doors behind himself.

I lit my noxious weed, thanking my lucky stars that my mother was not here to see me: (a) smoke on the street; (b) eat on the street; (c) sit on a cold marble step. Any of which would have horrified her.

Because ladies *never* did (a) or (b), only sluts below reproach did, and (c) gave you hemorrhoids—all from the Gospel According to Roberta "Doll" Ball, Our Lady of the Rummage Sales, as handed down to me from birth and cut in stone.

Give my mother the child until the age of six and she will return to you a woman who would rather risk eternal hell than wear slacks to church.

That's why when Edgar swooped down and grabbed my doughnut, I was sort of grateful. Eyeing me warily, he tugged and pulled at the gluey pastry until it began to ooze sickly yellow filling. With a triumphant cackle he sank his bill into it and chowed down.

"Edgar," I said, "you are becoming a junk-food junkie."

He dipped his tail at me and kept eating, watching me as if afraid I wanted that doughnut back. It occurred to me that the crow might have been the only witness to Findlay Fish's death.

"Who did it, Edgar?" I asked.

"Colonel Mustard with a candlestick in the conservatory," Edgar replied.

I nearly jumped out of my skin.

Sam morphed himself from the shadows and the light, grinning evilly.

"If you weren't dead, I'd kill you all over again," I snapped, trying to make my hands stop shaking. "God, you gave me a turn! Car-stealing ghosts are bad enough, but talking birds—"

Sam inclined his head, his grin fading. "What's wrong?"

"Just ghosts stealing my car and dead judges turning up and finding out Friendly used to be real close to Hardass Hardcastle. No, nothing's wrong. Everything's just peachy perfect! Where's my car?"

Edgar, perhaps not liking ghosts or my tone of voice, picked up the rest of the doughnut and lifted off to his nest.

Sam draped a weightless arm around my shoulder. "I didn't *steal* your car. I just *borrowed* it. I needed it to run into Watertown on an errand."

I was suddenly aware of a bone-crunching weariness. "Well, that was really stupid. What errands could a ghost have? Where is my car now?" I knew arguing with Sam was really stupid, too. He always seemed to win, mainly by relentlessly wearing me down. I quickly changed the subject. "What are you doing here? You don't happen to know who killed Judge Fish by any chance, do you?"

"Can't help you there," Sam said. "But there might be somebody who can."

From out of the darkness, Smollet Bowley appeared with a sheepish grin. "Hi, Hollis." He waved.

I turned and looked for Sam, but he was gone.

"I didn't do it, Hollis, honest," Smollet whined, shifting away from me, as if he expected I would hit him.

"Do what?" I asked irritably. "Kill Judge Fish, run away from the jail, what? And speaking of *what*, what the pluperfect hell *are* you doing out of jail?"

Smollet shifted uneasily. "That fella you was with said it was all right," he said hopefully.

"What fella? You mean Friendly? Big, tall guy?"

Smollet shook his head. "Na, that dark-haired guy in the blue shirt. The one you was just talking to. Where'd he go? He was just here."

"Sam told you it was all right to walk out of the jail? Are you sure it was Sam? A dead guy, sort of about five-ten, dark hair, blue eyes, blue shirt, tan pants?"

My head was spinning. With Smollet, simple communications are impossible. He goes all over the place and back rather than tell you a simple fact.

"I guess that was him, if you say so. See, I was just settin' there, waitin' to be processed, and all of a sudden, Bry and Wink and everyone runs out and I'm just settin' there, and then that guy was just here comes in and says, 'You may as well go on out to the Wal-Mart and get a toothbrush and whatever you need, because by the time they book you in it'll be tomorrow morning.' Was that Sam?"

"You can see Sam?" I asked, amazed. The talent to communicate with ghosts was not something I would have ascribed to Smollet Bowley. His type can barely communicate in sophisticated grunts.

"Well, why wouldn't I be able to see him? I ain't blind, am I?" Sam asked indignantly. Before I could reply he continued, "Because I figured he knew what he was talking about and I just headed out the door. And found this."

From behind his back, Smollet produced a familiar-looking decoy. My heart sank.

"Where did you get that?" I asked.

"I *said* that I found it. It was stuck over there in that ivy thing," he repeated patiently, pointing toward an old wrought-iron trellis mounted into the brick courthouse wall. Reaching from the foundation to the roof, it rose past the open chambers windows. In the summer it was covered with ivy and trumpet vine, but now, thick, leafless vines twisted about the ironwork in a skeletal death grip. Somewhere in there, the crow had a nest, but it was well hidden in the thicket of tendrils and branches, even in winter. "It was sorta stuck in the branches. It looks like it's a real old decoy. Maybe one of them duck carnival people lost it. Do you suppose there's a reward on it?"

"Lemme see that, Smollet." I grabbed for it.

Smollet jerked back from me. "It's mine," he snapped. "If there's a reward, I want to collect it. I found it." He cradled it against the front of his bony chest.

"You better give me that," I snarled, grabbing it from him. I pulled the bird from him and inspected it closely.

Then wished I hadn't.

It was the Scratch Wallace snow goose all right, but someone had dipped it in something wet and nasty, like red paint.

"What the hell did you do, Smollet?" I growled. "There's wet stuff all over it!"

"That ain't stuff," Smollet said thickly, peering over my shoulder. "That there's muck."

Even by the dim light of the streetlamps, I could see the nasty red stuff was all over the bird. It was also smeared all over me. Ugh.

"What the hell did you do with this thing?" I grumbled.

"I didn't do nothing," Smollet said sullenly. "I barely touched it!"

"I'm sorry, Smollet, but honestly—" I spluttered. Then I looked closely at the bird.

"Smollet, that's *blood*!"

He peered at the decoy. "Yeah, that's blood all right," he pronounced. There was sanguinary stuff all over the tail end of it, and it looked pretty banged up. There were fresh splits in the old wood and it was splintered, as if it had been smashed against a hard surface.

Like Fin Fish's head?

"How did blood get on this?" I asked him suspiciously. A terrible thought entered my mind. "Smollet," I hissed, "what have you done?"

"I didn't do nothin'! Why does everyone always think *I* always did it?" he whined.

"Because generally you did," I replied mean-spiritedly. I pulled some wet wipes out of my pocketbook, wiping the stuff off my hands, trying not to worry about AIDS.

"Why would I smear blood all over a fine decoy like that?" Smollet demanded, full of indignation.

"Why do you do anything, Smollet? Smollet, did you kill Judge Fish with this decoy?"

"Why would I wanna do something like that?" Smollet whined reasonably. "Why, I didn't even *know* the man."

"Because someone bashed the back of his head in and it looks as if they did it with this damned Scratch Wallace decoy!" Using the wet wipes, I picked it up by the neck. Like I was really preserving prints on it or something. I took a deep breath.

"Look, Smollet, you stay here. Don't move, don't do anything. Just stay here. Wait for me to come back," I commanded, feeling like I was hot onto something. "We're gonna straighten this mess out; you hear? I've got a friend who's a detective for the state police, and he'll help us out—I'm going to get you out of trouble—" I was backing away toward the door. "Everything will be all right. Just stay right where you are!"

"I ain't goin' nowhere," Smollet promised.

Mentally cursing Sam, I raced back into the courthouse and up the stairs gingerly holding the bird as far away from myself as I could.

Friendly was on the phone in the clerk's office when I came flying up the stairs, out of breath, waving my bloody discovery like a bowling trophy. He raised his eyebrows at me, then looked at the thing in my arms. Athena Hardcastle was nowhere to be seen, I noted.

"What've ya got?" he asked. "Is that the missing bird?"

"I've found the murder weapon, I think," I said with barely concealed triumph as I carefully set the goose on the desk.

Friendly gave me a look that should have peeled my paint, and then glanced at the decoy. "Gotta go," he barked, replacing the phone in its cradle.

"I think we have the murder weapon," I repeated breathlessly. "Check it out!"

He gingerly took the decoy from me, holding it by the wipes as he set it, bloody mess and all, on the desk. He studied it for a full minute. Only then did he allow himself a shrill whistle of astonishment. "Well," he said succinctly. "I'll be damned. Done in with a decoy, huh?"

"It looks that way, doesn't it?" I was rather proud of myself.

"Where did you find it?"

"Smollet Bowley found it. He's sitting outside on the steps. I told him you'd help him out."

"Smollet Bowley? You left him sitting on the steps? You're kidding me!" Calling to one of the uniforms to keep an eye on the evidence and get some prints lifted or whatever, Friendly took off down the stairs. "Smollet's not going anywhere—" I said. I rushed to follow Friendly down the steps and out the front door. Although it took only a few seconds to hit the street, it seemed as if it took forever.

And, of course, Smollet was gone. Vanished into thin air. Nothing but cold, empty marble steps where once a Smollet was.

Sam, you'll pay for this, I mentally promised. Aloud I said weakly, "Well, Smollet *was* here."

Friendly looked like he wanted to have another major outburst. For a guy who said he ran a loose ship, he was getting real Captain Bligh on me tonight.

"Look, I don't know what kind of a game you people are running on me, but let me tell you, Ms. Hollis Ball, I do not appreciate it! Murder's a damn serious business, and all of you people seem to think it's some kinda goddamn joke. I oughta run your ass in."

"For what? I was just trying to help you!" I retorted.

"Obstructing, to start with," Friendly said. "And after that, a whole lot more. Enough to put you on ice till I can get this thing straightened out."

"Boy, and you had me fooled into thinking how laid back you were," I muttered defensively, looking under the bushes as if I really expected Smollet to be hiding there.

He had vanished. Just like Sam. Before I could stop to wonder if there was a connection there, and if so, what it was and how I was going to explain this to Friendly, the man himself started going ballistic again.

"I do run a loose ship," he growled, "until someone or a whole bunch of someones start to jerk my chain. *Then* I start to feel real pissed off." He glared at me, green eyes sparking.

"I guess it wouldn't help to say you're cute when you're angry?" I ventured with a weak grin.

"No!" Friendly replied, but the corners of his mouth turned up just a little. He took a deep breath, then shook his head. "So. You came down here to have a cigarette, and Smollet Bowley just strolls up with the decoy?"

"Yeah," I said meekly. "Something like that. I think he was hiding in the shadows, by that trellis. He said he was sitting down at the jail waiting to be processed, and everyone was busy, and then someone came along and told him to go get some stuff together and come back tomorrow because they probably wouldn't have him in a cell till early morning. That's what he said, anyway."

What was I supposed to tell him? That the ghost of my ex-husband had, for whatever Sam's reasons, told him to take a hike? Oh, right. Friendly was really gonna believe that, wasn't he?

He turned and threw the courthouse door open. "Get a move on!" he yelled inside. "While you're hanging around with your dicks in your hands, Bowley's been spotted!"

That certainly had the desired effect. I never saw so many people move so fast in my life. Even Sherwood motivated his doggy self.

"Where would he go?" Friendly asked me.

"I don't know." That at least was the truth. I couldn't think of any logical reason to mention my car again. Try telling a man that a ghost may have stolen your Honda and then helped a convicted criminal escape. See how far *you* get.

Needless to say, the long, exhaustive search of the immediate area didn't turn up any sign of Smollet. I sat wearily on the steps and watched, smoking too many cigarettes and wishing I was home in bed asleep or at the very least had a book to pass the time.

"You know more about this than you're letting on, don't

you?" Friendly asked me when he finally decided there was nothing more we could do here.

"Frankly, I'm glad Fish is dead. His sexist bigotry and careless stupidity caused a lot of trouble for a lot of people, and at least one of them, that idiot teenage girlfriend of Sneed's, is dead because of Fish's caveman attitude toward justice," I steamed.

So I'd lied. So what? Friendly leaned against his truck and looked at me wearily, fumbling for his keys.

"Rule number one," I said flatly, "everybody lies." I shivered, even though the temperature had risen considerably since early evening. "Person A pulled the trigger, the gun just went off and killed B by accident. Councilperson X has no financial interest in the new strip mall, even though the land is in a paper trust that leads directly to Mrs. Councilperson X's bank account. Mrs. Y is not boinking Mr. Z at the Cocky Locky Motor Lodge out on Route 50, and doesn't understand why Mr. Y tried to run over Mr. Z in the Santimoke Yacht Club parking lot last Saturday night."

I lit a cigarette and inhaled, watching him unlock his door. "Even when people don't lie, they don't always see what really happened. Witnesses aren't always reliable. I may see a green car, you may see a black truck. Delegate Z may have said 'yes,' but I might hear 'no.' Reality is frequently a matter of chance or choice. And I'm glad Fish is dead. I just wish I knew who killed the son of a bitch. I'd give 'em a medal."

Friendly leaned across the seat to open my door. His face was very close to mine; I could see the pores in his nose. "The Eastern Shore's not a fucking region, it's a cult," he whispered.

We rode back to Toby's in silence. We were both too tired to talk, let alone argue.

I was totally unsurprised to see my ancient red Honda sitting alone in Toby's deserted lot, the engine still warm. Wherever Sam had been, he knew better than to jerk my chain one more time that night.

After grunting a farewell at Friendly and being grunted at in return, I drove home, filed my story, then collapsed into a deep and dream-filled sleep where Harry Truman, the old water-man, not the dead president, chased me around the courthouse with a live snow goose.

FIVE

•

No Good Deed Goes Unpunished

The shriek of the bedside phone cut through my sleep like a fork through a crabcake. Cranking one gummy eye open, I grappled for the receiver. The clock, I noted, showed an ungodly 7 A.M.

"Wha?" I croaked.

"Hollis, it's Friendly," growled a familiar voice. "Are you awake?"

"Should I be?" I croaked. "By any reasonable standard, I have hours more sleep coming to me."

If I was expecting a snappy comeback, I was disappointed. "Look, Hollis, I've gotta make this quick. We paid an early morning visit to Lenore Currier's house."

"How Gestapo of you," I snuffled, yawning. "Did she kill Fish?"

"Never mind that, she was already up and about," he replied airily. "Look, I've got to make this quick because I need to check out her movements last night after she left the courthouse. But she's going to be calling you, and I want you to go along with whatever she wants."

"What? You've got a suspect and you want me to work her over with a rubber hose for you?"

"Very funny. Look, just play along and report back to me, okay?"

"What have you done for me lately? I've still got a story to file."

"You've got until Monday morning to file it. Your rag has

no Sunday edition, and we're keeping a lid on this for now. I'm trying to locate Fish's ex-wife and Barry Maxwell and a couple of other likely witnesses. It sounds like a lot of people really hated this Fish guy."

"I think you could safely say that," I admitted. "But who hated him enough to kill him?"

"It also seems like everyone and his mother has a key to the courthouse." Friendly sighed. "Look, Hollis, play with Lenore for me, and I promise, I'll give you the exclusive, inside-track, straight poop."

"Friendly, what the pluperfect hell—"

"Just keep her busy and I'll explain it all later. Okay?"

"Okay. But I want the exclusive."

"You've got it, hon."

Disconnect.

Just as I was drifting back into blessed sleep, the phone rang again. "Hollis? Is that you? Thank God you're home! It's Lenore Currier," said a brisk voice, sounding far too damn chipper for this unreasonable hour. "I'm sorry to call so early, but it's something of an emergency."

The events of last night came back to me and I struggled to sit upright and sound as if I were wide awake and aware of the outside world. "That's all right," I croaked, reaching automatically for a cigarette and my notebook. Even half awake, I could sense this story.

"Lieutenant Happy was at my house this morning, telling me about Fin Fish. I was terrified! And all the questions they asked me, as if I would know anything! It's weird, isn't it? But of course, no one liked him, did they?" Her tone was matter-of-fact, as if he'd been stricken with a twenty-four-hour virus.

"It's not pleasant," I replied cautiously. I was scrabbling for a pen and trying to light a cigarette all at once and succeeding at nothing.

"Hollis, can you tell me one thing?"

"Well, I'm not really at liberty to discuss anything specific," I replied a trifle pompously. I could have, but I knew if it got back to Friendly, I would be toast.

"I understand. God, this is so inconvenient. I just can't

believe it! Hollis, you've got to tell me one thing, please. Lieutenant Happy wouldn't tell me, and I *need* to know." She really sounded desperate, as if she were having an anxiety attack.

"Uh, okay." Not that I knew much.

I could hear her taking a deep breath, forcing the words out, as if the thought were too awful to bear.

"Is the Scratch Wallace decoy damaged?"

When I could speak again, I admitted, "It's not in great shape."

"Oh, my God!" she moaned. "The Scratch Wallaces are among the most valuable decoys in the world! Any damage to that bird would be disastrous! We were counting on having it out for display today at the Santimoke Inn. Decoy mavens are pouring into town, you know, and having a Scratch Wallace is the highlight of this year's Decoy Jamboree."

"It's evidence in a murder case now," I pointed out, in what I hoped was a reasonable tone of voice. "Someone used it, they think, to bludgeon Judge Fish."

"Can you imagine?" she asked indignantly. "Of all the things in that room you could use, to vandalize a priceless decoy! I just hope it isn't damaged beyond repair!"

I had to bite the inside of my lip to stifle a laugh.

"Well," she continued, sounding annoyed, "the handsome policeman who was here earlier, Lieutenant Happy?"

"Detective Sergeant Ormand Friendly," I said, hacking up my first toke of smoke along with about half my left lung.

"Well, I knew his name sounded like he was one of the seven dwarfs." Lenore sighed impatiently, oblivious to my barely suppressed laughter. "But, he said the police couldn't release the decoy to the Jamboree Committee, even though I *explained* that the Scratch Wallace goose was the major exhibition, that famous people were coming in from all over and we'd advertised its presence at the event for over a year! Can you *believe* he said he didn't care?"

"Yes," I said, but that didn't stop Lenore from plunging right along. "Fin would have wanted it this way! He would have wanted the goose on display! I told Lieutenant Happy that, but it didn't seem to register."

"No doubt," I replied solemnly. "I'm afraid Detective Sergeant Grumpy just doesn't understand the vital importance of having a Scratch Wallace murder weapon on display at the Decoy Jamboree."

"I'm so glad you understand," she breathed. "I *knew* I could count on you to help us out."

Uh-oh. "Help you out with what?" I asked cautiously.

Lenore Currier drew in a deep breath. "Well, since you're friends with Lieutenant Happy, I thought perhaps you could explain to him that the decoy is absolutely *necessary* to the Jamboree. It will be on display in the lobby of the Santimoke Inn, in a locked glass case, where there's *always* someone to watch it, and we promise we'll return it to the police Sunday night, just as soon as the Jamboree is over. I mean, what could be more secure? God, Hollis, Fin's death is bad enough, but not having his decoy on display is much, much worse. Decoys were his ruling passion. I'm sure we could borrow another Scratch Wallace, but there just isn't time!"

His ruling passion. Oh, Lord. "Well, you know that and I know that, but nothing I can do or say will move Officer Friendly to release a suspected murder weapon." I forced myself to sound sober and serious.

I saw no reason to add that I was acting as his agent and spy. But she'd stroked my ego with her assumption that I had any influence over anything. Hell, I couldn't even get a parking ticket fixed in real life.

"But he did mention," she said thoughtfully, "on his way out, that you might know an undiscovered old-time carver. His name was Millard Fillmore or something like that?"

"Harry Truman?" I exclaimed, astonished. "Not the dead president but the old retired waterman?" I sensed where this was going, and felt highly amused, in spite of myself. I was awed to think of Harry in the same sentence as "undiscovered old-time carver." He was a smelly old bachelor who lived in a trailer down by the harbor. So this was what Friendly had in mind. But where did he think it was going, and why did he need me?

"Well, I thought I knew *all* the modern carvers, but this man is a new one on me," Lenore said waspishly. "Lieutenant Happy said as far as he knew, this man never does shows, but I simply can't imagine a carver who doesn't do the shows."

A carver who did not seek fame and fortune was completely outside her comprehension. But then again, she didn't know Harry Truman. If it weren't for the call of whiskey, the man would avoid humanity altogether.

"You're not from around here, are you?" I asked.

"Good Lord, no!"

Out of the corner of my eye I noted, with annoyance, that Sam had materialized in the rocking chair beside the window, where his form was illuminated by a shaft of sunlight. I wondered how long he had been there. He grinned a mocking grin at me.

"Where the hell have you been?" I demanded. "Why did you take my car last night?"

"A mission of mercy," he said mysteriously.

"What's that? What's that about your car, Hollis?" Lenore's voice, high and piercing, zinged through the phone.

Sam whispered. "Take her down there and introduce her to Harry Truman. Then Lenore'll owe you a huge favor. You never know what she might know about Fish that she hasn't told Friendly. She looks like a prime suspect to me. Wouldn't it just bust Friendly's chops if you got the inside skinny on who killed Fish all by yourself?" He leered at me, the morning sun shining right through his toothy smile.

"How do you know so much about all of this?" I hissed at him. "Have you been eavesdropping on my life? Sam, you promised not to—"

"Hollis, please. I'm asking this as a personal favor. I'll tell you everything I know about Fin Fish if you'll help me out. And I know quite a lot," Lenore bargained. "I mean, you *are* a reporter, aren't you? This *is* a story, isn't it?"

The thing is, it always seems like a good idea at the time, then the next thing I know, I'm ass deep in alligators.

I inhaled and put the phone up against my ear again. "Listen, Lenore, I think I have an idea."

"That's right!" Sam sulked. "Claim credit for it."

I chose to ignore him. "Suppose you could bring in this great undiscovered decoy carver no one ever heard of before?"

"You've got to be kidding! These are experts! We can't just stick any old block of wood in there, they'd know in a minute!" She paused; I could hear the wheels turning. "Besides," she said in a resigned voice, "how do I know no one's ever heard of him before?"

"Because he's Harry Truman. He shuns publicity," I said. Like Count Dracula shuns sunlight.

"Can you give me his e-mail address?"

I laughed, imagining Harry Truman getting e-mail. "Well, he doesn't even have a phone. If you want to talk to him, you have to go to his trailer."

"No e-mail! How does he cope?" she demanded incredulously.

"Pretty well, I think, for an old bachelor trapper. Look, if you meet me down at his trailer on Beddoe's Island, you can talk to him. He knows me, so I think he'll talk to you. He's the best, ah . . . undiscovered carver I know of." And the only one.

"What about your father? Isn't he from Beddoe's Island? Wouldn't he know this Millard Fillmore's work? How come Perk never discovered him?"

Because my father, being the honest sort of man he is, thinks Harry Truman's an old fraud, I thought but did not say. Instead I said, "Well, Harry's not much on showing or selling stuff. He just sort of does it for, ah, food money." Whiskey being mother's milk to Harry, this wasn't really a lie.

"If I could just meet this new carver . . ." Lenore was thinking out loud. "Discovering a new carver would be a coup almost equal to a Scratch Wallace. . . ."

"I'll introduce you to Harry. He's one of those characters we haven't used yet, if you know what I mean. He's probably the last of the old-timers who live off the land."

Lenore gave a reluctant chuckle. "In this business, you deal with no one else but characters! Just for the record, Hollis, I'm an honest broker; my whole reputation's built on it! I don't dare even *think* about reproductions. There are already too many fakes on the decoy market."

"There are?" I tried to sound shocked.

"You'd be amazed," she said darkly. "When I first started brokering decoys, lots of people must have thought a woman couldn't know the first thing about forgeries, because they brought them in by the bushel basket. Why Fish tried—" she broke off, recovering herself. "But we need a replacement. Even an undiscovered carver would be better than nothing at all."

"I don't even think he's ever been to the Decoy Jamboree. He's sort of like a hermit." And Elizabeth Windsor is sort of like queen of England.

"After this show, I'm retiring from decoy brokering forever. I've been offered a job appraising folk art for a major New York auction house, and I intend to take it. Meanwhile, I'd like this to go off without a hitch, so I'm willing to pay Mr. Truman and pay him well, if he has a body of work to show. It doesn't even have to be fabulous. We just need something, *anything* new in that case by tonight."

" 'Morality is not something that concerns those of us who are already in hell,' " I quoted. Sam squirmed in the rocker and gave me a sharp look.

"Something like that." Lenore Currier laughed bitterly. "It's all show business, Hollis. You know that. What you do, what I do, it's just show business. But if this ever gets out, I'm fried."

"They won't hear it from me," I promised, giving her directions to Harry's.

"I'll meet you there at nine. I've never been to Beddoe's Island so this should be interesting all the way around."

We disconnected.

"There's a star for your heavenly crown," Sam said as I hung up the phone.

When I looked up, he had vanished. The empty rocker swayed back and forth in the sun.

It's true what they say. No good deed goes unpunished.

* * *

An hour later, in jeans, rubber boots and a heavy jacket, I stumbled out of my house. A single sullen, milky cloud covered the morning sky, and a thin steel breeze from the bay gusted across the empty soybean fields.

I live in an isolated cedar-shake two-over-and-two-under on a piece of hardscrabble farmland on Crazy Woman Creek, one of the thousands of tributaries of Chesapeake Bay. I rent from the farmer, my distant cousin, whose house is about a half a mile away from mine across the woods and fields. According to him, he's spent his whole life doing for other people. Most of those people would tell you he's spent his whole life doing for himself at their expense, but that's another story.

Vestiges of last night's ice and snow still lay in scraggly patches across the fields. The watermen say when snow lies on the ground like that, it's waiting for more to fall. I could believe it; the air felt like more weather was coming. I shivered as I climbed into my car and tossed my purse and notebook on the passenger seat. My car smelled more stale and unwholesome than usual, and I wrinkled my nose.

As I turned the key in the ignition, I heard a new sound that made me wonder what was going up on the old car now. It sounded like a drunk drowning. I turned the ignition off, but the sound was still there. And it wasn't coming from under the hood.

Slowly, I turned around and looked into the backseat.

Smollet Bowley stirred, making an unpleasant hacking sound in the back of his throat as he struggled to sit up. "Good morning," he said thickly.

I just sat there with my mouth hanging open for several seconds, trying to find my voice. When I did, I said, "Smollet, what the pluperfect hell are you doing in the backseat of my car?"

Smollet hacked up some phlegm and wiped his nose on the sleeve of his Twisted Sister tour jacket. He regarded me blearily. "Well, your friend told me it was okay," he pronounced.

"Sam?" I asked dangerously.

"Yeah. That guy Sam. The one who come and picked me

up last night in your car?" Smollet was, I guessed, one of those hideously cheerful morning people. He gave me a toothy smile.

I winced. I hate cheerful morning people almost as much as I hate meddling ghosts. Last night was bad enough, but this was serious stuff.

"Sam, are you around here? You'd better get your ass in here now! Sam, you've got some explaining to do!"

Smollet beamed happily.

If I was waiting for Sam to materialize, I'd be sitting there until hell froze over. Whatever my ghostly, ghastly ex-husband was, he was keeping a low profile.

"So, what's for breakfast?" Smollet asked.

"Better let me ask the questions, Smollet. You're on thin ice right this minute," I growled. "Why didn't you stay put at the courthouse last night?"

He looked wounded. Smollet was very good at looking wounded. "I did! Except Sam come along again and told me to hop into the car. So I did. But I was so tuckered out, when he tole me to lay down in the backseat, so no one would see me, I went right off to sleep. And when I woke up, you was here, it was mornin' and you was firin' up the car."

"Sam came along where?" I asked as patiently as I could.

"Along of where I was settin', I told you that," Smollet replied. "I'm a mite peckish. Don't you have any food in the house?"

"Smollet, the day I let you in my house will be the day I lie down in the middle of Route 50 and let a Chinaberry Poultry Farms gut truck run over me," I said evenly. "Now. Where were you when Sam came along and picked you up?"

"I tole you. I was settin'. Listen, you got a candy bar or somethin'? I'm awful hungry."

"In a minute. Where were you set—I mean, sitting?"

"Alongside the courthouse, right where you left me!" Smollet's tone implied that I was dull witted at best.

"You were sitting where I left you, on the front steps of the courthouse, and Sam came by in a car and picked you up."

"That's what I said!" He rooted around in the fast-food

wrappers on the floor. "Any ole, cold stale fries? A piece of bun? A dried-up pickle?" he asked plaintively. "Iffen I'da stayed in jail, at least I woulda gotten a bowl a oatmeal and a cuppa instant coffee by now."

But I was coming to a rolling boil over the idea that Sam had not only stolen my car, but then stuck me with an escaped convict. Well, okay it was *only* Smollet, but still, it *was* Smollet, who smelled jailhouse funky and couldn't have given you a straight answer if his life depended on it.

"I'll kill that son of a bitch," I said through gritted teeth. But since he was already dead, that wasn't an option. "I wonder if I can get him exorcised. . . . Somewhere there's got to be an understanding priest, a witch doctor, maybe an extermi- nator. . . ." I was muttering to myself, but even Smollet could tell I was a tad perturbed.

"Sam tole me you might get upset. He says you get upset real easy," Smollet confided happily. "I said to him, I says, 'you know, Hollis is always been a real nice lady. She's always written me up real fair.' "

I threw him a thin smile; Smollet just brought out the mean- ness in me. "You don't know me as well as Sam does."

"Well, he seems like a real nice dude, and he likes you a whole lot. *He* don't think I killed Judge Fish," Smollet added piously.

"He doesn't, huh?" I was beginning to get the bigger picture here. Sam is perfectly capable, alive or dead, of dragging me into trouble. If he thought Smollet was about to be accused of a murder he didn't commit, Sam would have few qualms about helping him escape from custody, and even less con- science about involving me.

Also, it was beginning to dawn on me that Smollet didn't know that Sam was a ghost. If you ever saw the lovely and tal- ented Mrs. Smollet, you'd know our boy wasn't the most dis- cerning person on the Eastern Shore when it came to picking out his cohorts, but this was ridiculous, even for him. I toyed with the idea of wiping that stupid smile off Smollet's face by telling him he'd been taking advice from a dead man, but decided against it, for now.

The last thing I needed on my hands was a hysterical Bowley, especially one who had just escaped from jail. Believe me, a garden-variety Bowley is bad enough. In fact, the last thing I needed on my hands was anyone; I was due to meet Lenore Currier at Toby's in fifteen minutes and it was a twenty-minute ride.

I know, I know. There's real time and there's Eastern Shore time, which is about an hour later than you think it should be, but I like to be prompt when I'm interacting with murder suspects, don't you? On the other hand, if Friendly found out I'd been sheltering an escaped convict, I'd be in pretty serious trouble.

I pondered for only a second. The solution was obvious. I could dump Smollet off at Toby's and tell him he was on his own, and that would be that.

From Toby's, he could call some member of the Bowley clan who would come and get him and stash him away wherever they stashed fugitive Bowleys. Somehow, I had to get out of this mess Sam had gotten me into without implicating myself.

Thinking about what I could do to Sam, I informed Smollet of my plans. "And if you drag my name into it, I swear, Smollet, I'll track you down and deliver you to Miss Bertha myself."

"Well, I know Toby won't turn me in," he sniffed. "*Some* of them Beddoe's Island people are all right."

I chose not to reply to that as I bumped down the long lane to the road with my unwelcome passenger in the backseat.

"Smollet, why don't you just turn yourself in?" I finally asked.

"What? And spoil the fun?" he replied indignantly. "I can't wait to see what happens next!"

SIX

·

Lifestyles of the Poor
and Obscure

Did you ever wonder what would happen if you did things just a little differently? There's this theory that a butterfly flapping its wings in the Amazon Basin can ultimately be the cause of a huge tsunami on the Pacific Rim. The idea is that the smallest actions can have the most enormous repercussions.

To this day, I'm not entirely sure what would have happened if I'd just said to hell with it and gone back to bed. Probably my life would have been a lot easier.

But then again, maybe not.

Toby was just opening up the bar when I screeched into the parking lot. He barely raised an eyebrow when I pushed an escaped convict out of the car.

"You stay here till I get back," I commanded Smollet. "Toby, don't even think about letting him go anywhere!"

Before either of them could say anything I tore off down the road toward the harbor. I mean, I thought, if I can't trust Toby to harbor a fugitive, who *can* I trust? I put The Problem of Smollet on the back burner.

Cedar Cove isn't much of a harbor, as harbors go. The sheltered cove lies between the village and some open, marshy land that juts out into the Santimoke River. It's a dirty and gritty place designed for working bay craft, not pleasure boats. Most of the workboats tied up here are weatherbeaten and rust stained with years of hard use.

The single-dredge boat anchored up against the windward

leg was hogged and forlorn, her life almost over. The great days of working sail on the Chesapeake were coming to a close.

Artists and photographers who prowl the Shore in search of the charming and quaint are invariably disappointed with Cedar Cove. Lenore Currier certainly was. She was standing beside a Land Rover, cell phone in hand, eyeing an empty beer can blowing across the grungy asphalt toward the water as if it were an unchecked virus, which maybe it was.

Lenore's expensive L.L. Bean drag looked oddly out of sync here. "What a ghastly place," she said by way of greeting, with a disdainful look at a discarded clam rig. "Why don't they clean this place up for the tourists?"

"Why should they?" I asked, glancing down at her two-hundred-dollar imitation workboots. "The path out to Harry's is sort of marshy in spots." I threw my arm to leeward to indicate the overgrown rivershore.

"You mean someone actually lives out here?" she asked incredulously.

"Harry Truman does. When his shanty out on the point burned down, some of the guys from the fire department found him a trailer and brought it out to the lot. He still doesn't have any plumbing, though."

"Where exactly does this man live?" Lenore squinted around.

I pointed out toward the end of the leeward leg of the harbor, about five hundred yards away, where a lonely hammock of pines rose up from the marsh. In the chaos of greenbriar and rusting appliances, you could just make out the faded silver of Harry's ancient Airstream. Patches of disappearing snow added to the desolation. Laundry flapped disconsolately on the line. One thing, though: He had a great waterfront view of the Santimoke River and the bay. I wondered how he kept from freezing to death when the wind blew down the water from the northeast. A faint trail of smoke from the jury-rigged stovepipe announced that Harry was at home.

"Good Lord," Lenore breathed. Not, I suspected, entirely irreverently.

"Shall we?" I asked, gesturing toward the faint path through the marsh.

I'll give her this: She was game to pick her way over the sinking corduroy path, and never complained when those two-hundred-dollar boots sank into the mud up to the tongues. The wind spurted across the open marsh, and the snowcapped grass flowed in waves. The fire department boys had gotten a barge and a crane to place the trailer on the foundation of the burned-out house; Harry's little bit of high ground was disappearing into the Santimoke, eroded away by the steady coercion of wind, waves and the overabundant muskrat population.

I wouldn't want to be out here in a hurricane. One good flood would sweep that poor old trailer down the river and into the open bay, out toward the Atlantic. A mental picture of Harry and his trailer happily floating on the Gulf Stream toward Mexico made me grin.

"Mind you don't step in any open traps. Harry traps muskrats, you know." I'll also admit that I was playing this for all it was worth.

When we got to the edge of Harry's overgrown, littered wonder of a yard, I stopped her. "I'm going to call out. We have to let him know we're here," I said in my best Ramar-King-of-the-Jungle-Mighty-White-Hunter-Guide manner. "Otherwise he's likely to think we're government people and blast us out of here with a shotgun."

"Good Lord!" Lenore breathed.

"Harry! Harry Truman!" I called.

The only answer was the dry rustle of the wind in the pines and the dull chime of an ancient sheet of tin rhythmically brushing the side of a rusted-out car door. Abandoned appliances, old mattresses, barrels of aluminum cans, springs, car seats and unidentifiable bits and pieces of postindustrial stuff were gradually decomposing back into their component elements. The door of the plastic portable outhouse, half obscured by a pile of old tires, swung open and closed on the wind. A duck whirligig nailed to a corner of the trailer caught a wind current and started to flap; we both jumped.

Harry Truman was nothing if not a collector.

Just when I'd decided that Harry was out on the marsh checking his traps, a rotting curtain twitched in the window, then the door slowly opened a crack.

The old man in all his magnificence appeared in the doorway. And was, I might add, a sight to behold.

Harry Truman's wizened visage peered out at us between a baseball cap and several days of gray stubble, all of it stained with food and tobacco juice. His winter-river blue eyes regarded us without expression. Slowly, one paint-stained hand reached up to scratch his bulging stomach beneath a tattered undershirt. "Yew got any cigarettes, Hollis?" he asked, completely unsurprised to see me.

"Sure do, Harry," I reassured him. "And I have a lady here who wants to look at your decoys."

Now, there are some around the island who say Harry's a bit slow on the uptake and a slice of cheese short of a reality sandwich, but I've never known him to miss a trick when it comes to business.

"I don't have no decoys," he quavered, suddenly sounding old and helpless. "I don't know nothing about no decoys. I'm just a poor old man." He added, "She ain't from the welfare, or the tax people, is she?"

"She wants to buy some decoys, Harry," I called. "And she's not from Social Services or the 'Infernal' Revenue."

He nodded. "Well, why didn't you say so?" He was instantly restored to his former chipper self. Harry Truman's twin bugaboos were interfering social workers who might move him out of his trailer, and tax men who might try to take a chunk out of his meager trapping and crabbing income. Harry was of the old school, who believed in neither giving nor taking from government.

While I was musing on this, Lenore stepped forward. "Mr. Truman? My name is Lenore Currier. I'd like to see your decoys. Hollis tells me they're quite beautiful."

I hadn't said anything of the sort, but I watched Lenore cast her spell. It was the same magic she'd used to captivate Edgar Allan Crow. And like the black bird, Harry Truman seemed helpless in her hands.

The next thing I knew, we were inside Harry's trailer. Personally, I would have been happy to stay outside in the fresh air. Inside, it was dark and enclosed, triggering my uneasy claustrophobia. There was an overwhelming essence of unwashed human, stale whiskey, rotting food and paint thinner. Like Harry's yard, it seemed to be crammed with every manner of trash, but I picked out the tools of his trade: hatchets, knives, cans of rustproof paint, ragged brushes jammed into an ancient coffee can, a half-carved duck head held in a C-clamp on the edge of the aluminum dinette table. The vise shared space with unwashed plates, old newspapers, ragged clothing and stuff I felt it better not to contemplate too closely.

None of it seemed to bother Lenore Currier. With an unerring instinct, she pointed upward toward the plate rack, where a wood duck peered back down at us out of the gloom and the junk. As my eyes adjusted to the darkness, I saw other birds piled carelessly up there. A pintail hen, a mallard drake, a trumpeter swan. A hooded merganser stared out at us from beneath a pile of dishes; a goldeneye leaned crazily against a pair of boots. The whole room was filled with waterfowl decoys. It was like one of those drawings on the kid's page of the newspaper. "There are seventeen decoys in this picture; can you find them all?"

A pair of skinned muskrats lay in a plastic tub on the counter, their bright red flesh soaking in salt water. A future meal, to be cooked in the greasy cast-iron spider on the stove, I thought, even though the oven was belching out heat.

"You're just in time for lunch," Harry chuckled, gingerly leaning over to open the oven door.

"I don't think—" I started to say, but Lenore Currier's gasp cut me off at the pass.

From the oven, Harry withdrew a Canada goose. No, what I mean to say is that he withdrew a wooden Canada goose decoy. With a little chuckle, he knocked some dishes aside with his elbow and placed it triumphantly on the counter. "When she cools off, you'll see the nicest aging of that paint you ever did see on a decoy," he said to Lenore. I may as well have been invisible. It was just the two of them in that stifling trailer, the old man and the young woman bonding with the birds.

"So that's how it's done," Lenore said in tones of awe. "I didn't believe you could achieve that crazed finish with heat."

"Heat and cedar chips," Harry said proudly, stepping back to admire the effect of his work. "And, of course, a secret ingredient all my own." He smiled, revealing black gaps where his teeth used to be.

"Amazing." From her pocket Lenore withdrew a jeweler's loupe and examined the still-steaming bird closely. "Simply amazing. Why, if I didn't know better, I'd say this was an old Shang Wheeler decoy!"

"I was hopin' for Creighton Hooper," Harry Truman said. "When I was a boy, many's the hour I sat in his workshop, watchin' 'im and all th'other old men carve 'em birds and tell each other bigger and better lies."

Lenore stepped back as far as she could in the crowded room to examine the goose from a distance. Even in the dim light, she seemed to find it impressive. "Yes, yes, you're right. It *does* look like a Creighton Hooper. You've really captured the style of Hooper's heads. What's the body made from? Pine?"

"Old trapper's blocks, heart pine. You don't find no more heart pine, not since I was a boy; they logged it all away. I find 'em out on the marsh sometimes. From the olden, olden days, when they used to use them ole big blocks as deadfalls for trappin' muskrats. They get buried down in the mud, and they keep up real good."

"I'll say they do. Posthole beetles and brackish water are an unbeatable combination. You can fake a lot, but you cannot fake authentic aging of wood."

Behind her back, Harry Truman grinned, but he said nothing, merely winked at me. I knew for a fact that Harry had a trick or two up his sleeve that he'd take to the grave.

"That ain't nothing, compared to what I can do," he said, however. He disappeared behind a blanket hung in a doorway and reappeared with something in a cardboard box, which he placed square on the table. "Take a look at that, Missus."

Lenore leaned over the table and slowly put her hands into the box. Carefully, she withdrew a duck. "Oh, my God," she said. "This is a Scratch Wallace."

"Is it? Or did I carve it?" Harry asked her. He was not smiling now, just sucking in air between the gaps in his teeth.

"Oh, my God," Lenore Currier breathed. If she were holding the Holy Grail, she could not have been more reverent or look as awed as she did at that moment. "A Scratch Wallace canvasback."

She turned it over and examined the bottom. "The lead weight is certainly authentic," she pronounced. "And the initials are carved right into the bottom." She held it at arm's length. "The paint looks old and the colors are correct for the time period. Of course, I couldn't verify it without an X ray, but it looks like original paint. It is certainly in the style of Scratch Wallace. I'd have to say it *was* a Scratch Wallace, just looking at it."

"Yeah, but is it a real Scratch Wallace or one a mine?" Harry Truman repeated, chuckling.

The sound of a gunshot shattered Lenore's reply. Harry pitched forward, dragging the vinyl tablecloth with him. Plates, 'rats, tools and decoys tumbled to the floor. Glass eyes scattered across the filthy linoleum. Lenore clutched the decoy; I ducked for cover.

Judging by the string of innovative curses, Harry wasn't damaged. He sprang to his feet, surprisingly agile for an old guy, and headed out the door. "See what happens when I don't watch what I'm up to?" he cried, hustling out into the yard, where an oil drum was merrily spouting ten-foot flames into the cold air.

With a longer string of curses, Harry slapped a lid down on the flaming drum and held it there for several seconds while Lenore Currier and I hovered in the doorway trying to put the pieces of the scene together. Apparently there'd been some kind of explosion in the barrel.

After several seconds Harry cautiously removed the lid

from the drum, releasing a cloud of toxic-smelling smoke into the air. With a pair of tongs, he reached right down into the barrel and brought something out that looked like a badly charred roast of beef.

With a grunt, he plunged it into a tub of water. We could hear it hissing as he swished it vigorously around in the water.

Triumphantly, Harry held it up on the fork of the tongs. "I thought I'd left it in there too long when she blew up, but it's just about perfect!" he crowed.

"What is it? A new decoy?" Lenore asked.

Harry shook his head. "Lunch," he announced, and then I saw that it was another muskrat. A nuked muskrat, but a muskrat nonetheless. "You all like to stay to supper?"

I swallowed hard, but Lenore was made of sterner stuff. "What else do you have in that barrel?" she asked, hopping down the crumbling cement steps.

"Jes' some new bodies," Harry said. "I paint 'em and put 'em down in the ash to age 'em up." He slapped the blackened 'rat carcass on a dirty-looking plate that just happened to be lying there. "Sometimes, if I don't get to it right away, the chemicals in the paint blow right up."

"What do you use for paint—" Lenore peered into the smoking barrel.

"That there's my trade secret," Harry Truman gloated.

"Oh, you can tell me," she said. Or rather, she cooed.

"Awww," Harry demurred. I could have sworn he was blushing.

Oh, those two were just having a great time.

But Harry was not completely enthralled by Lenore Currier. In spite of all her blandishments, the Decoy Jamboree just didn't appeal to his finely tuned sense of larceny.

A while later we were sitting at the somewhat reorganized kitchen table. Harry had offered us beer, and since we figured there was nothing he could do to ruin something bottled in a nice clean brewery, we had accepted. I'd forgotten he had no electricity; the beer, cooled in the river, was ice cold. Harry drank Crab Orchard whiskey from a dingy plastic glass.

"Naw, you ain't gettin' me to that damn duck carnival," he said firmly.

"But think of the *accolades*," Lenore said.

Harry, cutting his scorched 'rat into bite-sized pieces with a buck knife and a plastic fork, spent some time gumming down his lunch. His side dish of canned sardines, eaten directly from the container, smelled oily and rank. He glared at us as he gummed, and there was lèse-majesté in those blue eyes.

"I'm thinkin' of all them ole carvers and hunters and watermen that made 'em there decoys in the olden times," he finally growled. "Now these here rich assholes buy 'em all up to set 'em up on the shelf and stare at 'em. That's all they can do, stare at 'em! Can't hunt no damn more! When I was a boy there was some ducks! The sky was black with 'em! Now, there ain't none left. Them damn rich people come in here and bought up all the damn land and closed off the water and ruint it for the birds. Ain't a duck left nowhere. And now the crabs and the oysters are goin', and ever'where there used to be open land there's houses and more damn houses. Used to be a man could roam where he wanted to roam, do what he wanted to do, put up a blind where he wanted, but now it's all No Trespassing and Posted and Keep Out! To hell with it."

Well, I could have corrected him on a few historical points, but what good would it have done? He was an old man; he was entitled to his worldview. Maybe he knew better than I did what it had been like when he was young and the Eastern Shore was an isolated backwater.

"Now they want our decoys. It's got so a man can't live off the land no more, 'cuz them rich sons a bitches got it all screwed up, ev'r which way. I lived off the land ever sinct I was a boy, just like my dad done, and his dad afore him, and I'm damned if I go in there now and suck up to these here foreigner sons a bitches! Let 'em buy all the damn decoys they can! And I'll keep on foolin' 'em all!" Harry gummed his blackened muskrat angrily.

"But I can make you rich and famous!" Lenore exclaimed. "It's the American dream!"

I truly believe that it was outside her ken that anyone should not want these things, since most Americans, myself included, hold that fantasy so dear.

"Then I guess I ain't every damn Amurrican!" Harry huffed. "What do I need with bein' rich and famous? I'm happy with what I got. Besides, I hate rich people!"

"You sound like a communist." Lenore sighed. She was feeling pretty frustrated by then. She'd been working on him for the better part of an hour.

"I ain't no damn communis'!" Harry growled truculently. He stabbed a piece of sardine to prove his point.

"I don't think that's what Lenore meant," I said quickly, just to smooth his feathers down. "I think what she meant to say was that—"

"I think Harry and I need to talk alone, if you don't mind," Lenore said to me meaningfully, so I took my beer and went outside.

The morning tide was going out, no doubt taking a little bit more of Harry Truman's precious high ground with it. I found an ancient enamel lawn chair down by the water and brushed the snow off the seat. Nursing my beer, I stared moodily out across the Santimoke toward the bay. The waters were gray and whipped with whitecaps. The wind had picked up, cutting through my coat, but I welcomed the fresh air after being stuffed into Harry Truman's malodorous Airstream.

Which is doubtless why I lit a cigarette. The better to contemplate nature. It's better seen through a nicotine haze.

After a while, Lenore came out of the trailer. She looked triumphant as she picked her way through the rusting traps and the cast-off hubcaps. "Well, I did it," she announced, with a toss of her blond hair. "Harry and his decoys are coming to Decoy Jamboree."

"How?" I asked.

Lenore smiled a small, sourly edged smile. "Everybody has a price," she said mysteriously. "You just need to find out what it is."

Before I could ask her what Harry Truman's was, she picked up an old bushel basket and emptied the junk out of it, right into the brown grass. "Help me carry some of his decoys to my Rover, will you? We haven't got a whole lot of time to get him and the birds into Watertown, and once I get him there, I've got more work to do." She looked at her watch. "I'll tell you this, Hollis. Discovering an unknown carver like Harry, an authentic primitive character, is going to make losing that Scratch Wallace goose look like nothing." She hoisted the bushel basket up on her shoulder. "It's quite fortunate that Fin Fish was killed," she said casually as she walked toward the trailer. "Harry Truman is even better than a Scratch Wallace!"

I was still pondering this remark while Lenore loaded an unprotesting Harry and two bushel baskets of decoys into her Land Rover down at the harbor.

"Really, Hollis, I can't thank you enough," she was saying as she fished her car keys out of her pocket, leaning out the window of her shiny Rover. "And if you want to drop by the Jamboree this evening to see the results of your labors, I'll leave your name at the door."

Normally, as I've said earlier, I'd rather spend an evening in hell than go anywhere near the duck carnival, but mindful of Friendly's admonition to keep an eye on the Decoy Queen, I agreed.

"Great!" she smiled. "We'll see you there. And if you want to bring a date, it's black tie. If anyone needs me, I can be reached at the Santimoke Inn!"

Her words hung in the air as she gunned the engine and peeled out of the parking lot. The last thing I saw was Harry Truman's stubbled face grinning at me as he rode away toward fame and fortune.

Dark suspicions about just what Harry's price might be crossed my mind. However, one of the maxims I live by is this: Some things are better left uncontemplated by humankind's fragile and precarious intellect.

Like what to do about Smollet Bowley.

I was pondering this as I headed back toward Toby's and pulled into the parking lot next to a lemon yellow Coupe de Ville just pulling out.

Which may have been why it took me a second or two to

realize that someone else had decided to solve this for me. As I glanced at the Cadillac, Smollet Bowley's face appeared in the passenger window. He waved happily out the window.

"Follow that car!" Sam yelled, suddenly materializing beside me. "She's kidnapped Smollet!"

SEVEN

•

Miz Fish and the Good Ole Boys' Network

As I watched, mouth hanging open, the bright yellow car peeled out of the parking lot and headed up the road toward the mainland. All I could see was Smollet and the top of some very small person's blue head above the steering wheel.

"What are you waiting for," Sam yelled. "Go after them! She's got Smollet!"

I floored the Honda and made for it.

It was not exactly what you might call a high-speed car chase; both of us were slowed down considerably by a Patamoke Seafood Cap'n Fike's Flash-Frozen Breaded Clam Strips truck heading to Watertown. On the two-lane blacktop that connects the island with the rest of the world, it's best not to be in a hurry, since the road blindly twists and curves all the way to town.

"What happened?" I demanded as I followed the yellow de Ville up the road at a heart-stopping forty miles an hour. "And what did you have to do with it? Do you know how much trouble I'm going to be in if Ormand Friendly finds out I have not only failed to turn Smollet in but allowed him to escape? I'll be toast! Jailed toast!"

"We were just sittin' there, having a nice friendly Bloody Mary, you know, Toby and me and Smollet and Scr—well, anyway, when this bluehead came in and took Smollet off with her."

"Bluehead?"

"You know, a white-haired lady with a blue rinse. A bluehead," Sam said impatiently. "She just came in, waved this little gun around—"

"She had a gun?"

"Holl, this is America. Everyone's armed and dangerous!" Sam said impatiently. "So, anyway, the bluehead asked which one was Smollet and when Toby said 'That one' she grabbed him by the ear and took off. She said she was going to liberate him!" Sam was grinning as he recounted this, which irritated me more than anything else he could have possibly done. Well, almost anything.

"What do you know about all of this?" I asked suspiciously.

"What do you think I know?" Sam asked innocently.

"Did you take my car into town last night and pick up Smollet?"

"Well, yeah, I did."

"Sam, have you lost your mind? Why?"

"Watch it, she's gonna turn right down Razor Strap Road," he exclaimed, neatly changing the subject.

Since she'd put on her signal about a year before she turned, this was unnecessary information, but I slowed down and followed her onto an even narrower back road that wound through old woods and open fields. If she knew I was right behind her, it didn't seem to faze her; she had slowed the eight-cylinder behemoth down to a snail's crawl. I couldn't have lost her unless I stopped and took a nap.

"Where is she going?" I wondered out loud. "She can't be a Bowley; none of them could afford a Caddy even if they stole it."

"Oh, I'm pretty sure she's not a Bowley," Sam breathed. He hunkered down in his seat and stared out the window at the passing landscape. "Looks like we might get some more snow," he remarked. "Look at those clouds over to the west there."

"Sam, Smollet thinks you're real-life," I said. "And I think you conned me into this mess. I don't know what you're up to this time, but, I'll tell you right now, I don't intend to—"

"Watch it, she's turning again!" Sam exclaimed with a great deal more excitement than the fact warranted, since once again, she had her turn signal on about half a century before she made a leisurely left down Red Toad Road.

"I think we're gonna end up down in Devanau County," I said. "The line's just over the Suicide Creek Bridge."

"Maybe so," Sam agreed. "Turn the heat up; it's a little chilly in here, don't you think?"

"How can a cold-blooded ghost get cold?" I asked, swinging along behind the Coupe de Ville as we moved in stately progression over the old wooden bridge that crossed Suicide Creek.

Sam had folded his long legs up on the dashboard and closed his eyes. Not a care in the world, that one. His eyes slowly closed, and a gentle, rhythmic breathing emanated from his ethereal chest.

"How can you sleep now?" I yelled, but he ignored me. I know he was just pretending; if he really wanted to avoid my wrath, he'd just discorporate. So I bounced along the back roads, following Smollet Bowley and a bluehead lady in a yellow monstermobile.

"It's a nice day for a car chase in slo-mo, and I have three quarters of a tank of gas and nothing else particularly pressing to do." I lit a cigarette, keeping the banana yellow car in sight.

"If they had a sign saying 'Smollet on Board' in the back window, it couldn't have been any easier to follow," Sam remarked sleepily. I pushed a tape into the deck and Cecilia Bartoli sang selections from *Cosi Fan Tutti*.

"So what happened with Lenore Currier?" he asked. "Did she confess?"

"Hell, no. She co-opted Harry Truman. Can you believe it? He's on his way to the Decoy Jamboree even as we speak."

"No shit!" Sam actually opened one eye for that one.

We drove on in unhurried silence for some minutes, twisting down long and winding roads. "I've never been back around here before," I said. "We must be somewhere near Bethel, but I don't know where exactly."

"She's going to turn left down that road there," Sam said suddenly. "Where the sign has that duck on it."

I saw what Sam was talking about; a big, ornately incised

house sign framing a mallard decoy hung from a post by the side of the road.

FISH

was incised in large, gold Chancery italic bold right above the bird. With a big, waddling dip of its wide rear end, the Cadillac turned into the drive.

"Sam, is this where Fin Fish lives?"

We followed the Fishmobile up the long oyster-shell lane flanked by twin rows of ancient Atlas cedars.

"Lived," Sam shot back.

"You don't think Fish is a ghost, do you?" I asked, even though I knew the answer. If Fish had come back as a ghost, he could tell us who done him in.

"You know it doesn't work that way," Sam replied priggishly. "The Rules state very clearly that that would be cheating."

The Rules. The Rules were the reason Sam was still here— something complicated and cosmic about the way he died and making amends for his many sins. Given Sam's past, I was probably going to be stuck with him for some time, according to The Rules as I understood them.

"Damn The Rules! I think you make them up as you go along, anyway. I think—"

What I thought didn't really matter, because we were in sight of the house now. It was just what I would have expected from chez Fish; big, colonial and white, fronting an isolated section of some picturesque backwater creek.

We pulled up behind the yellow Caddy in a hail of gravel.

"See ya later," Sam said cheerfully as he discorporated into a mist.

"Coward," I snarled, jumping out of the car.

Smollet had crawled out of the Cadillac and was assisting the tiny driver to alight. She was indeed a bluehead. In the cold winter sunlight, her feathered, carefully coiffed hair was a canescent sapphire. She was wearing a tailored camel's hair coat and the ineffable air of the prosperous upper-middle-

class matron. Both she and Smollet turned to look at me as I
ran toward them, my mouth open and ready to start asking
questions.

"It's all right, Hollis," Smollet said cheerfully. "Miz Fish
here wants to help me ex-cape to Brazil."

"That's absolutely correct, my dear," said Mrs., I mean,
Miz Fish. He was not a tall man, yet he loomed over her protectively, a ludicrous stringbean of a man in his stained and
bedraggled Twisted Sister tour jacket. "Smollet has done me
the favor of a lifetime by killing that swine I was married to
for forty years," she added mildly. "I think I owe it to him to
help him flee the country."

"But Smollet didn't, I mean he couldn't have killed your
husband—" I stammered.

"Miz Fish, I'd like to have a word with Hollis, if you don't
mind," Smollet interjected, with meaningful looks at me.

She smiled benevolently upon us, and patted his shoulder.
"Of course, Smollet. I'll go and make us some hot chocolate.
It's such a brisk day, a hot beverage should make us all feel
better." Miz Fish turned and walked into the house, leaving
me to face the man who was fast becoming my least favorite
escaped convict.

"For God's sake, Smollet, what the pluperfect hell are you
up to now?" I demanded.

"Aw, Hollis, I ain't up to nothin'," he whined. "I was just
settin' there with the boys at Toby's, and Miz Fish come in
and said she heard I was hiding out from the law there. Well,
at first, when she pulled out that gun—"

"She really did have a gun? My God, Smollet!"

"Well, she had a gun with her. Well, it weren't much of a
gun, just a little ole pearl-handled single shot, one a them
garter guns ladies used to have to avoid a fate worse than
death. Like you see in alla them ole movies with that actress
with the big eyebrows—"

"Okay, okay! So she walked into Toby's and she had a gun.
How did she know where you were?"

Watching Smollet's face mirror the inner workings of his
mind was an interesting experience, but one I had no patience

with right at this moment. "Okay, okay, we'll figure that out later. So what happened? She had the gun and then . . ."

"She looks around and she says, 'Which one of you is Smollet Bowley?' Well, I like to pee in my pants right there, but Toby just points to me and Sam starts to laugh—"

"*Sam?*" I replied in a truly awful voice. "Did she see Sam?"

"Well, I dunno, I mean it all happened so fast, yeah, him and Toby and this other guy Wally or Itchy or somethin', except he wasn't sayin' a whole lot, he was just settin' up in the corner and—"

"I might have known Sam was involved in this somehow." I stewed. I looked down the empty driveway at the last bit of melt dripping from the Atlas cedars. "Sam, I know you're here and I know you can hear me, and I just want you to know when I get my hands on you, I'm gonna kill you all over again!"

"Well, Jeez Louise, Hollis," Smollet said reproachfully. "There ain't no need to yell at *him*. He can't hear you, he ain't here! I mean, one look at Toby and you knew he was gonna drop for that sawed-off shotgun he keeps under the bar, so maybe I done the right thing."

I took a deep breath. I took several deep breaths. "Okay," I said slowly. "What happened then?"

"Well, Miz Fish, except I didn't know she was Miz Fish then, she says 'Smollet Bowley, you done killed my soon-to-be ex-husband two days before the divorce was final, and you done me the biggest favor a human bean could do for another. So, I am going to reward you by spiriting you off to Brazil where they don't have no extra diction treaty.' She says, 'In Brazil, you can live like a king on five dollars a day and they have some great beaches, so come with me.' Well, I wasn't gonna argue, gun or no gun, so's I got on my coat."

"What did Toby say?"

"He said that if Miz Fish was on the level, and he for one had no reason to believe that she weren't, then a man would be a fool to turn down the offer, and he wished he had offed the judge because he was a damn bad judge to begin with, and he,

Toby, would like to spend the rest of his life layin' on some
tropical beach with wimmen in string bikinis drinkin' rum out
of a coconut shell."

I smiled in spite of myself. Save for the gender in the string
bikinis, it did sound all right. "So, Toby advised you to take
Miz Fish up on her offer?"

"He said as far as he was concerned, he'd never seen me. I
guess what he meant was if the man come lookin' there for
me, he was gonna say he never seen me. But hell, ain't no one
on Beddoe's Island gonna tell the po-lice nuthin' anyway."
Smollet smiled beatifically at me, as if this explained it all.

Well, if you were from Beddoe's Island, it made sense.
Trust me on that one. Beddoe's Island settles its own problems. No one there likes interference from the law.

"And why does Miz Fish want you to go to Brazil?"

Smollet looked at me as if I were truly stupid. "Because she
thinks I killed her husband and she's grateful, so she wants me
to ex-cape! Aw, Hollis, come on, be a friend! This is my big
chance to go to Brazil! Hell, I ain't never been no further than
Baltimore before," Smollet pleaded. "An' that was just to testify before a grand jury, so I didn't get to see nothin' like
Harbor Place or Camden Yards or nothin'! I bet Brazil's a
hunnert times more excitin' than Baltimore!"

Smollet shook his head so hard, his greasy blond locks flew
back and forth. "But she thinks I killed her husband, and she's
grateful. Come on, Hollis, be a pal! It's a free trip to Brazil! I
wanna lay up on that tropical beach with a Bud Light and git
a tan!"

Larceny was never far from the surface with a Bowley.
Neither was rational thought. I threw up my hands. "I don't
know who's crazier, you or Miz Fish!" I exclaimed.

"It's you that's nuts, if you ast me," Smollet said sullenly.
"I'd like to see *you* turn down a free trip to Brazil. Anyway, by
the time spring comes and I come home, they'll have caught
the real murderer and my mother-in-law will be out of the
house. And," he added with a sudden happy thought, "the
duck carnival will be over!"

"The kettle's boiling, my dears," called Miz Fish cheerfully from the house. "And I've got some Pepperidge Farm cookies!"

It sounded like a good plan to me. I was not only confused, I was freezing.

Miz Fish bustled around a long pine-plank table, setting out mugs and cloth napkins. Both, I noted, featured waterfowl motifs. She made the real cocoa of my childhood, from the brown and silver Hershey's tin, heated with milk and sugar. It was a warm and pleasant room, large and low beamed, with a big window that looked out upon a frost-browned winter herb garden. A fountain in the middle, surmounted by a bronze mallard peering into the bowl, was dry and full of leaves. As I slowly defrosted, feeling warmth course back into my numbed toes and fingers, I began to note that the decor was very heavy on the waterfowl motif. In fact, it looked as if the Fishes' decorator had had a nervous breakdown at an Orvis outlet. Decoys patterned the wallpaper and the curtains. The tiles over the sink and the stove were painted with geese and ducks. Drawer pulls on the antique china cabinet, refrigerator magnets, potholders, all sported the winged waterbirds. The Canada goose and the mute swan roamed over the placemats on the table. A row of plates around the wainscoting displayed the aquatic aviana in full color and full flight.

When I happened to look up at the ceiling, my eye fell upon a wrought-iron wheel chandelier with stamped-out you-know-whats in flight all around the edge.

"Now that's a real man's art," Smollet breathed reverently.

"Yes, isn't it?" Miz Fish sighed as she passed the Pepperidge Farm Mint Milano cookies. "That's the first thing I mean to change." She stirred her cocoa with a spoon before sipping. "I've been looking at some of these Martha Stewart decorating books. I think I'll call the decorator just as soon as I can get the estate settled."

She gestured into the hallway and I turned to look at the series of decoys lining the walls, each on its own little shelf.

"The whole house is filled with them," Miz Fish remarked with distaste. "Of course, *he* wanted the ducks in the divorce, and the house, too. And because he was so connected, and so clever, he might have gotten them, too, along with everything else. I'm still finding out where he hid all his assets. My dear, I advise you never to marry a lawyer. They're bottom feeders of the worst ilk."

"Don't worry, Miz, I mean Mrs. Fish," I was able to say in absolute truth, "I never would."

"That reminds me of the time that my friend Snake Wingate got a divorce from his wife, down there in Wingo, Virginia," Smollet said around a mouthful of cookie. "Snake and his lawyer was standing in front of the courthouse after the hearin', and Tammi Wingate come around the corner in her little pink pickup and run right up on the curb toward 'em. When Snake an' his lawyer jumped back, Tammi threw 'at ole Toyota into reverse and screeched back toward 'em again. When it come up to Big Court, she said she was aimin' for Snake's lawyer, not Snake. When the judge asked for proof, Tammi stands up and says 'Well, Judge, everyone knows you don't back up and hit a snake twice!' "

Miz Fish let out a merry little tinkle of laughter. A sweet blush of color filled her wrinkled cheeks. "That's very good, Smollet dear. I shall have to tell that one to my bridge club! Have some more Mint Milanos."

I was trying to imagine her married to Fish and couldn't really see it. The poor dear, I thought, patting her hand. "It must have been utter hell for you, trapped in a marriage to an abusive man for all those years. What made you decide to finally get out? Was it a woman's group? Or did he finally just beat you up so badly you couldn't stand it anymore?" I asked sympathetically.

She blinked at me.

"Oh, no, my dear," Miz Fish said gently. "Findlay never laid a hand on me. He wouldn't dare! Why, he never even raised his voice!" Her tiny, fine-boned hand reached out and closed comfortingly around mine. "It was the decoys, dear. I finally told him, it was me or those damned, dead ducks. And Findlay chose the decoys."

Tears stood on her lashes and her lower lip trembled. "Can you imagine what it was like for forty years with those dreadful birds staring down at me from every nook and cranny in this house? I thought it would drive me mad! Every time I turned around, he'd buy another one. He was obsessed with them! He was spending our retirement money on those stupid, stupid birds!" She turned and beamed at Smollet. "So, when I announced I was getting a divorce, he starting hiding the assets, our assets. And he would have gotten away with it, too, if dear Smollet hadn't bashed his head in with that awful Scratch Wallace thing! That's where he was hiding his assets. In those awful decoys. He was cashing in all our stocks and bonds and putting the money into more birds! He thought I was too much of a silly woman to realize what he was up to, but I knew!"

My fantasies of a domestic-violence victim's life for Miz Fin Fish seemed to have been popped. I sat there with my mouth open, for once in my life, utterly speechless.

"When yew ass-ume, yew make an ass of yew 'n' me," Smollet snickered, but I kicked him under the table, so he shut up and consoled himself with another cookie.

"Was there another woman? Was he running around with Lenore Currier?" I tried a new tack.

"That little blond girl? Ha! If only it were so! No mere human woman could compete with Fin's lust for ducks," Miz Fish said, pouring cocoa from a Chinese export porcelain chocolate pot featuring an Asian Baikal teal drake. "I wish he had drunk or chased women or gambled or something the average male does, forgive me Smollet."

"No offense taken," Smollet replied cheerfully, pouring his cocoa into his saucer and blowing on it. "I done alla them things before I found religion."

"Where did you lose it?" I asked nastily, then felt bad because Smollet gave me such a wounded look.

"I belong to the First Church of Elvis, over to Slaughter's Crossroads," Smollet said in mawkish tones.

"No, Findlay had to be a collector," Miz Fish continued, oblivious. "Fin ate, slept, breathed decoys, don't you know? That was all he thought about. The children and I may as well have not existed. Decoys, decoys, decoys!" She suddenly broke off and peered at me. "Aren't you Hollis Ball?"

"From the Beddoe's Island Balls," I countered defensively.

She nodded thoughtfully. "But, my dear, weren't you a Wescott? Weren't you married to H. P. Wescott's poor dead son? The one who blew up in that terrible sailboat accident?"

Well, I didn't know about poor and dead, but as to the rest, I said, "I'm afraid so, Miz Fish."

"You know, I'm a Daughter of Historical Devanau. And your sister-in-law is Claire Wescott Dupont, president of the Daughters of Historical Santimoke, isn't she?"

I agreed warily and sipped at my cocoa, not certain where all this was going. My former sister-in-law gives fresh depth and dimension to the word *bitch*.

Miz Fish, having established my credentials by marriage, nodded. "And you were the one who wrote all those things about Fin when he sentenced that man to six months in jail when he killed his wife?" She regarded me without expression.

"Yes," I said. I had no idea where this was going, but I was prepared to defend myself to the death.

"Why didn't you call me? I could have told you why he gave that terrible man such a short sentence. Harmon Sneed collected decoys. Although, of course, nowhere in Fin's league, but then, who was? They're a fraternity, my dear, these decoy collectors."

"Fish gave Harmon Sneed six months in jail because the guy was a fellow decoy collector? Are you serious?" My eyebrows were up in my hairline, I'm sure. Could anyone be that fatuous? A collector could, I answered my own question.

"If only you'd asked me, dear, I could have set you straight," Miz Fish said matter-of-factly. "Of course, then the man got out of jail and murdered that teenager, that Tiffany Crystal child. What were her parents thinking of when they named her that, do you know? She sounds like a bridal registry! Terrible! Well, young and silly is trouble looking for a place to happen, as my mother used to say, but I really don't think one should have to die for it, do you? I suppose Mr.

Sneed will be away for quite a while now. Fin was, of course, utterly unrepentant. The idea that he could be wrong about *anything* was totally foreign to him." She shook her head sadly. "More cocoa? Yours looks like it needs to be warmed, Smollet. Have some more Mint Milanos. You know, the last thing I was expecting last night when I came home from my bridge club was a policeman on the doorstep, telling me someone had done Fin in with a decoy!"

She sipped her chocolate delicately. "Fin *was* a terrible judge," she confided. "Of course, in Devanau County, who noticed? It's all a part of the good old boy network. He was, after all, a Fish." Her mild eyes scanned my face. "I couldn't find a decent local lawyer to take my divorce. They're all friends of Fish, you know, or terrified of him. So, of course, he was going to get away with everything. It's the code of the good old boys network. He even wanted my grandmother's silver, and that, as you can see, is repoussé. It's Old English Rose, and heavy, too, not like that hollow-handled stuff young brides order these days."

Looking down at my spoon, I could see that it was indeed Old English Rose. In Miz Fish's world, as in my mother's, your ancestral silver is not only everything, it's the only thing always passed down in the female line. If Fish had tried to rip off his wife's great-grandmother's silver, she could have drilled him at high noon in the center of Bethel and no jury of Shorewomen would convict. But apparently, her bridge club gave her an alibi. I was grateful she'd volunteered the information. Somehow, asking her where she was last night while Fish was getting conked on the judicial head seemed rather tacky, even for me.

While I was considering all this, Miz Fish beamed. "But Smollet saved me from all of that, didn't you, dear?"

Smollet beamed. There were crumbs in his teeth and a smudge of chocolate on his chin. "Yes ma'am, Miz Fish," he said agreeably. "And I sure do want to go to Brazil, too."

"And we're going to work on that, aren't we?" she returned. As if she had suddenly realized that I was there, she turned and looked at me. "Hollis, dear, I really hope you won't feel constrained to report this to law enforcement. After all, you wrote so . . . well, indignantly, about Fin and Harmon Sneed—such an unspeakable man, I couldn't agree with you more about Fin's utter stupidity—so I just can't imagine that you'd be devastated if Smollet went away to a nice, warm country—"

The two of them smiled at me brightly.

I wondered if they were both on Prozac.

I was about to reply that as far as I was concerned, I didn't care what they did, but I needed to find out who killed Fish by Monday morning deadline. Happily, I kept my mouth shut.

And right now, Miz Fish was looking like she had motive aplenty. But I just couldn't see her hoisting a decoy with enough force to cave in the back of her husband's skull. Poisoning his cocoa, now . . . I pushed my cup away.

Just then, Smollet Bowley's pointy little ears pricked right up. "Is that a car?" he asked, pushing himself away from the table with the palms of his hands, looking around as if he expected a SWAT team to break down the door.

Neither Miz Fish nor I had heard a thing, but she rose. Smoothing down her pearls and the back of her Fair Isle sweater, she looked out the window. "Oh, for heaven's sake," she said, "It's just Frosty Froston." She frowned. "The decoy grapevine must be in high gear; he's quite a collector, don't you know."

"Maybe Smollet and I ought to disappear," I suggested, while my faithful escaped-convict companion nodded violently.

Miz Fish beamed. "What a good idea! We really don't want Dr. Froston to see you here. It could really spike our Brazil plans. Surgeons are so gossipy, don't you know, and he's chief of staff at Bethel Memorial Hospital. I volunteer there, don't you know." She waved us toward the stairs. "Go on up there and look in the second bedroom on the right. My son Chipper was about your size, Smollet. I'm sure you can find a change of clothes up there. Since he joined the Hare Krishnas, all he wears is those silly peach sheets, so he won't miss anything." She wrinkled her nose. "Besides, Smollet, you could really use a shower, if you don't mind me saying so, dear." Miz Fish's talent for understatement was a marvel to me.

As we were moving toward the stairs, the sound of quacking ducks filled the house. "Frosty's ringing the doorbell now," Miz Fish said, waving us up the back staircase. "You run along and I'll let you know when the coast is clear. Oh, this is so much fun!"

"I'm glad she thinks so," Smollet growled as we headed up the narrow, twisting staircase. "All I wanna do is git to those warm Brazilian beaches!"

While he occupied himself looking through the absent Chipper's closets, grumbling about the Fish scion's conservative tastes in gentleman's furnishings, I leaned over the stairwell and spied on the goings-on below the stairs.

A very large, very middle-aged man in a tweed hat stood in the hallway, radiating insincere concern as he rubbed his gloved hands together. Looking down, I thought he resembled no one so much as Sydney Greenstreet, if the late actor had run through Eddie Bauer with a magnet.

Then I realized that I had seen him before. I just couldn't remember where.

"Ah, Caroline!" he boomed in a voice so loud the bas-relief flying geese on the wall shook. "We were at the Decoy Jamboree cocktail party and we just heard the terrible, terrible news this morning! So sad about it all, and such a mess, too. Most dreadful, I heard! Poor old Fin! Marjorie wanted me to drop by and bring you one of her stringbean, mushroom soup and Durkee's onion ring casseroles . . . and ask if there's anything we can do . . . anything at all. Say, isn't that a new pair of fulvous whistling ducks? They look like they might be Cigar Daisy's. . . ." Shoving the casserole dish at Miz Fish, the big man crossed the room to peer through thick glasses at a matched set of decoys on the hall table. "Magnificent! Simply magnificent! Look at the carving on those heads! Do you mind if I just pick this one up and look at it?" Without waiting for Miz Fish's assent, he picked the duck up and flipped it over to study the signature on the flat bottom. From some inner pocket of his tan field coat, he whipped out a magnifying glass and proceeded to study the bird micrometer by micrometer, making little, delighted sounds in the back of his throat. "Yas. Um-hum, yas . . . ," he hummed while Miz Fish stood by holding the casserole dish, all but forgotten. "Mmmmm hmmmm, yas . . . yas! Yas, interesting. Very interesting! Look at that comb work! What detail! Magnificent! Truly magnificent."

She wouldn't have to tell me he was a collector. Even from afar, I could sense the obsession, feel the twanging vibration of covetousness, watch his hands start to shake with excitement and his expression grow distant and glassy. Froston was emanating collector's lust like a room deodorizer.

"It's very nice of you to stop by, Frosty, and you will thank Marjorie for me, won't you? Unfortunately, I have so many things to do right now that I can't really stop to visit. . . ." Miz Fish might as well have been talking to a brick wall. Froston had cradled the duck in the crook of his arm and was now looking at its mate. "As nice a pair of decoys as you'd ever want to see," he was wheezing. "Almost as fine as those Corb Reef surf scoters he bought last July . . ." He looked up over his glasses at Miz Fish with a vulpine gaze. "Now, Caroline, it's a fact that you don't want these birds, so I'd like you to think about selling them to me. You know I'd offer you a good price for the lot . . . especially the Scratch Wallace!"

"I'm sure you would, Frosty," Miz Fish replied with commendable politesse, "but that nice policeman told me that the Scratch Wallace decoy was the murder weapon."

Dr. Froston clutched at his heart. Well, actually, he gathered up a great deal of coat in his thick fingers. "It didn't hurt the decoy, did it?" he breathed.

"I really don't know," Miz Fish replied dryly. "You'd have to ask that nice Detective Sergeant Friendly, who's in charge of the case. I sincerely hope so!"

"Caroline, this is not a joking matter! Scratch Wallace decoys are pearls beyond price!" Frosty Froston gasped, as if she had committed blasphemy, which maybe she had. At least by his lights. "There are only eight known Scratch Wallace birds, and that was the only one still in local hands!"

"Oh, I know what Fin paid for it, don't you worry," Miz Fish replied briskly.

"Dear Lord, what madman would use a Scratch Wallace to bash in a heavy object like Fin's head?" Frosty Froston fretted. "The damage could be incalculable! Why, that could bring the price of the bird down to five figures!"

"My feelings exactly," Miz Fish snapped.

"Oh, Caroline, don't tell me they picked it up by the neck?" he asked in tones of abject horror. "If they broke the head off—" Froston shuddered at the thought. "Imagine! Abusing a Scratch Wallace!"

"Well, I really don't know how broken up it is and what's more I didn't ask. The deed was done, that was all I cared about," Miz Fish said briskly. "Now, if you'll excuse me, Frosty, this *is* a house of mourning. . . ."

But Dr. Froston sank dramatically into a chair. "A couple of hysterectomies, that's all it would have cost," he groaned. "Why, oh why did I hesitate when Lenore Currier told me there was a Scratch Wallace on the market? Imagine, it's been handled by . . . by a philistine! Splintered! Paint ruined with blood! You can never get blood and brain out of something as porous as old wood!" He choked. "Caroline, I am not well. A Scratch Wallace, manhandled like that! Dear Lord, is nothing sacred?"

"Apparently not," Miz Fish replied cheerfully. "Now, Frosty, if you don't mind, I've really, really got to—"

At that moment, there was more quacking.

"Now what?" Miz Fish said, unceremoniously slamming the casserole dish on the hall table. Several decoys bounced and one wobbled on its perch. Frosty made a good save, still cradling the whistling duck protectively in his arms.

Miz Fish made a *tsk*ing sound in her throat. "It's Loop Gareau! Now whatever can he want?" she asked as she opened the door.

"Caroline!" A short, dark man with a lean, funereal aspect

appeared in the doorway, bearing a foil-covered cake plate. I knew him, too. But from where?

"I just came from the Decoy Jamboree! We heard the terrible news that Fin passed on last night and—" He stopped, staring balefully at Dr. Froston. "You!" he snarled. "I might have known that you'd be here. I thought that was your car in the drive!"

The new mourner was small, beyond thin and well into cadaverous. His dark overcoat hung on his bony shoulders as if he were a coat hanger; his smile was a rictus. "Barbara sent me over with a coconut cake and our condolences. . . ." His small black eyes roamed the room, scrutinizing the decoys.

"Good morning, Loop," Miz Fish said without much enthusiasm.

"Loop Gareau! You damned buzzard, you're too late!" Frosty Froston said bitterly. "Someone used the Scratch Wallace to kill Fin!"

The short man drew back a pace. What color there was drained from his face. "Did it hurt the decoy?" he demanded. "Damn it, man! Speak up! *Did it hurt the Scratch Wallace?*"

It must be nice, I thought, peering down into the hallway, to have such concerned friends. It was a good thing Fish was dead; this might have put a hurting on his ego.

Speaking of ghosts, I turned to see Sam standing beside me. He was also watching the business in the hallway.

"Weren't those two guys hanging around the courthouse last night?" he asked.

I turned to look at him. "That's where I saw them—" I started to say, but he put a finger to his lips. We silently listened as Miz Fish patiently reiterated that the decoy had been used to bludgeon her late and unlamented husband to death and, no, she had no idea how much damage the decoy had sustained.

"Someone-used-a-priceless-Scratch-Wallace-decoy-as-a-weapon?" Loop Gareau hissed.

"Don't tell me you're letting Loop Gareau act as your estate lawyer, Caroline!" Froston sputtered. "Why, he'll rob you blind! You know all he wants is to get his hands on Fin's decoys!" Still cradling the whistling duck, he glared at the other man.

"Oh, for God's sake, Frosty! Be a man!" Loop Gareau snapped. "And put that bird down! The oil in your skin will ruin the paint! Good Lord, Caroline, are you *sure* it was the Scratch Wallace?"

"I'm not using Loop as my probate attorney, and for heaven's sake, will the pair of you stop whining about that decoy?" Miz Fish asked reasonably.

"I know why Froston's here!" Loop Gareau growled. "He wants to buy Fin's decoy collection! What's he offered you, Caroline? Whatever it is, you can be sure it's not what it's really worth! Oh, he'll try to cheat you, all right! Whatever he offers, I'll double it, no, I'll triple it! I *must* have Fin's birds! I must!"

"You liar! I was prepared to offer Caroline a good price! Very damn good! You shouldn't even consider letting Loop touch a tailfeather of them, Caroline! He isn't worthy!"

"Worthy? Worthy? I'd like to see you own some of the birds I have! Oh, you'd give your eyeteeth for my Elmer Crowell king eiders, wouldn't you?"

"You might have beaten me out on those John Blair cinnamon teals, but you won't get Fin's collection. And lay your hands off that there Harry Jobes or I'll sue you for assault!" Loop Gareau fizzed as he reached for the decoy cradled in Frosty Froston's arms. When he was excited, his sibilants grew more pronounced. He sounded like an angry blacksnake.

"Harry Jobes? Harry Jobes? This is a Cigar Daisy, you idiot! You heard him threaten me, Caroline!" Frosty roared, jumping back. "You wouldn't sell up those birds to a pissant like Loop! It would be an insult to Fin's memory!"

"Unhand that duck, you, you butcher!" Loop howled, reaching out again to grab the decoy away from Frosty. Collector's lust shone from him like a cheap cologne. Too bad there's no twelve-step program for decoy collectors; these two could have used it.

The two men struggled for a moment while Miz Fish looked on, making little sounds of distress in the back of her throat. It looked like Frosty was going to win; Gareau had the disadvantage of holding a cake plate.

"Arggggh!" True to his attorney's instincts, he used his weakness as a weapon and hurled the cake at Frosty's face. The foil worked loose and butter-cream coconut icing and yellow cake flew everywhere, but mostly all over Frosty Froston, M.D., F.A.C.S., who howled with rage, but still clutched the duck to his ample chest.

"Wow," Sam whispered admiringly, "I haven't see a brawl like that since Douglas Southall Freeman and Bruce Catton got into it over the length of Robert E. Lee's beard a couple of months ago! Lee himself had to settle it by getting his whiskers measured and—"

"Stop it!" Miz Fish was saying angrily. "Stop it right now!"

I was ready to go down and break it up, but Miz Fish was not the frail flower you might have thought. She picked up that stringbean casserole dish and dumped the semifrozen contents on the combatants. Something had to give, and it did. The effect was similar to turning a hose on fighting dogs. The surgeon and the lawyer jumped apart.

The trouble was, the whistling duck jumped apart, too. The head of the duck separated from the body, and both parts, loosened by the greedy grips of the doctor and the lawyer, flew across the room in a rain of cake and casserole, collectors still attached.

Froston had the body, but Gareau had the head.

"Now, see what you've done, you damned fool!" Froston roared, wiping icy cream of mushroom soup off his glasses. "You've broken the head off!"

"And you'll pay for the repairs, you moron! I'll sue you until your teeth rattle!"

"Don't lawyer me, Loop! I'll personally see to it that you're taken off the Jamboree Committee! Expunged! Erased!"

"And speaking of sponges, you malpracticing sot, who left one in that old woman's stomach last December, hey?" Gareau spat stringbeans. "I'll have your hospital privileges revoked!"

"You and what army, you courthouse barnacle?" Froston

retorted. "You call those few pathetic blocks of wood over in your house a decoy collection? Why, you wouldn't know an Umbrella Watson from a Ben Holmes if it snuck up from behind and bit you on the ass!"

"Everybody and their mother knows you can't tell a gadwall from a mallard!" Gareau retorted, picking an onion ring from his dripping vest pocket. He took a deep breath and hissed, "What's more, *everyone* knows that half your birds are forgeries!"

Those must have been fighting words. Dr. Froston pulled himself up to his full height and puffed out his chest. He opened and closed his mouth several times, nonplussed. In lieu of speech, he waved the body of the duck in the direction of Loop.

To his credit, Gareau held his ground; he glared at Froston, jaw outthrust, the decoy head clutched defensively in his hand.

"If there are fakes around, then they're in your collection, not mine!" Froston yelled, finding his words again. "At least they were until you realized you'd been fooled and started passing them off to others as the real thing!"

"Are you accusing me of duplicity?"

"I'm not accusing you, I'm telling you what I know! You're the one who auctioned off those fake Ira Hudson redheads at the Jamboree last year! Fakes! Fakes! Fakes! I put them on the X-ray machine at the hospital and debunked them! Fakes!"

"You were the one who did that? You moron! You don't know what you're talking about!" Gareau squealed. "They were the real Hudsons! Are you telling me I don't know a real bird from a reproduction? Me?"

"I'm calling you a con artist and a thief! Lawyer this, Loop!" Froston raised the middle finger of the hand not clutching the decoy at Gareau.

Just then, Smollet, wrapped none too appealingly in a towel, appeared in the doorway of the bedroom "Hey!" he yelled. "Where's the shampoo?"

"Out! Out!" Miz Fish shouted. When ruffled up, she had a big voice for such a tiny woman. "My . . . my son's here, and if you don't get out, I'll have him come down and escort you

out. Now, leave, both of you! Ghouls! Fin's still on the mortuary slab and you're fighting over his decoys. I wouldn't sell them to either one of you for all the tea in China after this display! Shame on both of you! *Out! And I mean right now!*"

She threw open the door and pointed down the driveway.

To my surprise, the doctor and the lawyer slumped like a pair of naughty fifth-graders. As she pointed angrily toward the door, they grinned sheepishly and shuffled outside. Miz Fish slammed the door and leaned against it, breathing hard.

"That was a close call." She sighed.

Still, you could hear them spatting all the way down the driveway, doubtless trailing stringbeans, butter-cream coconut icing and onion rings behind them.

The head and body of the poor decapitated decoy lay abandoned on the table.

"I swear," Miz Fish sighed, looking at the mess on the floor. "I ought to donate the whole collection to charity!"

It was while she and I were mopping up the hallway that I had my brilliant idea. "You know there will be more people coming," I pointed out, swabbing the floor with a mop. "And your children will be coming home, too. You can't hide Smollet here."

"Well, Lisa's in the Antarctic with a National Geographic expedition looking at some Russian lake or something. As far as you can get from phone and fax and heaven knows when they'll return to base camp. I left a message but it may be weeks before her team returns and possibly more weeks before she can come home." As she mopped up blobs of cake, she sighed. "And of course, Chipper's with the Hare Krishnas, and almost impossible to reach, but I did leave a message at the ashram in West Virginia. They said he might not be able to call back for a week, that he was between airports. Not, I suppose, that either child will be heartbroken. Fin was not a prime candidate for 'father of the year.' Parenting took time away from his decoys." She wrung out a rag in a bucket. "Drat the man! He's as inconvenient dead as he was alive!"

It was at that moment that my brilliant idea struck me. "Miz Fish, does Chipper have a shaved head?"

"I suppose so. He did the last time I saw him. He was chanting in the terminal at BWI." She looked up, brushing a stray wisp of blue hair away from her forehead. "Why, dear?"

I sat back on the steps and lit a cigarette, flicking the ashes into a brass goose ashtray. "Well, if no one's seen him in a while, and it seems like they haven't, all they'd be expecting to see would be a shaved head and a peach-colored sheet, right?"

Miz Fish nodded.

"Well, we don't have a peach-colored sheet, but suppose we shaved Smollet's head . . . ," I whispered evilly.

"Hide in plain sight!" she exclaimed.

Smollet, as you can imagine, had other ideas about having his long, lank blond tresses shaved off, and was quite free about vocalizing his objections.

"I been growin' my hair sinct I dropped outta high school! It look just like Tommy Lee now and you wanna shave it all off!" he howled.

But I more or less held him down on a kitchen stool while Miz Fish made for him with the electric shears. "I used to clip the dog before poor old Whiskey finally died," she said cheerfully, but I don't think that made Smollet feel any happier. At least he smelled better since his shower.

As his thin locks fell on the newspaper beneath his stool (the *Bethel Call*, I was interested to note, not the *Watertown Gazette*) he mournfully sniffled.

"I look like a damn skinhead!" Smollet whined. "What would my family say if they saw me now?"

"They wouldn't recognize you, which is precisely the point," I said.

And it was true. With his shiny new shaven head, attired in Bajwhan Projabawah "Chipper" Fish's old chinos, broadcloth shirt and crew sweater, Smollet had a whole new image. He could indeed pass as a son of the Fishes, recently deprogrammed from Krishna and reprogrammed into Calvin Klein. "You actually don't look too bad, for a Bowley. Which is to say, you look like you could walk erect and communicate in sophisticated grunts," I told him while he studied himself in the mirror in the downstairs bathroom. "Just don't open your mouth and all will be well where the gene pool meets the cement pond." Actually he looked like a skinny plucked chicken, but I wasn't going to be the bearer of bad news.

"The cement pond!" Miz Fish exclaimed. "Of course! I can put Smollet in the pool house and he can guard the ducks. Come with me, my dears."

She draped her coat over her shoulders and led us outside. Smollet was still grumbling under his breath about the loss of his heavy metal hairdo.

On the other side of the brown, barren garden, down beside the creek, a small glass-and-brick building was nestled amid the boxwoods.

"Yew din' hafta cut my hairs so I could hide in the shed," Smollet growled, rubbing his bald pate as we halted before the building in question, which was anything but a shed.

Using a key she had withdrawn from her pocket, Miz Fish unlocked a heavy wooden door. The overwhelming smell of swimming pool—chlorine and mildew, heat and humidity, old towels and rubber flip-flops—assailed our noses from the dim interior. It was so unexpected, so out of context, that I felt a momentary stab of confusion.

"You gotta see this," Sam whispered into my ear. He had materialized beside me in a mist. "It's amazing."

I held a finger to my lips and shook my head. Sam faded into the shadows, so only I could sense his presence.

Outside, it was winter. Inside, it was summer.

Miz Fish flipped some switches and light flooded the room. We saw a good-sized swimming pool, as blue and steamy as a David Hockney painting. She flipped some more switches, and with a distant humming sound, the blinds that had been used to shut out the world slowly rolled toward the ceiling, exposing long, high glass walls and a glassed-in ceiling, all framed in exposed wooden beam.

The walls were filled with horizontal narrow wooden shelves, and the shelves were jammed and packed with carved birds. I'd never seen so many kinds of bird in my life. There must have been at least a thousand of them. Probably more.

Loons, grebes, herons, auks, puffins, geese, swans, rails, crakes, hawks, falcons, plovers, terns, ducks, songbirds, crows, quail, even a woodpecker or two and at least one huge horned owl—they were all around the room, all positioned on their shelves. Wood, canvas, cork, ivory, feather, clay, plastic, rubber, every species, every medium, every carver, every culture must have been represented in that collection. I'd seen some decoys, being Perk Ball's kid and all of that, but I'd never seen anything remotely like this assembly, even in a museum. When I looked up, I saw more, suspended on monofilament from the beams in the ceiling. It was like being in an aviary of dead ducks.

"It looks like the inside of Roger Tory Peterson's head," Sam commented, while I tried to ignore him and stifle an unexpected giggle.

"This," Miz Fish said, oblivious to Sam's ghostly cracks, "is the main body of Fin's collection. The jewels in his night crown heron, one might say. He used to like to come out here and float the working decoys in the pool. Rather like a small boy playing with his rubber ducky." She walked across the tile toward the back of the building, the heels of her low pumps making a hollow, clicking sound on the tiles. "There's a small guest house back here, with a bedroom, bath, and a wet bar and kitchen," she said, throwing open doors and turning on lights. Her voice echoed against the vaulted ceiling. "I think Smollet would be quite comfortable here, don't you, Hollis? And he can keep an eye on the decoys. I wouldn't put it past Loop and Frosty to try to sneak in here in the middle of the night to try and make off with some of the birds—they're that mad about collecting. Many of them are quite rare, you know. The decoys I mean, not Frosty and Loop."

But Smollet and I were still in the doorway, unable to move. Both of us stood there with our mouths open, just staring at the birds. I know I'd never seen anything like it, and I'd bet the farm Smollet's experience was even more limited than mine. Dark avian shapes, still and eerily silhouetted against the pale winter sky, the birds seemed to be looking mockingly back at us. That Hitchcock film flickered through my mind. I had a momentary vision of all those decoys coming to life and attacking us in revenge for human hunting of their real-life counterparts. I closed my eyes and shuddered. It was just too weird, even for my perverted little mind.

"Wow," Sam breathed reverently, as he faded to nothingness. "Art Ducko!"

EIGHT

•

Scratch Wallace Gets a Clue

The devil, they say, is in the details. Happily, I'm more of a big-picture person. You'd think that would put me on the side of the angels, wouldn't you?

Wouldn't you?

Having forced Smollet to give his word, for what it was worth, that he wouldn't try to rip off Miz Fish, or open his mouth in front of any visiting mourners and expose his true identity with his atrocious English, I left our favorite escaped criminal and the merry widow to entertain each other while they opened up the guest cottage, or as Miz Fish happily called it, "Smollet's Hideout, just like in a Western!"

Munching a Mint Milano, I climbed into the car, changed the tape to the Five Blind Boys singing "The Rough Side of the Mountain," lit a cigarette and waited for Sam to materialize with an explanation.

"I know you're going to chew me out for dragging you into this mess" was the first thing he said when he corporated into the passenger seat. "It's a wise ghost who knows when to stay disappeared, but here I am."

Before I could start in, he narrowed his eyes, glaring at me. "What's this business between you and that Friendly guy?" he asked.

"Whatever it is, it's none of your business," I replied, momentarily thrown off course.

"It's my business because your health and well-being are my business; that's why I'm a ghost, remember? Are you really gonna go out with him?"

I looked straight ahead. "He's asked me and I've said no." *So far* I thought but did not say aloud.

"You don't want to get involved with a cop," Sam offered shortly. "I'll bet he's got a babe in every town."

"Right now, I don't want to get involved with anyone," I replied primly.

"Yeah, that's what you say."

Time to change the subject. Neither of us was going to give an inch, and it wasn't getting us anywhere with the Fish thing.

"Art Ducko!" Shaking my head, I drove the Honda out of Devanau County and back across Suicide Bridge, toward home and my comfort zone. Just when I'm ready to kill Sam all over again, he says or does something so funny I forget to be mad at him. "What's this really all about, Sam?" I asked in a more reasonable frame of mind.

"Rescuing Smollet from himself, if nothing else. I don't think he did it, Hollis," Sam murmured thoughtfully.

"I'm at least sure about that. It's just that murder isn't Smollet's thing. He's bad, but he's not evil. Did you tell him to walk away from the jail, Sam?"

"Well, I don't think he did it, and I think your cop pal would like to pin it on him. We've temporarily solved The Problem of Smollet," Sam shifted breezily. "Neither of us thinks he did it. So who did? Turn what's left of your mind to considering Miz Caroline Fish, Dr. Frosty Froston, M.D., and Loop Gareau, attorney at law. Knowing the whereabouts of any of the above last night would be interesting."

He settled airily down on the surface of the seat, so transparent that I could see the flat and empty fields through his profile. "Miz Fish is a lovely woman, one of those iron butterflies that women of a certain age become in the South, don't you think? She says she was playing bridge, and we'll assume your pal Friendly is checking her story."

I chose to ignore that swipe at Friendly. "I could have called my journalistic colleagues at the *Bethel Call* and learned some little-known facts about well-known people that would never see the light of print, libel suits being what they are," I mused. "But, in return, I would have had to give them at least some of the straight poop on the untimely demise of the Honorable Findlay S. Fish. Professional courtesy. However, much as I like my colleagues at the *Call*, I'm not about to let them scoop my story."

"Okay," Sam agreed.

"Besides," I added self-righteously, "I promised Friendly I'd keep a lid on it until Monday. How do we dig the dirt on three promising non-Smollet suspects?"

"The answer, Holl, is so transparently obvious that I wondered why I hadn't thought of it instantly," Sam pronounced. "Perk."

"My father?"

"Your father and a font of all information on things Art Ducko. Right about now, he should be adjourning to Toby's for his afternoon coffee and catch-up on island gossip."

Glancing at my watch, I turned the Honda back toward the island. Sam was right on target. I just wished I'd thought of it first.

The parking lot at Toby's was not yet full, but it would be jammed later that afternoon. I remembered again that it was Decoy Jamboree weekend, and cursed, knowing that the place would soon be filled up with duck-obsessed fun seekers, pouring into the county for the big event and surrounding hoopla. I took a deep breath and marched in the door, sensing the invisible Sam behind me.

I wasn't surprised to find the usual suspects hunched over their favorite beverages, their bleary collective gaze glued to the Theater Vision screen overhead, watching something involving men, a lot of running, and a ball.

I was able to find a stool as far down the bar from the TV as possible, well into the darkest corner of a very dim, very warm room. Toby, never taking his eyes off the screen, shoved a can of Diet Pepsi in front of me, sighed loudly and disappeared before I could open my mouth.

I knew I was getting the hissy for having involved him with The Problem of Smollet, and I also knew that until he was ready to calm down and listen to my cheap excuses, there wasn't much I could do.

I closed my eyes, resting my chin on the heels of my hands as the morning caught up with me.

"You're looking in all the wrong places, you know," someone said from not too far away, and I opened my eyes on a dim form in the darkness next to me.

Another ghost, of course.

I blinked, but no one else seemed to notice the dim presence in the darkness, no more than a blink of dust motes if you weren't looking for it, something half seen out of the corner of your eye that's not there when you turn and stare at it.

"If you want to know the truth, you have to start at the beginning of the story," said the ghost's voice, thick with the stopped glottis and swallowed consonants of the old Shore. A battered slouch hat was pulled down over his eyes, and he was hunched up into an old boiler jacket, the collar turned up so I couldn't see much of his face. Between the hat and a thick, untrimmed beard, what was visible was gin-blossomed and weather-beaten, reddened skin carved into a thousand tiny lines. His eyes held me; pale blue, that winter river color, sheltered by thick, bristling eyebrows. His hands, thick knuckled and blunt, knotted and unknotted in his lap. They were callused and scarred, a waterman's hands. The old shade spoke so softly that I had to strain to catch each word.

"Oh, my honey, when I was growin' up down below, the sky was black with ducks all winter. You could have made from here to Swann's Island on the backs of them ducks out there. Black duck, mallard, canvasback, redheads, teals, they was all out there in them days. Shoot 'em? Sure we shot 'em. Shot 'em with them big old punt guns, loaded up with chain and shot and every damn thing. We cut down fifty, a hundred ducks at a time! Sold 'em up to the big hotels in Baltimore, that's how we fed ourselves all winter. . . ." He smiled; his teeth were large and even. *"We'd lay out there on the river with them big guns and cut 'em down. There were always more ducks. Oh, my honey, I grew up with a gun in my hands, proggin' around them marshes. Ever' chance I git, I'd make for them marshes.*

*I loved them ducks, thought they was about the prettiest thing
there was."* His voice was full of the sounds of endless wet-
land and open water, the wind in the scrub pines, the flapping
of a thousand wings, the distant hum of cold winter wind
across the river. *"We lived off the land in them days; that's
just what everyone did. Hunted and fished and trapped, maybe
did some farming if you had some land that weren't too
marshy. You traded for what you needed. When the war come
along, I hid in the swamp to avoid the Yellowbellies and the
damn Yankees both. Wasn't my fight on either side, nor any
other Shoreman's. We never had no slaves, not us! They was
lots of boys hid in them holes and cripples in the swamps.
That's when I started to carve, to pass the nights. It gets awful
lonesome out there. And them birds just seemed to come to life
for me."* He smiled again, a thin, ironic grin that showed those
big teeth. *"Seemed like I could carve almost any old bird 'coy,
and make it look real. Course, my mama could draw some;
she'd had some schooling, you know. Mebbe it run in the
family. Mebbe I coulda been one of them artists, up to Baltimore if things had been different. . . . But when the war was
over and I done come home, I still liked to carve 'em ole 'coys,
paint 'em up to look like real ducks, hunt over 'em. By then,
the skies weren't so black with ducks no more, and the rich
men were comin' over from the city to their fancy hunting
clubs."* He chuckled and his laughter was the rustle of the
wind through dry leaves. *"Before then, I made 'em for myself
to gun over, but them rich city boys just loved them 'coys I
carved. Oh, they loved comin' over here, they loved the
huntin' in a dry comfort blind with a marsh man like me to
carry 'em. And they loved my 'coys. Bought 'em all up and
carried 'em away for themselves. They'd take a shine to a
really good one and take it back to the city with them to put up
in their office, remind them of a good day's gunning."*

He leaned closer toward me, but he was still no more than a
few dim lines, like spiderweb, in the deep shadows. *"This is
what yew got to understand, so listen careful, 'cause I don't
have a lot of words like you do. Them boys loves 'em 'coys
because it takes 'em back to the soul of a man, when there*

wasn't no suits and ties and no offices and wives and huntin'
clubs. A time when every man lived off the land and his wits,
and ate what he could hunt or fish. " One of his rough, scarred
hands reached out and touched my wrist, no more than the
brush of snowflake against my skin. *"A 'coy's a fake bird*
made to lure in a real bird. So what's a 'coy of a 'coy? Figure
out that one, honey, and sure as my name's Albanus Wallace,
you'll have your puzzle answered—"

Albanus Wallace?

"You gonna drink that Pepsi?" Sam's matter-of-fact voice
cut across my thoughts and I started. Where my companion
had sat, there was a vacant stool. I put my hand out; it passed
through empty air. Sam slid easily through my hand, grinning
at me. Stupid ghost tricks.

"Did you see him? The other ghost?" I whispered, looking
around. Some sort of fracas with the ball on the TV kept the
boys at the bar happy and occupied and oblivious to the dead.
I could have stripped on top of the bar and no one would have
noticed.

"That was Scratch Wallace." Sam's eyebrows went up
slightly. "Albanus was his real name."

"Scratch! Of course! That's what Smollet had meant when
he was nattering on about some guy named Wally or something at the bar. Well, for heaven's sake!" I looked around, but
the famous carver had faded away until his motionless outline
was barely visible in the dark corner.

"Scratch Wallace? Oh, yeah. He always shows up here
around Decoy Jamboree time." He leaned closer to me.
"Scratch takes a personal interest in the price of his work at
these auctions. All those old-time carvers do, dead or alive. Of
course, ghosts can come to Toby's, but they can't move
around like I can. Something about an old Indian burial
ground or something. It's all in The Rules, but I forget exactly
where."

Just then the door swung open and a clump of writers and
photographers filtered in with a flurry of flashbulbs and rustling
notebooks. They were following my father like ducklings.

"Decorative carvers? We don't need none of that sissy

stuff! We're talking about the Decoy Jamboree—real honest-to-God working decoys, ducks a man can hunt over—not about some pseudo–art form for interior decorators!"

"Woman, behold your father," Sam laughed. "Damn, Perk does love those cameras, doesn't he?"

I turned around to see my father perching on his favorite stool at the other end of the bar, still holding forth to his media acolytes. They were hanging on his every word. I counted at least three still cameras and two camcorders. I don't count freelance writers; they're too thick upon the ground around here to number.

If my mother, Doll, is the Rummage Sale Queen of Beddoe's Island, then my father, Perk, is the community's Media Mouthpiece. Ever since he was elected president of the Beddoe's Island Waterman's Association last year, we have discovered that our previously taciturn father, husband and friend has the soul of a genuine publicity hound. He just *loves* those media people, and will hold forth on any subject at any time, as long as he has an audience who will sit still to listen. The world's thirst for Chesapeake Bay lore and culture has become such that many have sought him out for words of watermanly wisdom.

I guess explaining us to the outside world is a tough job, but someone's got to do it.

"When I was a kid, you could make a living all winter trapping muskrat off the marsh," Dad was saying. "Before these animal rights people got all upset about it, muskrat coats were quite fashionable. Back then, it used to be that black muskrat pelts went for four or five dollars apiece, brown ones for three or four. You could lease a marsh for about two or three hundred dollars a year, and take twenty or thirty pelts a day."

"Ugh! How cruel!" a woman in a suede coat shuddered. "Those nasty steel traps."

"Just as nasty as shooting waterfowl," Dad replied triumphantly. "What did you think was the function of these decoys? They weren't designed to sit on someone's mantelpiece. They were created to lure ducks in to be killed. Gunning ducks and carrying hunting parties was a big fall and winter industry around here for years and years and years. I put my daughter through college by carryin' hunting parties. When it was too cold to go oysterin', men fed their families by carryin' parties and trapping muskrat. Till two years ago, as a matter of fact, when they put up the moratorium on gunnin' migratory geese, you could still make some money at it. The ducks are long gone, just a short season on the sea ducks, although who'd want to shoot what you can't eat, I don't know," he said contemptuously, with a glare at a well-known sea duck guide at the end of the bar.

"And an opinion's like an asshole, ever'body's got one," Sonny The Sea Ducker shot back.

Sam chuckled, but I knew my father couldn't hear him.

Dad, unfazed by Sonny, signaled Toby for his ritual afternoon coffee. "The oysters are going, and soon the crabs will be gone and then we'll all be gone from here, where our families have lived for three hundred years, with nothing left but weekend people and tourists, and they won't care. But my point is, around Beddoe's Island, there have been very few men who've ever drawn a paycheck until the past ten, twenty years. So when I say that the Decoy Jamboree brings some money to the island, I know what I'm talking about." This last was directed at me, I knew. Since the duck carnival is one of the many things I've failed to show proper reverence for, I just waved my diet soda at him and grinned.

"There's the daughter I put through college now," Dad said mournfully. "She works on the newspaper in town." I prayed the next thing he said would not be about how I should get married and settle down, something that concerns Dad and Mom a lot more than it concerns me.

The pack of photographers and writers for the gloss and puff magazines turned to stare at me. A Japanese tourist took my picture. But my turn in the spotlight was brief, for Dad started up again with the nickel tour, pointing out Toby's collection of stuffed birds and decrepit decoys displayed around the plate rail, giving a brief talk on each one. It was only then that I recollected that one of his chores as vice co-chair of the Decoy Jamboree was shepherding the visiting press and important collectors on the decoy tour. God only knew what it involved; I have long felt that there are some things humankind was not meant to contemplate, and the details of Decoy Jamboree fit that niche nicely.

I nursed my Diet Pepsi quietly until Dad wound down his speech on Preserving Our Decoy Heritage, An Eastern Shore Way of Life.

From time to time, Sam, invisible in the shadows, shifted and sighed, but I was mostly able to ignore him. The last thing I needed was to have people see me carrying on a conversation with someone who was, to all intents and purposes, dead, not to mention invisible. No one else seemed to be aware of his presence, except of course Toby, but my cousin was pointedly ignoring us as he vended beverages and snack food to Dad's happy campers, dollar signs dancing in his eyes.

"Toby's pissed off at me, too." Sam sighed. "It wasn't my fault. How was I to know Miz Fish had a gun?"

"How did you let her know Smollet was here?" I asked out of the corner of my mouth. I looked at my reflection in the back bar mirror. Beside me, Sam reflected back a thin mist like stale smoke.

"I appeared to her in a dream," he said sarcastically.

I turned to look at him and he had the grace to drop his eyes. "Actually, I told Smollet to call her. I'm doing pretty okay with the driving stuff, but phone and fax are a whole 'nother story. If I could just get on the Net I could . . ."

"Never mind." I sighed. As I said before, some things are better left unexplored. The idea of Sam hacking into the Internet was scary, especially since I hadn't figured out how to do it myself yet.

"But I did catch up with Loop Gareau and Frosty Froston in the driveway," he said, continuing the conversation we'd had on the way over in his usual jumpy fashion. "They were fighting. Loop threatened to sue Frosty and Frosty threatened to get Loop's HMO canceled. Bad blood there, very bad blood, it sounds like. They compete for the same decoys, or so it would seem." He cast me a sideways look.

"I have the feeling you know more than you're saying,

Sam, but then you always seem to know more than I do about what's really going on, whether you do or not."

"Consider it part of my charm." He grinned.

"If you weren't already dead, I'd kill you all over again," I hissed.

"We ghosts prefer the phrase 'living impaired,'" Sam retorted primly.

At that moment, my father's disciples headed out to the harbor for a look at the skipjacks, the last working sailcraft in America.

"How about 'intelligence impaired,' you creep?" I hissed.

With a toss of my head, I picked up my soda can and eased on down the bar. The finish of the thing with men doing a lot of running with a ball had pretty much dispersed the regulars into the great outdoors or to the pool table. The juke punched up some neon action and the nasal plaint of Vince Gill flooded the dim and smoky room.

"Hi, Dad," I said, leaning over to kiss his leathery cheek. My father's mustache quivered slightly and he turned to gaze at me through mournful eyes.

"Don't 'Hi Dad' me, young lady," he sniffed. "Your mother and I are right put out with you."

I ran through a mental list of all the reasons why I had fallen into parental disfavor and decided it would be best to keep silent and see which of these had offended them the most. I was almost sure it was my failure to show up for church and dinner last Sunday, but just in case, I waited for him to play Name That Sin.

"You know, when something big like Fin Fish gettin' killed happens, and you're there, we'd like to hear about it from you, not from some stranger. What good is havin' a kid who's a reporter if she don't report the big news to us first? Now Frosty and Loop will get first refusal on his decoys!"

"Dad!" I exclaimed. "Don't you be a ghoul, too!"

"Your ma's making a pineapple upside-down cake for me to take down to pore ole Mrs. Fish right now," he said dolefully. "But I had to hear about it this morning from rumor! I expected better from you, Holly."

I swallowed back any possible guilt I could have felt. I should have known that Dad would want a crack at Fin's collection. Of course, he couldn't compete with the bottomless checkbooks of men like Froston and Gareau—"too high end," he would say with a sigh—but he was good at using that professional Eastern Shoreman act to get what he wanted for *his* collection. I could just hear him pleading with Miz Fish to sell him the best pieces "just to keep our shore heritage on the shore" or some such. In his own way, Dad was as obsessed a collector as either the doctor or the lawyer.

But I didn't think he'd kill for a 'coy; too much like work, as he would be the first to admit.

"As a matter of fact, that's why I'm down here," I said glibly. "I was looking for you to tell you. But I don't know, Dad. If I told you what really happened, I don't know but what you'd tell all your acolytes out there. After all, Dad, I promised Detective Friendly I wouldn't go mouthing the details of the murder around." I leaned in confidentially.

"To hell with the murder!" my father said indignantly. "I just want to know if that Scratch Wallace is all right! That's a damn valuable decoy!"

I could have sworn that I heard Sam and Scratch Wallace chuckling somewhere in the smoky atmosphere, if shadows and shades can be said to chuckle.

Turning my back on them, I pointedly reassured my father that I'd had a good look at the bird and I was pretty sure it was okay, except for the blood and brain matter.

"Well, then, that's okay." He sighed, relieved. "You can wash that stuff off, you know. It's the paint and the damage to the bird I was worried about. There aren't too many Scratch Wallaces around, and original paint's important!"

Before he could start fretting about the blood and tissue ruining the damned original paint, I had to move fast. "Look, Dad, I need to know everything you know about Frosty Froston and Loop Gareau." I gave him a highly edited version of my visit with Miz Fish.

You can bet that the words "Smollet Bowley" never crossed my lips in the telling.

My father leaned toward me, grinning, eyebrows working. "Are they suspects?" he asked hopefully.

"Everybody's a suspect," I replied confidentially. I didn't know how right I was about that, but I would, all too soon.

"Frosty Froston and Loop Gareau." My paterfamilias sighed, the way he does when he's thinking about how to make a good story even better. "Now there's a pair." As if by magic, his coffee cup was refilled, and Toby, who's just as nosy as anyone else in my family, stopped to hear the story Dad was about to unwind. Behind me, I could sense Scratch Wallace and Sam Wescott listening. You know he's good when even dead men want to hear his tale.

"Frosty and Loop and Fin used to all be butthole bunkies," my father started out. (Immediately I have to digress here to explain that uniquely Eastern Shore parlance doesn't mean what you might think, in the latter half of the twentieth century. It just means that they were guys who liked to go gunning together.)

"Frosty, Loop and Fin Fish. Sounds like three different kinds of kid's cereal." Sam snorted, and Scratch Wallace giggled. Toby made a noise in the back of his throat. I was caught up with an unexpected snort and blew Diet Pepsi out of my nose.

My father looked at me reproachfully as I wiped my face and my sweater with a handful of those tiny, flimsy bar napkins.

"I didn't know there was anything funny about duck shooting," Dad said. Anything to do with ducks and geese is right up there with Mom, Apple Pie and the Flag for him. "It put you through college, young lady!"

"Allergies," I muttered, daring to turn around and cast a quick, evil look at the Deadly Duo. Sam and Scratch, I realized unhappily, were having just a wonderful time.

They grinned back at me, the pigs.

"As I was saying," my father continued narrowly, "*if* you're interested—"

Quickly I turned back to him. "I'm all ears, Dad." And I was.

He sipped his coffee. "Froston, Gareau and Fish were huntin' buddies with old man Tolliver, Oliver Tolliver, the millionaire. Had that big ole yacht he named *Seafood*, remember that? Fella made all his money in those big ole fish canneries they used to have down to Bethel, but he was before your time, Hollis. Tolliver had himself a gunnin' club down near Elliott's Island, and those boys used to go out with him. Your cousin Cephas used to look after the place and carry 'em on out, and he said they done as much drinkin', card playin' and lyin' as they done shootin' down there. Of course, knowin' Cephas, he was right in there with the rest of 'em."

"Cephas did like to party," Toby said, adding coffee to Dad's mug. My father thoughtfully stirred in his milk. When he tells a story, it's best not to push him; he has his own rhythm for these things, and as he warms to his themes, he moves into broad dialect. When the coffee was lightened to his liking, he sipped, then cleared his throat.

"Well, old man Tolliver upped and died—this was about twenty, twenty-five years ago—and Mrs. Tolliver, well, I guess she was the second or third or fourth Mrs. Tolliver, by then. The older he got, the more his wives kept gettin' younger and blonder and bigger through the chest, and this one wasn't much interested in hunting anything bigger than a diamond bracelet. Cephas inherited alla old man Tolliver's guns, though, and he had some nice ones, so it weren't a complete waste of time for him."

"And lost ever' damn one of 'em playin' cards," Toby put in with a small grin. I knew that's how *he'd* come across a couple of his shotguns, but I didn't say anything.

"Cephas is a fool," my father said abruptly. "But here's the point. Old man Tolliver left that hunting club property to Frosty, Fin and Loop. On condition."

"What condition?" Toby and I naturally asked, and in the shadows, I sensed, rather than heard, Sam and Scratch Wallace waiting for the answer, too, their shades suspended like an intake of breath.

My father's eyes sparkled, and beneath his mustache, his lips quivered as he leaned in close to us. "The old man left a codicil to his will that said they could have the lodge; two pit, two off-shore, and three shore duck blinds; and a hundred acres of prime marsh and old-growth woods if they'd agree to one thing." He held up one finger to illustrate. "See, old man Tolliver just *loved* his gunnin'. So he had himself cremated, and had his ashes stuffed into a couple of great big old decoys he had the Ward brothers make up just for that purpose. They were a couple confidence decoys, whistling swans, I believe. Had to be big to store up alla them ashes. The deal was, they had to shoot over his decoys, and I mean literally his, old man Tolliver's, decoys, on every single trip."

"No!" I protested. I thought until that moment I'd heard of everything, but this was a new one on me.

"Old man Tolliver was the duck hunter's duck hunter," my father said with great admiration for an idea at once so simple and yet so poetic.

"Ain't that something?" Toby asked, lost in awe.

"Talk about your stuffed decoys." Scratch Wallace cackled hollowly and he and Sam went off into guffaws.

I managed to restrain myself.

"I hope you all remember that when my time comes," Dad was saying. I thought about my mother's reaction and tried to develop instant amnesia.

"Now, the deal was, and this was all spelled out in the will, which I happen to know about because Cephas told me all about it one time when we were sitting out in a shore blind," Perk continued, careful to get his sources straight, "as long as Fin, Loop and Frosty carried old man Tolliver's ashes gunnin', they had the hunting club. If anything happened to his decoys, and they couldn't hunt over him anymore, it was to be sold up, and the profits donated to Ducks Unlimited. Well, that would seem like a good deal. The upkeep and the taxes weren't too much for two lawyers and a doctor, you'd think. Of course Fin hadn't run for judge then, but he was still a courthouse barnacle."

"So what happened?" I asked.

"I'm just about to get to that," my father said crossly. "Anyway, for a couple of years everything went along just fine. They gunned over old man Tolliver every season, and had themselves a fine old time down to the gunning club."

"I bet you and Cephas were having a fine old time gunning their blinds when they weren't around, too," I said disloyally.

"Who's telling this story, you or me?" my father asked and I humbly shut up.

"Now," he resumed, "around about that time, decoys were starting to get real collectible. You know, not the old working decoys at first, but those decorative pieces them old boys like Harry Truman's father and uncle used to carve for the sporting clubs. Some of them were trading and selling for a good price, and when they got to be out of sight, any old wooden working 'coy got to be pounced on. Of course, Fin, Frosty and Loop were right in there, collecting and trading. They'd drive around all over the Shore and find old people too poor and too old to hunt anymore and buy their decoys up for a song compared to what they were really worth on the collector's market. And many a poor country widow not knowin' any better, she'd take what little they offered and say thank you. They didn't know back then." He grimaced. "Course they do know now that it's too late, but then, you know, no one thought anything of it. They were just old decoys, and everyone was going to plastic."

I stirred restlessly, and Toby flicked a speck of dust off the bar with his bar rag. "Well, sir," Dad continued. "Course, old man Tolliver had some nice working 'coys, maybe seventy-five or a couple hundred of 'em all layin' up there in the shed down to the club, forgotten. Chopped out by all them ole carvers and outlaw gunners and watermen and what not. Nobody ever thought they was anything special till someone over to the Smithsonian or somewhere declared the working decoys folk art, then it was 'Katie, bar the door!' Before, you couldn't give 'em away, and all of a sudden, any ole block a wood with a duck's head on it become valuable! Those ole decoys were worth hundreds of dollars. Apiece. Even the factory-made 'coys and the cork ones, people who'd never been near a blind wanted to pay good money for 'em."

"I'll bet Cephas wishes now he inherited those decoys, instead of the shotguns," I ventured.

"Cephas didn't want them ole wooden 'coys when the new plastic ones were so much better," Toby pointed out reasonably.

"But you can bet that Fin, Loop and Frosty carried those old wooden decoys away one by one for their personal collections until there was nothin' left to hunt over. Then they got to fightin' over who was doin' the most work and payin' out the most money. Oh, it was tragic." My father sighed. "When they weren't huntin' over old man Tolliver, those two ashy decoys sat up on top of the mantelpiece down to the clubhouse. Then, one night, after they'd been playin' cards and drinkin' Wild Turkey, it actually came to a right nasty feathering up."

"Tsk," Toby said, like he'd never been in a bar fight in his life.

"And what with one thing and another, somebody knocked those decoys over and all that was left of old man Tolliver went right into the fireplace."

"No!" I exclaimed, horrified, but not for the reasons Dad thought.

"Talk about getting your ashes hauled!" Sam slapped Scratch on the ghostly back and the two of them went off into hollow hoots. Toby snorted. Remember, the sign over his back bar says he doesn't serve unpleasant people, but there's nothing about dead ones.

Oblivious to the irreverent revenants in the corner, Dad just shook his head sadly. "Well, old man Tolliver was just set in there with cork stoppers," he observed mournfully. "And when he fell out all over the floor and blew onto the fireplace, they couldn't tell him from the wood ash, so that sobered 'em up all right. They had to sweep up the whole mess and stuff it back into the swans. But old man Tolliver's lawyer found out about it, so they lost the club. Some corporation from Delaware bought it as an executive retreat, DU got the money and Frosty, Loop and Fish have been blaming each other ever since. Well, I guess they won't have Fin Fish to blame anymore. Poor sumbitch never did have much luck with those decoys."

"That's real interesting, Cap'n Ball," said a familiar voice.

"Cheese it, the cops," Sam muttered. "Come on, Scratch, let's get outta here."

"Hey, hang around, you don't want to miss this," Scratch replied. "This cop's something else."

Ormand Friendly had entered Toby's bar at some point during Dad's narrative and had been listening quietly as the sorry tale unfolded.

My father turned around. I felt that as a native Beddoe's Islander, it was his sacred duty to find out this guy was a cop and give him the brush-off, but no. His face lit up like Christmas.

"Friendly! How the hell are you?" he asked happily, slapping a cop on the back as if they were best friends.

Toby, that traitor, was already pulling him a draft as Friendly slid himself up on a barstool, nodding affably at me. "I'm glad I got to hear that story," he said, "because I just came in search of you, Cap'n, looking for whatever you knew about Dr. Froston and Loop Gareau. Doesn't anyone around here have a normal name like Steve or Doug?"

"Hell, no, Orm." My father grinned. "Say, you hear anything about the Scratch Wallace decoy? It didn't hurt it, did it?"

"How do you two know each other?" I asked suspiciously.

They both just looked at me like I was nuts, which maybe I was, trying to figure out why everyone but me seemed to think Ormand Friendly was so fabulous. He was wearing a spectacularly wrinkled tweed jacket with the elbows out, a blue dress shirt that had seen better days and a necktie that featured, I swear, the Three Stooges.

"So," Dad said, "are Frosty and Loop suspects? Lord, I wouldn't put anything past those two, if decoys are involved."

Friendly sipped his beer gratefully. "Not at liberty to say." He grinned. "But I've been out talkin' to them. No one's seen Smollet Bowley, have they?"

"Not recently," I was able to reply with utter honesty.

Toby shot me a fierce look, as if he'd just remembered why he was mad at me. "If I see that little prick in this bar again, it'll be too soon for me," he growled.

Friendly shrugged indifferently. "Boy, I hate this case," he said sadly. "A homicide and an escaped prisoner. You wouldn't believe the paperwork involved. Forms, forms, forms. All I do is fill out forms. You all gonna be at the Decoy Jamboree Carving Contest tonight?"

"I'll have to be there," Dad said. "I'm one of the vice co-chairs." Of course, he wouldn't have missed any of the ceremonies for all the Scratch Wallace decoys in the world, but try to get him to admit that he was going to go somewhere and actually have fun.

"I gotta hold down the bar," Toby said. "This is one of the biggest weekends of the year for me."

Friendly turned to look at me. "How about you, Hollis? You comin'?"

"Oh, yeah. I promised Lenore Currier I'd come." Quickly I sketched in my morning with Lenore and Harry Truman, then gave him the heavy-edit version of my visit chez Fish.

I'm pleased to say that I had everyone's attention, including Friendly's. He merely whistled and made some notes, but Dad and Toby definitely had opinions.

"That old forger! What're they trying to do? Turn this into a sissy decorative carving tea party?" Dad howled.

"That old dude owes me a bar tab from here to hell!" Toby roared. "What's *he* doin' right to get to be wandering around with a blond babe while I'm stuck behind this damn bar all weekend?"

Poor old Harry Truman. He couldn't win, as far as the island was concerned.

"Well, Hollis," Friendly said, grinning at me, "before you go off to the Decoy Jamboree, you need to stop by the state's attorney's office. Teeny Hardcastle wants to talk to you. In person."

"Why?" I asked irritably.

Friendly slid a look at my father and Toby. They were entirely wrapped up in marveling over Lenore's interest in

Harry Truman, and couldn't have cared less about me. Friendly raised and lowered his shoulders and shook his head in a "beats me" gesture.

"She thinks you're a suspect," Friendly informed me. He wasn't smiling either.

"Why?" I demanded when I could catch my breath again.

"Well, apparently, you pounded Fish pretty heavy on that Harmon Sneed thing. She got ahold of all your old clips from the paper."

And, I imagined, Rig Riggle, the editor from hell, was more than happy to open the newspaper's morgue up for her perusal. "Give me a goddamn break!" I sputtered. "I was just doing my job! Just because I thought the man was human scum doesn't mean I killed him!" Although, I thought, I could have if I wanted to; the opportunity to sneak back upstairs and bludgeon His Dishonor had certainly been there. I thought about the person who had rushed past me in the darkened hallway. The person only I had seen.

Oh, yeah, there was one other witness. A ghost almost no one else could see.

"Admit it, you had motive and opportunity, Hollis. And it was no secret you were outraged by the six-month sentence."

"If that's the case, then about half the women in America are suspects."

Friendly shrugged again. "It's you she wants to see, though."

"But I told you everything I knew! Three times! What can I tell her that you don't already have in my statement?"

"She's the top cop in Santimoke County," Friendly said. "She's got a right to question you. And she can get a warrant on you to bring you in."

"Oh, for heaven's sake!" I hissed angrily. "It's Saturday! Doesn't that woman have a life?"

"Not when there's a murder involved. I don't think she's been home to sleep since last night," he said thoughtfully.

"Well," I said snippishly, sliding off the stool, "I guess you'd know all about that, wouldn't you?" I was amazed at my own nastiness. Why did I lose it when he said that?

My father and my cousin halted in midsentence to turn and look at me. Great, I thought; now my family knows I'm ass deep in alligators. Again.

My father was already looking at me as if all of his worst suspicions were confirmed. I waited for him to tell me that if I found a decent man, got married and had some kids, I wouldn't find myself in these situations, which is what he usually says when something like this happens. Never mind that my marriage to Sam ended deplorably, that my subsequent relationships have been serial reenactments of the *Titanic* vs. the iceberg. Never mind that my ex-husband's ghost was sitting, invisible to my father, not five feet away; Dad's solution to all my problems is marriage and children.

At that moment, I happily could have killed all of them just for being in Toby's Bar and Grill at the same time I was. Instead, I sighed loudly in the tones of the eternal female martyr.

"I'm outta here," I announced stiffly from the door. "This place is suffering from testosterone poisoning."

Unfortunately, Dad's duck disciples chose that moment to breeze back in, oohing and aahing over the dredge boats and the beauties of the Chesapeake Bay, totally squishing my little drama as they brushed past me in search of hot coffee and more atmosphere.

"Whoa," Scratch Wallace breathed in sepulchral tones. "This is turnin' right serious, Sam."

No one else even noticed my exit.

NINE

•

Hardass Points a Finger but Edgar Gets the Beak

"It doesn't get any better than this," I muttered sarcastically as I circled the block around the courthouse one more time, looking for a place to park. Decoy Jamboree had filled every slot within a five-county radius. The center of Watertown, usually comatose and deserted late on a weekend afternoon, was crammed with happy Jamboreers, wandering from duck exhibit to goose exhibit in attitudes of reverent bliss, as if on pilgrimage.

"If you'd just let me drive, I bet we'd find a space," Sam offered.

"I bet we would, too," I replied. "At the hospital psych ward, when people see me in a car with no driver, rolling around town."

The likely space I had spotted ahead was quickly filled before I could even get near it. "Protestant Mardi Gras indeed," I huffed, as my circles around the courthouse grew wider and wider, and my temper grew shorter and shorter with each parked-up street I cruised.

"Socrates," Sam pointed out pedantically, "said the un-examined life is not worth living. I'd like to bring him back just so I could lock him in a room with someone who's spent too much time recovering their lost memories so they can get in touch with their inner child in cognitive group therapy for people who swim with the sharks. In short, there's no reason to get bent out of shape, Hollis. It's just a parking space."

"If Socrates had been leading my life, no one would have to

force him to drink hemlock; he'd *beg* for it. I've spent the past decade trying to avoid poking at my life with a sharp stick, and look what's happened to me since you landed back in my life. Within the past six months, everything I've been avoiding has risen up to haunt me. Literally," I retorted.

"Temper, temper," Sam soothed. "Athena Hardcastle only wants to talk to you, not beat you with a rubber hose."

"We'll see about that," I sighed gloomily. "I'll bet she's got that hose all ready to go right about now."

"Deep breaths, Hollis," Sam commanded. "She can try to eat you, but she can't kill you."

"The second most irritating person in my life has summoned me to a grilling over the murder of a really, really annoying judge. I think I have a right to be anxious, don't you?"

"Could it be that you're just a little, oh, I don't know, *jealous*?" Sam asked.

"Jealous?" I demanded edgily. "Whatever for?"

"Well, you don't know if you want Friendly, but you don't want anyone else to have him either, which makes absolutely no sense whatsoever, especially since Hardass Hardcastle and he were apparently a thing of the long ago past before you knew either one of them. Besides which, Friendly is hardly worth the effort. I know you are, shall we say, morally elastic, but remember, getting involved with a cop who's a source is a real conflict of interest for a journalist."

"*You're* calling *me* morally elastic? You had—*have* the ethics of a politician!" A thought crept into my mind. I glanced at Sam's profile. "I think you're the one who's jealous. Jealous of Friendly!"

Sam rose a half inch off his seat and floated in the air, looking at me from wounded puppy dog eyes. "Jealous? *Moi?*" he demanded indignantly. "Ghosts are above such petty emotions."

"See what I mean? It doesn't pay to examine some things in my life too closely. You can get burned yourself!" I trumpeted. "Look! There's a space right there!"

Even as I sighted the empty slot, the Volvo following me

pulled out, zipping right around my Honda. The driver grinned, cutting me off with inches to spare as he made for *my* empty space, blinkers flashing, horn whining.

"Hey!" I cried.

"The trouble with some people is, they have no manners," Sam sighed in a world-weary tone.

"Don't do anyth—" I started to say but it was too late.

I watched as the car picked up speed, hurtling into the space nose first. Tires squealing, it jumped up on the sidewalk, slamming with a loud crash into a parking meter.

"That should teach him a lesson in highway safety." Sam grinned as we passed the Volvo. "Don't look back, Holl."

I didn't.

In the end, I parked my car in one of the spaces behind the courthouse reserved for the judges. I knew Fish wouldn't be using his. I wondered if they had parking problems in Hell.

As I carefully checked my makeup and my hair in the rearview mirror, Sam said, "When you have to confront someone or something unpleasant, it is wise to groom and dress yourself as best you can."

Since my next stop after this particular piece of unpleasantness was to be Decoy Jamboree, I'd chosen to wear my black velvet Chanel knock-off dinner suit. Copy or not, it had still cost a fortune, but it was well worth every hard-earned cent I'd put into it because I looked great in it.

"Knowing you look good gives you confidence to cope," Sam pointed out.

"I need confidence to cope," I said, making sure my grandmother's pearl earrings were in place. "This is my gospel armor against Hardass Hardcastle's uncanny ability to make me feel like homemade inferiority."

"You'll be just fine," Sam promised. "I'll wait for you outside. I've got to talk to someone." In a small burst of light, he discorporated. He was there, then he wasn't there. It was one of his parlor tricks that always surprised me, no matter how often I saw him do it. Still, his words had given me the confidence to face the dragoness in her lair.

With my mental loins well girded, I hurried into the court-house behind a chill wind and the fading sunlight. I smiled at Carl, the baby trooper still on door duty, when he told me I looked good enough to eat. "Hardass's in her office." Carl unlocked the door to let me inside. "Don't that woman ever sleep? She's been there since eight this morning," he confided plaintively. Baby troopers get all the scut jobs.

Madam Hardass herself was on the phone when I walked in, her desk piled with the endless folders and forms of law enforcement work. She looked up as I came through the door, waving me toward a chair. I preferred to wander the office, distracting her.

Athena Hardcastle had added her own touches to the state's attorney's office. Horace Pippin posters and a Joyce Scott sculptural piece decorated her walls, and blooming orchids added surprising life and color to the room. Blue twilight passed through the narrow windows, but she had not turned on the lights yet, leaving the room in a pleasant, shadowy light.

I glanced at some photos on her desk of Fish lying dead on the chambers floor. And I looked away again quickly. Real-life violence doesn't get any easier filtered through a camera's unblinking eye.

A drawing on the wall caught my attention and I moved closer to study it. It seemed to be charcoal on lined notebook paper, a somewhat primitive rendering of a child's happy face. It was only when I was right on top of it that I saw that the child's happy smile was more like a scream of unbear-able pain.

"Visionary art," Athena Hardcastle said, replacing the phone in the cradle.

I turned to look at her, questioning.

"Art by untrained artists. That was done with burnt match heads. The artist is a seventeen-year-old boy I helped convict after he killed his stepfather, his mother and his half sister with a butcher knife. He sent it to me." Her tone was matter-of-fact, as she briskly gathered up the papers on her desk, sorting them into neat piles. But I noticed she didn't look at me when she spoke.

"The family was quite religious. When he first started exhibiting signs of paranoid schizophrenia in early adolescence, most people would have taken him to a doctor for a thorough physical and psychiatric workup. His family took him to their church, where the stepfather was a self-ordained minister. He attempted to beat the demons out of his stepson with a large wooden cross. When that didn't work, the boy was locked into his room and chained to a bedstead. The beatings and prayers continued for several years. One night, the kid got himself loose. There were a hundred and thirty-seven wounds in the stepfather alone. The kid was in general population at the prison in Somerset, but I finally got him into Perkins, where he can get some kind of treatment. That, Hollis," she concluded dryly, "is a self-portrait. A thank-you present."

I somehow felt as if she had already won this round without even firing a shot.

Her eyes swept over my black dinner suit; I instantly felt wrinkled. "Nice outfit," Athena said, as if she had pulled the compliment out of herself with pliers.

"Oh, I clean up real good," I replied brightly.

She smiled; it was thin and bleak, never reaching her eyes, but it was a smile. Athena, of course, looked fabulous in an ultramarine worsted frock ("dress" just would not do for this garment) with chunky gold and silver jewelry at her ears and neck. And, of course, not a hair or a thread out of place, even on a Saturday night with a heavy homicide on her hands.

"On your way to the duck thingie over at the Santimoke Inn?" she asked, gesturing me toward a seat. With the light at her back, her face was in shadow. I couldn't read her expression, but I could feel like I was getting the third degree.

"I told my father I'd meet him over there," I replied with a pointed look at my watch. "He's one of the contest judges."

"We'll try to make this as brief as possible, Hollis," she retorted crisply as I sat down in a chair just slightly lower than her own.

Athena leaned forward and placed her elbows on the desk, peering at me. "Tell me what happened from the moment you walked into the courthouse yesterday morning. Try to remember

as many details as you can, or anything you might have noticed that seemed odd or unusual. Sometimes things fall into
place in retrospect."

I started at the beginning, went on to the middle and came,
as the Red King suggested, to the end. Athena listened
intently, from time to time making a note on the yellow legal
pad in front of her. Since you already know everything I knew,
there's no sense in picking it all over again. Suffice to say, I
edited out any mention of aiding and abetting your favorite
escapee and mine, Smollet L. Bowley.

It was only when I got to the part about the lights going off
and being pushed into the statue of the Unknown Waterman in
the courthouse hallway that Athena seemed to get really interested. "Someone brushed past me in the dark. Knocked my
bag off my arm and scattered my stuff all over the hallway," I
repeated. "I heard, rather than saw, them run to the door and
push it open, then all I think I saw was a shape."

"Who?" Athena asked. "Chances are good that person was
the same one who pulled the Johnson bar and closed down the
power."

"Why?" I asked. "Why kill Fish? Who had motive and
opportunity?"

"Well, you did, for one, Hollis." Athena's voice was again
curiously matter-of-fact. She pulled out a fax sheet with all the
Gazette clips from the Harmon Sneed flap and pushed them
toward me. "It sounds, from these clips, as if you really went
after Judge Fish two years ago. Your editor sent these over to
me, at my request. Did you kill Findlay Fish, Hollis?"

I couldn't see her face in the shadow of twilight. Was she
serious? Did she really think I offed Fish?

"Not bloody likely," I replied, my voice more even than my
emotions, or so I hoped. "Unless I was having blackouts or my
evil alter personality Sunny was running amok again. For one
thing, murder's not my style, and for another, I wouldn't know
how to turn all the power off in the courthouse. Besides, if I
had, wouldn't there be blood all over my clothes? Everyone
saw me on the street, and then down at Toby's Bar, including

Ormand Friendly. If I were covered in blood and brain matter, someone might have noticed."

"You could have bludgeoned him without getting a drop on yourself, according to our forensics experts," Athena said coolly.

"You mean the murderer could have," I snapped.

"The murderer could have," she agreed.

"Well, how about Lenore Currier?" I huffed. "What is *her* motive? Have you looked into that?"

"Lenore Currier was at the Santimoke Inn after she left here, attending the pre-Decoy cocktail jamboree with Mayor Goodyear, Sheriff Briscoe and about five hundred other folks." Athena shook her head. "Mayor Goodyear called this office this morning just to provide Ms. Currier with an alibi." Was there a little dry humor peeking through the gloom? I wasn't sure, but I persisted. At least here we were on equal footing, two women trying to solve a mutual problem. "Ms. Currier has no motive and some powerful friends."

"Yeah, but she could have snuck back here and done the dirty deed," I pointed out. "Half of those present at the cocktail party were too potted to know if they were there and the other half are only interested in getting themselves seen at the right parties. The Santimoke Inn is only a block from here. She could have made it here, walloped El Fisho and been back in seconds, well before anyone missed her."

"Mmm?" Athena made a skeptical noise.

"Well, minutes," I conceded grudgingly. "If, as you say, it's possible to bludgeon someone from behind, and not get blood all over yourself, no one would have been the wiser. She could have told everyone she'd slipped into the ladies' room for a couple of minutes. But why whack Fish? He was buying a decoy from the estate of a rich Japanese businessman, and she stands, or stood, to make a huge commission brokering the sale! In fact, her future career as a curator depends on the successful outcome of this sale, from what she told me."

"That's something to look into. But get back, for a minute, to opportunity. The courthouse was locked and Bailiff Winters made sure that he let everyone out before he took Mr. Bowley over to the detention center."

"Bob could have done it." Oh, that was low, and I knew it. But you never know. Bob Winters wouldn't murder anyone, would he? "Naa," I said aloud. "Bob didn't have a beef with Fish. Bob's the kind of man who loves everyone. You know, he'd say 'Oh Hitler, well sure, he killed eight million people and involved the world in total war, but once you got to know him, he was a pretty okay guy.' " But who knew how far Fish had pushed him, or what their history had been? Naaa. Of course, he could have done it when he returned to "discover" the body. . . .

"Besides, Bob would have had to do it with Smollet chained up beside him," Athena said thoughtfully. "And even Smollet would have noticed that, wouldn't he?"

"Hard to tell with Smollet." I sighed. "He's got the intelligence of a small appliance bulb."

"Well, did you know that Smollet's first cousin was the woman Harmon Sneed murdered?" Athena asked coolly.

I tried not to sit bolt upright. "No!" I said, more in wonder than disbelief.

"Lucinda Wells Sneed, Harmon's wife, was a first cousin to Oder and Smollet Bowley," she said, looking at her notes. "They have the same maternal grandmother. So, you see, after some idio—someone carelessly allowed Smollet to walk out of the detention center, he could easily have ambled back here and killed Judge Fish. I don't have to remind you that Smollet has five priors for breaking and entering. He knows how to pick locks, it would seem, so he might have been able to undo his own shackles and unlock a courthouse door. These locks are a joke, you know. I've let myself in with a credit card when I've forgotten my keys."

I knew she was studying my expression, even though I couldn't see hers. I made an effort to maintain a poker face, but inside I was beginning to feel anxious. "Smollet wouldn't kill anyone," I repeated. "It's just not the Bowley style. The Bowleys are crooks, but they're not violent crooks; they're not into crack or any of that crap. Besides, everyone around here is related to everyone else. I'm related to both Myrtle Goodyear and Bob Winters, for instance. But I frankly don't think either one of them would kill to avenge my death, nor I theirs."

Of course, if anyone tried anything with me, my father, my brother and Toby might flatten them, but I didn't need to tell her that, did I?

"Well, there's also Caroline Fish, the judge's wife, who, I understand, was in the process of divorcing him. Too many ducks, it would seem." Athena leaned back in her chair. "Or at least that's what she told the detectives when they interviewed her. She also says she was at her bridge club at the time of the murder with seven other ladies. But her bridge club met here in Watertown, on Flood Street, just four blocks away from the courthouse. Like Currier, she could have snuck out when she was dummy."

I shook my head. "Miz Fish had plenty of motive, but opportunity? Hard to picture her creeping around a dark courthouse turning off lights. Or having the physical strength to whack Fin Fish with a decoy; she must be in her sixties. In fact, I doubt she's ever even been in Santimoke County's courthouse."

Athena shrugged. "Airtight alibis always make me suspicious. Apparently, Judge Fish was not a well-liked man. You're not the only one who protested loud and long about the Sneed sentence. But before we start fanning out, I think it's wise to concentrate on the nearest suspects. Statistically speaking, that's generally where the perps are found."

She pushed a pencil through her neatly tied-back hair. "If only the butler did it!" She did crack a smile then.

So, I quickly sketched in what I knew about Dr. Froston and Lawyer Gareau, for her edification. "It's sort of strange that they were outside the courthouse last night. Even if you consider that they probably do hate Fish—*did* hate Fish more than they hated each other, what were they both doing down here, going astray from the cocktail party? Froston even had a glass of whiskey with him, as if he'd just gotten the news and couldn't wait to yell at Fish for getting the decoy—except Fish bought it first. In the cranium."

Athena was not amused, and I was not surprised.

"Frosty Froston and Loop Gareau!" I rushed on. "Poor Larry and Curly; now that Moe, the third Stooge, is dead, what's their game plan? Do they still blame Fish for losing the gunning club? Plenty of motive. Kill him, get his ducks for their collections. Where were they last night? Could one or the other of them have snuck away from the cocktail party? Either one of them could have slipped out and done in the Fish."

"Do you really think they would kill for decoys?" Athena asked dubiously. "That seems like a stretch."

"Collectors will do anything, anything at all, to get what they want. Look at the guy who stole the Van Gogh. He couldn't hang a famous painting up on the wall for all the world to see. He had to keep it in a secret room where only he could visit it. But it didn't matter, he wanted it, he got it, and that was that. He sat there for twenty years secretly looking at his Van Gogh. Collector's lust is a whole different kind of covetousness."

"I take it the state police CID will be running a background check on those two," Athena murmured, taking notes. "But I'll make a note of them just the same. Of course, we're looking into the jury and the courthouse employees, but there's no connection so far that we have been able to establish. We're also looking into the whereabouts of Lucinda Sneed's and Tiffany Crystal Tutweiler's family and friends last night. Does *everyone* on the Shore go to the Decoy Jamboree?"

"This will be *my* first visit," I said. "I've avoided this thing like the plague for years."

"That's what Ormy told me." Athena leaned forward. "So why this sudden desire this year?" I could feel her eyes boring into me.

Ormy. I blinked. There, for a moment, I had forgotten that I disliked this cold, elegant woman and that she disliked me. With our heads together, reviewing the suspects, we had almost become civil. But with that single word, she snapped

me back into my bad head as if she'd used a rubber band.
What made me even madder was that I knew this emotion was
beneath contempt and totally unworthy of a hardened cynic
and a mature woman.

Oblivious, she was waiting for an answer.

"You really think I had something to do with this, don't
you?" I asked flatly.

"What makes you say that?"

God, she was good, I thought resentfully. For a minute
there, she almost had me believing we were on an equal
footing. But I knew that answering a question with a question
that implies you know more than you really do is one of the
world's oldest interrogation techniques. I'd used it plenty of
times myself.

"What led you to ask me the questions you did? Obviously,
you think I know something. Unfortunately, I'm as much in
the dark about who killed Fin Fish as anyone else."

"You know, you've got quite a reputation around here for
being in the wrong place at the right time." Again, that matter-
of-fact voice.

"What is that supposed to mean?" I asked, a little more irritably than I'd meant it to sound.

"What do you think it means?" she countered.

I rose. "My, how the time flies when you're having fun!
You know, you missed a great career in clinical psychology,
Athena. I've got to run now, but call me if and when you catch
Smollet. And the real killer."

"Don't worry," she promised. "I'm sure you'll already be
there."

What the pluperfect hell was that supposed to mean? I
fumed as I made my way past another baby trooper guarding
the front door. He must have been there since early that
morning; he was drowsing in his folding chair, a copy of the
Baltimore Sun, folded to the comics page, falling from his
limp fingers. Yellow crime scene tape was strung across the
staircase leading up to the circuit courts.

He never even stirred as I tripped past the statue of the
Unknown Waterman. The heels of my black patent pumps

clicked, echoing on the marble floor as I pushed open the big front door and let myself out on a gust of cold blue wind.

There was no sign of Sam outside.

It was almost dark in these short days of early winter, and the sky was jet black and starless, threatening more foul weather. The courthouse clock tolled the half hour, and I threw my big challis shawl around my shoulders, warily assaying the long cold block between the courthouse green and the Santimoke Inn.

Waiting, I lit a cigarette and puffed away like a troll under a bridge. I was steamed about being considered a suspect, and even more, stewing about Athena's attitude.

"Naw! Maw!" croaked a familiar voice, and I took a step back as black feathery wings brushed past my face.

"Edgar!" I exclaimed, looking up. Sure enough, Edgar Allan Crow was circling my head, eyeing me with profound dissatisfaction. As I watched, he soared toward the second story of the courthouse and landed on his feeding station outside the chambers window. There, he perched for a moment, flicking his tail irritably before hopping to the heavy wrought-iron trellis.

"Naw! Maw!" Edgar cackled, hopping back to his feeding station, then back to the ivy trellis again. "Naw! Maw!" He repeated this little dance three or four times, pausing each time to glare at me. "Naw! Maw!" he croaked.

"You're mad because they're disturbing you, aren't you?" I asked him. Crows, I suddenly remembered, are diurnal birds, only active during the day. Unless disturbed after dark by noise and lights, they pretty much pack it in at dusk. Poor Edgar; this murder thing must have been really hard on him, with all these people running around and making him crazy with their lights and their noise. Obviously he was still upset, or he would have been curled up in his nest in the ivy, feasting, no doubt, on the detritus of clam strips and fried oysters left behind by the Jamboree street vendors. "Where's Sam, Edgar?"

As I watched, he continued to hop from the trellis to the window, muttering and cackling and glaring at me as if I were to blame for his discomfort. "Naw! Maw!" he called, then strafed me again, flapping around my head like a tiny, angry Wicked Witch of the East.

I poked around in my pocketbook and found a half-forgotten roll of stale wintergreen Life Savers. Carefully, I unrolled them and placed them on the courthouse steps. "This's all I've got, Edgar." Great, I thought, first ghosts, now here I am talking to a crow. What next? Animated dancing decoys?

Edgar did not seem appeased. He clung to the ancient ivy trellis, shifted himself until he was almost upside down and hung there, eyeing me distastefully. "Naw! Maw!" he squawked. "Naw! Maw!"

"What's the matter, Lassie? Is Timmy trapped in the old well again?" I asked nastily. Ungrateful bird!

"Naw! Maw!" A sudden brittle gust of wind caught me from behind and I wrapped my shawl tightly around my velvet jacket. Edgar swooped at me. "Naw! Maw!" he cried, tugging at my shawl with his beak.

"Cut that out, you feathered creep!" I exclaimed, jerking the fringes away from him.

He skipped to the trellis and began to climb up the vines. "Naw! Maw!" he hissed. "Naw! Maw!"

Swift thinking has never been one of my talents, but enlightenment finally dawned. Warily, I walked over and studied the trellis.

"Boo!" Sam said, materializing right in front of me. He was hidden in the ivy, not six inches from my face, grinning diabolically. "Of course, the window's closed and locked up tighter than Bill Gates's wallet now, but when it was open last night, anyone could have climbed up that trellis and gotten in."

I jumped, but he didn't seem to notice as he floated down to the ground. "Any possible footprints have been blurred and wiped out around the foundation by hundreds of large law enforcement feet, shod in black leather cop shoes, tramping back and forth," he said, a little out of breath. "But I think we may have a clue here, Holl."

Looking upward, I could see how someone with murder in mind could easily climb up the heavy iron-and-vine structure, bolted sturdily into the brick wall. Protected by the shadows, they would not have been easily visible to a casual passerby.

"Just like climbing up a ladder," Sam muttered. "Then, when our murderer reached the second story, he or she could easily insert themselves right through the open chambers window to confront and do in the Honorable Findlay S. Fish!" He whistled.

"Naw! Maw!" wheezed Edgar. The bird lit on the step and began to crack wintergreen Life Savers as if they were nuts.

"Sorry, old man," Sam apologized absently. "It seems like everyone's been disturbing you lately. If only you could talk!"

"You mean you can't communicate with him?" I asked.

"Whatever Edgar knows, he's not telling. I think he's pretty righteously pissed off at all the disturbances." My ghostly ex looked thoughtfully upward, frowning as he placed his hands on his hips. "It's nothing for a ghost to do, but even the most out-of-shape mortal could climb up there and get in, you know," he murmured thoughtfully.

"Speaking of out-of-shape mortals, Frosty and Loop were loitering around out here in front of the courthouse last night," I pointed out. "And there's Lenore Currier, in her mud moccasins, pretty much in shape."

"Oh, I'd say she was in excellent shape," Sam grinned. "Lenore is a real babe, actually. Hard to believe Fish wasn't doing the nasty with *her*—"

"Athena just told me Miz Fish's alleged bridge party was held not more than four blocks away," I interrupted briskly. "And Smollet was hanging out right there when I saw him. That's where he found the decoy, stuck in the trellis."

"It was like Grand Central Station here," Sam agreed mindfully, still squinting up at the window. "Happy Jamboree goers, jurors, cops, our merry cast of suspects, even Fish his own self could have climbed out the window if he'd had a mind to."

"But why should Fish climb out the window? That doesn't make any sense. I could see any one of them climbing up that trellis. Even Smollet, for that matter, if you want to believe he did it, which I don't."

"Naw! Maw!" Edgar grumbled.

" 'Quoth the raven, "Nevermore!" ' " Sam sighed wistfully.

Dry, whispering leaves scattered across the brick sidewalks in the wind. I pulled my jacket and my shawl closer around myself. "I'm getting cold," I said.

"I wish I could. You know, feel cold and hot again. I miss those things." Sam draped an arm, light as a baby's, around my shoulders. We stood together for a moment, each wrapped in melancholy winter thoughts.

"Well," Sam said at last. "Shall we go on to the Santimoke Inn? Come, Watson! The game is afoot!"

"What do you mean 'Watson,' white boy? I'm Holmes here!" I said lightly, trying to break the sadness in his voice.

"No, I'm Holmes, you're Watson!"

The wind whipped our voices away with the leaves, and we argued all the way down the empty street.

TEN

•

Scenes from the Class Struggle in Santimoke County

"Hell-o! Welcome to the twenty-seventh annual Decoy Jamboree!"

It was, I figured, going to be *that* kind of a night. I just didn't know how much of that kind of night when I walked in the door.

A name tag was slapped on my left breast by a Barbie impersonator wearing camouflage short-shorts, boink-me pumps and not much else. "Hell-o!" she chirped. "Welcome to the twenty-seventh annual Decoy Jamboree!"

As she shoved a pound of printed literature into my hands, her beauty-queen smile was already directed toward more promising material, for a couple of rich-looking guys were right up behind me, sporting matching duck-winged base-ball caps.

"Hell-o, babe! Where've you been all my death?" Sam asked, although she couldn't see or hear him, and I was ignoring him totally. There's nothing quite like bringing a dead date to a big do. It nearly always adds to the fun.

"Yes, folks, here we are in the middle of Decoy Jamboree, right here in the reception rooms of the Santimoke Inn, Water-town's largest and most venerable establishment," Sam whispered as he trotted along beside me. "For the duration, the ersatz Louis XIV decor has been covered up with enough rough logs, phragmites and cornstalks to build duck blinds for the entire Russian army's ducking pleasure."

146

"Shhh," I hissed out of the side of my mouth, scanning the room.

"Oh, I see no sign of Ormand Friendly, although I did see a number of people, including Rig Riggle, your editor from hell, whose company you desperately did *not* seek," Sam remarked cheerfully. "Friendly, no doubt, is late as usual."

"Get lost, Sam!" I murmured through a stiff smile.

"Your wish is my command!" he laughed, and did his disappearing act.

Avoiding Rig, I spotted some carvers I knew through my father. Ron Rue and Harry Jobes both wanted to know what I knew about Fin Fish's untimely demise.

Just as I was explaining that they probably had already heard from my dad everything I knew, Eddie Dean came over and caught the tail end of my description of Fin's instrument of death.

"It didn't hurt the decoy, did it?" he asked.

Cigar Daisy, having given up his trademark stogie for health reasons, strolled past surrounded by adoring groupies. In this gathering, you could tell the carvers at a glance: They were the ones in jeans, borrowed sports jackets and anxious looks. Many thousands of dollars in prize money was at stake in tonight's decoy judging. With any luck, some of it would find its way into their pockets. Most of the bird boys probably would have been hung from the roof beam by their noses before wearing black tie, and yet this event was supposed to celebrate their work and artistry.

If the Jamboree theme was "Our Decoy Heritage," why not have this do down on the marsh? I hid behind Bobby Richardson and Ken Basile as Rig Riggle, the Editor from Hell, cruised past, sucking up to an important *Gazette* advertiser. You could tell by the way his lips were attached to her shoes that he was groveling real good.

"The *Gazette* will assure the advertisers that the Scratch Wallace will emerge without a scratch, heh, heh heh," he said, mopping his brow. "In the Monday edition, of course."

No sign of Friendly. Hopefully, he would turn up so I could

offload my trellis theory. Well, Edgar's trellis theory, except I knew damn well he wouldn't believe clues garnered from a crow.

Or a ghost.

People in black tie and long dresses moved gingerly and incongruously around the crowded space, doing their best to avoid physical contact with each other, exhibition booths and the brass quartet in the corner grinding out some version of "Muskrat Love" under a thatched-roof bandstand. Lined up along the walls in cagelike spaces, the exhibitors stared out at the free world like animals in a zoo.

Decoys? Everywhere, even in places you would normally not expect to see a decoy. This was the first and, I hoped, the last time I would ever see an evening gown with an embroidered decoy pattern or a tie-and-cummerbund set in high-jungle camo.

As I moved across the ballroom, I saw, in the middle of the floor, a large pool fed by a fountain featuring a regurgitating duck. In those limpid waters, several grown men in black tie were watching some wooden ducks bob around. I spotted Frosty and Loop immediately; their serious, sour expressions, as they inspected the decoys, gave not a hint that there was any pleasure in this event.

I blinked. Yes, that was my father beside the fountain, wearing a tuxedo and poking at a floating decoy with a pencil like it was a piece of prime livestock. I wished I had a camera; Perk Ball in black tie isn't one of those things you're likely to see every day, and it may have come in handy later for purposes of blackmail.

Instead, I snuck up behind him. "Dad," I hissed. "Where did you get that monkey suit?"

My father barely glanced at me, so intent was he on making little marks on a clipboard. "Your mother had it put back from the last Methodist Women rummage sale." He sighed.

"Any sign of Friendly?" I asked.

He shook his head. "No, but everyone's talkin' about Fin Fish. It's the hot topic of the show. Now, lookit that bluebill.

D'you ever see a bird ride that nicely?" He made a mark on his sheet.

"I never saw a bluebill ride anywhere," I answered quite honestly. Where was Friendly?

I cast a look at Dr. Froston and Attorney Gareau, about five feet away from us. They were studiously ignoring each other, also marking things on their clipboards. "Where's Lenore?"

"Around here somewhere. She's trying to Band-Aid the Fish killing. People are going into mourning over losing that Scratch Wallace. Promising everyone a big surprise later. But I'm wondering if Harry Truman's going to give her a big surprise."

Knowing how volatile Harry Truman could be, I was inclined to agree.

"We've got some fine carvers, here," Dad said, carefully picking up a goldeneye and turning it over to examine its bottom.

Grason Chesser came up and muttered something into my father's ear; both of them laughed as the Virginia carver strolled away, shaking his head in amusement.

In the tight little world of decoys, these guys were considered major celebrities.

"Jimmy Vizier, the Ragin' Cajun, just arrived," my father said. "He's not showin', he's shoppin' this year. We should get him to take Fish's place as judge."

"I doubt anyone wants to step into a dead man's shoes," I replied, keeping an eye on Frosty and Loop. I noticed the carvers gave them a wide berth, and I didn't think it was because you weren't supposed to interfere with the judges.

"Not well liked, those two, they've tried to cheat too many carvers out of a fair price for their work," my father muttered, as if he had read my mind. "Their whole premise is 'gimme a couple of your birds for my collection and I'll tell everyone you're a great carver and a good investment.' It's a kind of blackmail, but whataya gonna do? They're rich and they're big collectors; other people listen to their opinions. There ain't no carvers with waterfront estates, notice. When you get a five-, ten-thousand-dollar prize, that's a lot of money for people like us."

"Nobody's quit his day job yet, huh?"

"Precious few," my father replied. "But, if you win a show like this, and the one in Ocean City and a couple others, the price you can ask for a bird goes up considerably."

I nodded thoughtfully.

"Perk, ah, yas, Perk! I must remind you we're in the middle of an important judging," Frosty Froston called out repressively. He tapped his pencil on his clipboard and glared at us over his glasses.

"I know that," Dad retorted. "But do you know my daughter, Hollis? She's a reporter for the *Gazette*. She was there last night when Fin bought the farm."

The good doctor looked at me over his glasses as if I were a decorative decoy.

"Nonetheless, Perk," he started to say, when Loop Gareau, who had been listening to this conversation with great interest, bounded over to me, hand outstretched like an emcee on a game show.

"Ms. Ball!" he hissed. "I thought you looked familiar! Didn't I see you in front of the courthouse last night? Such a tragedy!" He smiled at me, pumping my hand while he shifted his clipboard beneath his elbow. He looked up at me. "You must tell me at once," he said. "Is the Scratch Wallace intact?"

Before I could reply, Frosty Froston had stepped in front of the smaller man. "Yas! The Scratch Wallace? Did you see it? Is it damaged? When will the police release it?"

Suddenly I found myself at the center of some unwelcome attention. Other people, hearing the magic name "Scratch Wallace" were coming closer to hear what I had to say.

"It's a terrible thing," a matron huffed, "when our precious antique decoys aren't safe! It's that man in the White House! I blame the Democrats!"

"This wouldn't have happened in the Reagan era!"

"Maybe," Loop said nastily, "you ought to ask Dr. Froston what he was doing lurking around the courthouse last night. Perhaps he knows what happened to the Scratch Wallace!"

"Me? Me?" Froston responded indignantly. "When I saw you sneak away from the cocktail party, I followed you! I knew you'd be up to no good! Perhaps a better question would be what do *you* know about the Scratch Wallace?"

"I saw you first!" Loop sputtered, oblivious to the crowd he was attracting. "I was keeping an eye on you! I knew you'd try to get to Fin first!" He shook his clipboard at the doctor. "Tried to make him an offer on the bird, behind my back, did you!"

"I didn't! But *you* did! You'd do anything to own a Scratch Wallace! *You'd* bash Fin's head in with it!"

"Only you would be stupid enough to do that!"

"So did you?" asked a familiar voice.

We all turned to see Detective Sergeant Ormand Friendly, resplendent in what took me a minute to realize was a tuxedo. The sapphire blue jacket was embossed in an allover coin pattern. His tie and cummerbund were a delicate shade of magenta. The effect was blinding, to say the least.

I was about to ask if his band was covering the top forty out at the Holiday Inn lounge, but he placed his hand against my shoulder in a warning gesture. "I'd like to speak to both of you gentlemen about your presence at the courthouse last night," he said to Gareau and Froston.

They both swelled in lèse-majesté.

Frosty Froston pointed at Loop Gareau.

Loop Gareau pointed at Frosty Froston.

"*He* did it," they both said at once.

"Is there a place we can speak privately?" Friendly sighed.

I was still contemplating the way Friendly glittered under the chandeliers as he escorted a protesting Frosty and Loop to the manager's office.

"This will only take a minute," he was promising them.

"Hollis! Hollis! Over here!"

Lenore Currier was rushing across the floor toward me with a welcoming smile. She was every inch the Empress of Duck Carnival, resplendent in shimmering teal silk. "I'm so sorry! I had to run out for a few minutes! There's always some last-minute detail you never count on, but I think I have everything under control now!" She was rosy and out of breath, as if she had been running. Her parka was still slung across her arm, as if she had just come in from outside.

"You've got to come and see what I've done with Harry Truman!" she exclaimed breathlessly. "It's going to be the highlight of the show."

She hooked her arm into mine and dragged me away from the Froston-Gareau action, threading her way through the crowd.

"Oh, Lenore, it's just awful about poor Fin Fish!" A gray-haired matron exclaimed, placing herself in our path.

"Do you know what happened?" an important-looking man asked her gravely.

"It didn't damage that wonderful bird, did it?" someone else asked.

"That's the question on everyone's lips," Lenore told me, after she'd calmed them all down with promises of a wonderful surprise this evening. Then we were on our way across the floor again. "Fish dead is much more exciting than Fish alive, it would seem. It's certainly jazzed this year's Jamboree up considerably!"

But another, and then yet another, group halted our progress, and it was a while before we were able to make our way to the little stage at the far end of the ballroom. The heavy velvet curtain was tightly drawn, but Lenore gracefully bounded up the proscenium steps, teal silk rustling as she drew back the curtain.

"I thought this would be so clever—" she said, beckoning me to the opening, then standing back to let me have a look. "We borrowed all this old carving gear from the historical society."

I peered into the stage. It had been done up like an old carver's workshop. Ancient wooden workbenches, pots of paints, brushes, vises and tools strewn creatively across a tastefully battered table. A large selection of what I assumed were Harry Truman's decoys were artfully displayed around the diorama. It was cute, I thought, but a little too neat and clean, a little too artistically displayed, as if *Architectural Digest* had gotten in there with a camera crew while the carver was sleeping it off one Sunday morning.

"That's really cute," I said tactfully, turning to Lenore, who was still standing outside the curtain. "Are you going to have Harry give a little performance?"

A crease appeared between her eyebrows, and her face drained of color beneath her foundation. Her lips drew back from her teeth, and she almost knocked me over as she whipped the curtain back to allow herself inside.

"Where is he?" she hissed, looking all over the display. She even stooped to peer under the table. When she stood up, her face was tight with fury. "Where the *hell* is he?" she asked again, seemingly of herself, for she gathered up her skirts and ran from wing to wing, even looking up in the flies, as if Harry might be hanging from a sandbag like a sleeping bat.

"Damn him all to hell!" she breathed, shaking with rage, long fingers curling and uncurling as she picked up a long, thin carver's knife from the table, gripping it tightly in her hand. "Damn!" she exclaimed. When she recalled my presence, she made a visible effort to calm herself.

"I'm sorry! It's just that I'm under so much pressure!" she breathed in a thin voice. "He was supposed . . . supposed to be here!" She made an effort to calm herself. "If he's slipped away and started drinking, it'll ruin everything!"

"Harry's been known to lift a few," I admitted. I really felt sorry for her. She was trying so hard to make this, her last duck event, a success and all she'd had so far was bad luck and homicide. "I'll go see if I can find him," I offered. "He can't be too far away. Harry's probably only been to Watertown about three times in his whole life, so he wouldn't go far. He's probably in the bar. Harry would find a bar blindfolded, bound and gagged."

The public address system shrieked and whined. "Ladies and gentlemen!" The dulcet squawk of Perk Ball's voice rang out across the ballroom. "Ladies and gentlemen, the judging is closed. The judges will confer, and winning carvers will be announced in two minutes. The winners will be announced from the stage in two minutes. Thank you." Shriek, crackle, dead silence.

Lenore spun around helplessly, as if Harry Truman would somehow mysteriously appear in the wings.

"I've got to find him! The curtain goes up right after the winners are announced!" she exclaimed, looking about herself in a panic.

"I'd better help," I offered.

Lenore shook her head. "No, go, you enjoy yourself. I'll look for him. He can't have gone too far away, not in the state he was in." She gripped my arm, and I was surprised at her strength as she pulled me down the stairs and gave me a prod. "I'm sure he'll turn up!" She smiled between clenched teeth.

Before I could protest, she disappeared behind the curtain.

I looked about uncertainly, hoping to see either Harry Truman or Ormand Friendly somewhere in the milling throng.

"My God, Holl, did you see Friendly's outfit? He looks like he's on his way to a high school prom. What did the rental place tell him that style was, Riverboat Medici?" Sam appeared behind me, and I nearly jumped. "Boy, this is a real geriatric crowd, isn't it? I thought a lot of these people would be dead long before I was!"

"Don't be such a snob!" I snapped, causing a middle-aged couple to turn and murmur an apology as they moved as far away from me as they could get and still be in the same room.

"Do you think the lug has found any clues with two hands and a roadmap?" Sam asked. "It looks like you and I will have to solve this one, too."

I shook my head slightly. "Not yet. Friendly's questioning Gareau and Froston, though. I think I'll try to see what's going on with that."

The tension in the room, as they waited for the winning names to be announced, was as thick as an August afternoon. I had thought to make my away across the floor to the manager's office, but it was like moving against a riptide; everyone else was pushing toward the podium, where my dad was tapping his microphone and wrestling dramatically with a piece of paper. Beside him, a smiling Barbie with solidified hair and breasts, dressed in a skintight camo jumpsuit opened to her sternum, held up a display board covered with fluttering prize ribbons.

"Wow," Sam laughed. "Check out your dad! Uh-oh."

"Uh-oh what?"

"I'll catch you later," Sam whispered and disappeared as quickly as he had appeared.

"Hollis, dear," said a genteel voice in my ear, and I turned to see Miz Fish, with a bald Smollet in tow. And he looked none too thrilled to be here either, even though he wasn't wearing a peach sheet or a black tie. In fact, both of them looked as if they were off for a nice sail; she was wearing a summery shift and Smollet was attired in chinos and a polo shirt.

"What in the world are you doing here?" I asked, not, I believed, unreasonably.

"We could ask you the same thing, Hollis," Smollet muttered, as surly as a teenager at a family reunion. "I mean, really, you swore you'd never turn up at the duck carnival. My head's cold," he added, rubbing a hand over his skull.

"Caroline, darling, we're all so sorry about Fin!" A red-faced man stopped in his migration toward the stage to take Miz Fish's hands and commiserate. "How lovely to see you here keeping his spirit alive, my dear."

"Oh, that's very kind of you, James, but not quite true. I'm here to announce that I'm selling Fish's collection and donating the money to the women's shelter," Miz Fish said evenly, smiling at me. "My son and I are on our way to the airport. We're taking a long trip."

"Chipper? Is that you? Why, I wouldn't have recognized you!" exclaimed a woman whose pearl-bedecked prow could have been featured in *Jane's Fighting Ships*.

"Hello. My name is Chipper Bagworm Projabawah Fish," Smollet repeated stolidly, as if he were a POW. Only his name, rank and serial number. "Hello. My name is Chipper Bagworm—"

"He's being deprogrammed," Miz Fish quickly explained, but I don't think anyone heard or cared about Smollet. They were all marveling over her decision to sell Fish's decoy collection.

I was able to drag Smollet aside from the school of sharks that were suddenly circling Miz Fish. "Bagworm? *Bagworm?*" I hissed. "What the pluperfect hell are you two doing here? Do you both want to go to jail?"

"Bagworm's about as close as I can come to sayin' his name, gimme a break," Smollet whined. "You already shaved my head, now you want me to be somebody with a name I can't say—"

"Smollet," I said after I took a deep breath. "What is going on here? What are you and Miz Fish up to? This place is crawling with cops!"

Well, I didn't know that for sure, but I did know it was crawling with a cop in a blinding sapphire blue tuxedo who would like nothing better than to recapture Smollet Bowley, escaped prisoner. And that was enough.

"Well, I would like to go to Brazil," he replied uncertainly. "Miz Fish dug up Bagworm's passport, and it's still good, it ain't expired or nothing, so she says I've gotta be Bagworm till we get to Rio."

"But what made you two show up *here*, of all the god-forsaken places on the face of the earth?"

"Well, it's like Miz Fish says, she don't want them decoys. So she's decided to get that duck woman to sell 'em for her, so we stopped here on the way to the airport so's she could give that decoy lady the key to the pool house. We're on a midnight flight outta BWI." Smollet grinned at me.

"Tonight?" I repeated stupidly. "Wow. Miz Fish doesn't waste time, does she?"

"Hot damn, Hollis! I'm goin' ta Brazil! I'm gonna lie up on the beach and sip 'em tropical drinks outta coconut shells. I'm gonna start a new life, Hollis. I'm givin' up this criminal crap. I'm goin' to get a real job and learn to speak the language and start a-new."

"What about your wife?" I asked.

Smollet shrugged. "She's better off without me. This way she can marry her first husband all over again and have the white wedding over to the First Church of Elvis jus' like she's always wanted. There ain't nothin' holdin' me on this damn ole Eastern Shore."

"Yeah, but—"

"But what? Spend the rest of my life like Oder 'n' the rest a my fambly? Always inna, outta jail, always scraping 'long to rip off some chump change and never have nothin' to show for it?" Smollet regarded me seriously. "This is my big chance, Hollis. My chance to begin again, make something a myself down there. Don't let me blow it. You know I didn't kill Judge Fish. And I'm pretty sure a nice old bluehead lady like Miz Fish didn't do it neither."

"Your attention, please. Your attention, please." My father's voice squeaked and rumbled over the PA system. "Will Harry Truman report to the stage area, please? Mr. Truman, report to the stage area."

I looked over the crowd to see my father and Lenore at the podium looking very worried.

Smollet wrinkled his forehead. "What're they lookin' for Harry Truman for? He's out in the parkin' lot with the low-enders."

"He is?" I clutched Smollet's arm. "Are you sure?"

"Hey, I know Harry Truman when I see him. I—"

But I was already pushing my way through the tide of people again, heading down the crowded room out a side door and down a long empty hallway through another door marked EXIT.

A whole new thing was going on out here; I took in the scene with a glance.

These were the low-enders, people who couldn't afford a $200 ticket to get inside, but loved those decoys and loved to collect. These collectors and traders gathered out here during Decoy Jamboree. No less obsessed than those inside, they just had less money. No Ward decoys out here, no Famous Guy

Carvers, although one could always hope for some undiscovered treasure amid the detritus. It was a big flea market. This was where the low-end birds and other hunting memorabilia appeared. Where working-class guys gathered in the open and the cold, sort of like the Decoy Jamboree Fringe.

They hunkered over their wares, goods displayed on blankets spread over the tailgates of their vehicles. Some warmed themselves with the heat from barbecue grills and huddled inside their coats.

Others wandered about the night asphalt, examining the goods, bargaining, visiting, exchanging ideas. Things offered here cost a fraction of what they did inside, I assessed quickly, as I walked between the cars looking for signs of Harry Truman.

You'd better believe decoys were for sale here, along with new works by novices on their way up, and the totally untalented. Decorative carvings were displayed of birds so realistic every feather was delineated. And stuff that would never fool a duck, let alone a hunter. All the grave goods of the vanished Eastern Shore were available in this back-lot bazaar. Stuffed deer heads and molting stuffed decoys. Old oyster cans, crab pots, hunting knives, traps, ammo boxes, tongheads, shotguns, oyster plates, reloaders and black powder; if it came from the Chesapeake Bay hunter-gatherer culture, you could teeter on your stiletto heels out here and bargain for it.

No bargaining inside. No smoking and God knows, no damn fun. But this, this was loud and cheerful and vivid. Give me low-enders anytime; they know how to enjoy themselves without draping their obsessions in pretentious cant.

No wonder Harry was out here. In spite of the cold and the dim light, people were actually laughing and having a good time. If anyone was taking themselves too seriously, I was missing it. But I was temporarily distracted by an old bail-handled Christy's oyster can with a sailor on the label who looked just like Elvis. If I weren't looking for Harry Truman I could have had a ball out here buying stuff I couldn't resist and could almost afford. But even I got distracted.

Rule of thumb: the amount of junk you have expands to fit the amount of space you have to store it. I still have a couple of inches to spare in what passes for my study at home. I was about to shell out ten bucks for that Elvis oyster can when I heard a familiar voice drifting across the trucks and vans.

"There I was, way out on the marsh. It were blowin' up a gale, and it were cold enough to freeze the tits off a witch when I come up on this ole decoy layin' out there—"

I found Harry right where I should have known he'd be, leaning against a pickup truck, holding a brant decoy and entrancing a bunch of young guys in white rubber boots.

Huddie Swann and Junie Redmond and Earl Don Grinch and Paisley Redmond, those boys from Oysterback, were spellbound as they leaned into the sides of Junie's '86 Chevy Sierra pickup, staring into the junked-up bottom of the flat-bed like the true meaning of life was to be found in some old nylon rope, a half dozen bushel basket lids and a bag of aluminum cans.

Harry and the boys weren't conversing, they were communicating in a series of sophisticated grunts and trying to keep their contraband out of sight, their wary watermen's faces hidden in the long shadows cast by the overhead lights that flashed on a bottle of whiskey going from hand to hand. My heart sank for poor Lenore.

Harry was three sheets into the wind.

"Cold? Oh, my honey, it like to freeze your balls to your backbone, it were that cold," he was saying. As he spoke, he dabbed with a dirty bandanna at his cheek. Lo and behold, he was shriven and shorn as clean as a baby, his hair was combed and he was wearing black tie. Lenore had fulfilled her promise to get him a room at the Santimoke Inn and get him cleaned up. Where she'd found a tuxedo for him, I do not know to this day, but Lenore Currier was a woman who seemed to be able to pull rabbits out of hats.

Of course, he'd added on an old orange hunting vest to his ensemble, the tie was long gone, his hair was frizzing up and the grizzled five o'clock shadow was coming back in, but I imagined that a couple of hours ago, he must have looked perfectly gorgeous.

"Oh, my honey, it were something right about—" he said again and broke off as he looked up and saw me. His old river-colored eyes snapped and spit fire, and the rye whiskey rolled off him in pungent waves. "Damn it, Hollis!" he hollered. "Why'n hell did you bring that woman around?" he spat. " 'At 'ere tater almost killed me!"

"Jesus, Harry, a bath and a shave isn't gonna kill you," I replied. "You've got to get back in there, all those people are waiting on you to—"

"No! Damn it, I mean that woman tried to kill me!" Harry Truman sputtered, taking the bandanna away from his cheek to reveal a long red gash.

"Damn, Harry, you oughta be more careful 'bout shavin' more'n once a year!" Huddie Swann laughed.

"I was settin' back there waitin' for the curtain to go up and she come back there and tried to stick me with a knife! If I had'na moved when I did, she woulda stuck that sumbitch in me!"

"Harry, there have been times when I have wanted to stick you with a knife," I replied, and the Oysterbackers laughed at the old silverback having it out with the girl reporter.

Since I'm related to the Redmond brothers, there wasn't much they could say.

"But you've got to come inside now, they're all waiting for you. You're going to be the hit of the evening, Harry. You're gonna be rich and famous!"

"Screw rich and famous," Harry growled, "I ain't goin' around that woman no more. She just wants to steal my 'coys, her and that damn judge." He patted the tailgate beneath him. "This is where I belong, out here with my buddies! Screw 'em, the rich assholes!"

The local boys snickered in agreement. Huddie Swann, always the gentleman, offered me the bottle, but I was too pissed off to take more than a little swig.

Gingerly, Harry slid down off the tailgate. "Come over

here, I want to talk to you," he said, drawing me a little aside from the Oysterback contingent.

"What is it? For God's sake, Harry—" I sighed impatiently. "People are in there waiting on you, you know."

"Lissen, I gotta tell ya somethin'," Harry Truman said with that utter earnestness of the truly drunk, swaying on his feet.

"God, Harry, get a move on, they're all—"

"That wasn't no Scratch Wallace," he breathed. "She paid me fifty bucks to make that decoy."

"What?"

"You heard me." Harry sighed impatiently. "She, you know, brought me a bird and said can you make me a snow goose in this here carver's style? There ain't a decoy made that I can't copy, I sez, and I done it."

"But how—?" My head was swimming now. Too many loose pieces and no way to make them fit together. People climbing into the courthouse on trellises and Lenore getting Harry Truman to forge decoys when they'd just met; it was all too much for my feeble brain.

"Well, how'n hell was I to know what she planned to do with 'em? Fifty bucks a pop is fifty bucks a bird! I never come around this damn shindig till you brung that 'ere tater around. An' if she pays people back by trying to kill 'em with a carving knife, I ain't comin' back none either!"

"You mean she really did try to stab you with a carving knife?" I asked stupidly.

Harry Truman glared at me. "I already told you that!" he growled. "Are you deaf?"

"If she really did try to kill you, and this isn't one of your stupid stories," I asked suspiciously, "how come?"

"Because she was sellin' off the judge's *real* decoys and replacin' 'em with the fakes I made! I thought you were supposed to be one of the eddicated Balls!" Harry sighed in frustration. "She thought she stabbed me with that carver's knife but it just went into my Therm-O vest!"

He turned around to display a slit in the back of his dirty old garment. A cloud of small, downy motes floated into the air as he pulled the cut open and I saw the gash in the fabric. "Snuck up behind me, she did! Probably thought she got me good, but all she got was my vest! Heh! Heh! Heh!" he chuckled. "That's when I figured it was time to get outta there. She left me for dead and I wasn't gonna tell her no different. As soon as she left, I picked myself up and got all the hell outta there! I was out here lookin' for a ride home when I run up against those Oysterback boys, and they had a bottle, and weren't above givin' an old man a drink, so—"

"Jesus, Harry, are you all right? It looks like you got cut right bad," I said, feeling slightly ill.

"It's just a scratch. Hell, I've had worse in the war and out on the marsh. Like the time I was gunnin' over old man Tolliver's blinds and he filled me fulla buckshot. Now, my honey, that was bad! I was jes' settin' there behind that stage, mindin' my own damn business when she come back and picked up that knife and stove 'at sucker right into my back!" His tone was mildly indignant, as if she had offended his dignity rather than tried to murder him. But then again, with Harry Truman, you never knew; it was probably the latest in a long line of attempts on his life. His had been a pretty rough career.

"She tried to kill you," I said stupidly. I was really confused now.

Hang in there; it gets even stranger.

"She tried to kill me when my back was turned!" Harry agreed. "Damn and all if I ever come to one of these shindigs again! I can get killed down on the island for free!"

"But why try to kill you?"

Harry blinked at me as if I were even stupider than I looked, which maybe I was. "Hell, I been copyin' decoys for her for years!" he growled impatiently. "She's been sellin' off the real ones and givin' him the fakes and now the whole goddamn thing's about to bust wide open!"

"You're not making this up!" I exclaimed.

Harry cut his eyes at me. "It's goddamn smart is what it is! Too goddamn smart for her own good. That way she got to keep all her good 'coys and have his money, too."

"But why would Lenore try to kill you? You're the goose that carves the golden decoys. Or something," I finished feebly.

Harry shrugged. "Lenore? Who said anything about her? I was talkin' about Caroline Fish!"

ELEVEN

•

Little-Known Facts About Well-Known People

"Miz Fish?" I asked stupidly. "Are you sure it wasn't Lenore?"

"Hell, no! It was Caroline Fish! That's what I said!" Harry Truman shifted, glaring at me with red-rimmed eyes. "Caroline Fish! Who'd you think I was talking about?"

"Are you sure?"

"Why wouldn't I be? I oughta know goddamn well who stabbed me!" Harry said contemptuously. "Came right up behind that damn curtain in there! The nerve of some people! Don't that beat all?"

"Harry, we've got to get you to a hospital and you have to talk to Sergeant Friendly—and we've gotta catch Miz Fish before she takes off for Brazil with Smollet—oh, my God, Smollet! She's got Smollet!"

All of a sudden, the loose pieces fell together.

"Miz Fish has been quietly selling off the judge's priceless decoy collection and substituting your fakes, hasn't she? That sweet little old lady?" I was stunned. And stupid, too.

"Sweet little old lady, my foot!" Harry Truman spat. "Caroline Tuckman was a tater when she was in high school fifty years ago and she's a tater now!" He staggered back to Junior Redmond's pickup and sat down on the tailgate, crossing his arms over his chest. "And I don't need no doctor. I just wanna go back to the island. This damn duck thing sucks!"

"Can you keep him here?" I asked the Redmond brothers.

"Holl, as long as there's a bottle," Paisley laughed, "you

can bet your ass Harry Truman's gonna be right along side of it."

Obviously, this was a job for Lenore. She broke it, she could buy it, I thought. Let her come out here and get him; I'd done my best, now it was in her hands.

Good little soldier that I am, I trudged back toward the inn, where wave after wave of applause washed out across the night toward me.

"A big hand for the first-place winner!" My father's voice, distorted and amplified, floated over the parking lot as I opened the outside door and stomped back into the corridor.

And came face-to-face with Caroline Fish.

I've been told that everything I'm thinking shows on my face.

I must have looked as frightened as I felt. Funny how a dear little bluehead lady doesn't look so dear when she's suddenly holding a tiny pearl-handled derringer right at your head. Tiny or not, I knew that baby could put a hurting on me; I've seen what a .22 bullet, fired at close range, can do to a human brain. It might not kill me outright, but it could scramble my brain badly enough that all I'd ever be good for was editing the social notes.

Uh-oh.

"So, you've found Harry," Miz Fish said conversationally, almost regretfully. "Well, never mind that. He won't say anything to anyone, as much as he hates the police. But whatever am I going to do about you? This is so inconvenient." She *tsk*ed.

I was just realizing that I'd missed a golden opportunity to wrestle that little pistol away from her when I heard her pull the hammer back. That click was very loud and very final.

"I really wouldn't even try it, dear," she said gently. "Years and years of golf and tennis have made me one very fast old lady."

"What did you do with Smollet?" I asked.

"Don't worry about him, Hollis, dear," she said soothingly. "He's taken care of, that's all you need to know."

"You're setting him up for Fish's murder, aren't you?" I asked.

"Oh, heavens no." She *tsk*ed. "But it seems that someone, perhaps your father, actually recognized him in there, so he had to leave."

Beneath the harsh fluorescent light in the narrow, featureless hallway, her face looked drawn and sallow, her features shadowed. I couldn't read her expression.

I also couldn't see the gun, but God knows, I could feel it, now pressed into my back, a sharp pain like a high thin whine.

"I suppose Harry told you, that filthy old drunk, that I'd been replacing Fin's decoys?"

"H-he said something about it. I didn't even know you *knew* each other."

"Not socially, but we *did* go to high school together. Haven't you ever heard that everyone's only six degrees of separation from everyone else? The odd thing is, Fin never even noticed I was replacing his birds, one by one. He thought he was so clever, you know, but he wasn't at all. I'd been taking them out of the pool house, two or three at a time, and having Harry copy them. Then I'd take the originals and sell them, far far away, where no one would recognize them as belonging to Fin's collection. Not that collectors are all that picky about the provenance of a decoy!"

"But he must have noticed!"

"Fin was very shortsighted, in more ways than one. I don't think he ever even glanced at them, once he owned them. Just like he never looked at me or his children." She sighed. "Fin really believed he was so clever in hiding all our assets in decoys. He thought he had me fooled."

"Wow, that's pretty clever!" I had to admire her nerve, if not her plan.

"Pooh. Fin thought everyone was stupid and he was smart. People who overestimate their own intelligence are the easiest to fool, you know. Look at you, dear, no offense."

"None taken," I said between clenched teeth. She had me there.

"Fin thought I'd end up with nothing, and he'd sell all those birds and live high on the hog!" She gave a genteel snort.

"I can see where you'd have a beef with him," I offered. I was perspiring, even though the hallway was chilly.

"A beef? Oh, you mean a *disagreement*. I am not at all conversant with this modern slang, you see. You really should avoid using it; it's quite unfeminine. Well, shall we go on?"

"Go on where?"

"I really hadn't thought about that," she said a trifle peevishly. "You did have to stick your nose into all of this, didn't you? And it was all going along so well, too! Let's walk, slowly, slowly out to my car and we'll take it from there!"

"What about Smollet?"

"Oblivious, as always. Of course, I gave him my word; can't go back on that, can I? Unless, of course, it's him or me." Miz Fish sighed regretfully.

"Look, I'm a lot of things, but I wouldn't go back on a promise like that, not even to Smollet. Especially not to Smollet. He—"

"Oh, nonsense, you have a fine criminal mind, I've noticed. Now, come on. And try to act as normally as possible, please, dear."

"What's normal?" I asked. "Normal is pretty hard to define, even under the best of circumstances—"

I was rewarded with a sharp poke in the ribs from her little gun for that one. I pushed on the sidebar and out we went.

Just then, the door at the other end of the corridor banged open and Ormand Friendly came running down the hall.

And kept on running right past us.

I didn't need the second poke from Miz Fish's gun to keep from screaming for help; I was the last thing on Friendly's mind.

He didn't even stop. His sapphire blue tuxedo shimmering, he was breathless as he all but elbowed us aside. "Have you seen Smollet Bowley?" he asked over his shoulder, as if it were an afterthought. "There was a rumor he's around here. Place's full of undercover cops—he can't get too far!"

Now, you would think that he might notice that I was being

held at gunpoint, but nooo. Instead, he thudded right on out the door, the tails of his hubba-hubba blue tux flapping right behind him.

I sighed as we stood back to allow three uniformed deputies, equally blind to the action, to rush past us. But what are you supposed to do with a gun in your spine? I was still hoping I could maneuver my way out of this mess, which will tell you something about my foolish optimism.

I yearningly watched them disappear into the low-ender crowd. "Where is a policeman when you really need one?" Miz Fish sighed.

"Where indeed?" I replied giddily. "This is getting to be like a Marx brothers movie."

"We'd best hurry along," Miz Fish said briskly. "Try to act normal. One false move and I'm afraid I'll have to damage you, Hollis dear."

The awful thing is, I knew she would. These little old blue-head ladies can be awful tough when they want something. We walked back out into the chilly parking lot again, past more scenes from the class struggle in Santimoke County.

"My car's parked over on Jefferson Street, about a half block away. Imagine getting a place this close to the inn! I guess we were just lucky, don't you?" Miz Fish asked brightly as we tripped along the sidewalk.

"I thought you were supposed to be at your bridge game. So, how did you kill Fish?" I asked. "Youth wants to know."

Oh, I'm funny, all right.

"You think *I* killed Fin?" Miz Fish gasped in horror. "But, my dear Hollis, I told you, I was at my bridge club! No, *I* didn't kill Fin."

"You didn't?" I asked doubtfully.

She shook her head firmly. "Heavens no! What do you think I am? Murdering Fin would have been entirely too tacky, don't you think? Of course Smollet did it. He had to! Who else could have?"

"Actually, I had been having a hard time picturing you

scaling a trellis in the dead of night to bash in the judge's skull, but the spouse is generally the most likely suspect."

"No, I'm sure it was Smollet. It had better be the boy! Whyever would he lie? This trip to Brazil is costing me a great deal of money!" Miz Fish sighed. "As for me, I played bridge last night and went right home!"

Had it only been last night? It seemed like a million years ago in another lifetime. As we walked away from the chaos of the parking lot, the sound of our heels on the brick sidewalk grew louder, echoing hollowly against the closed and darkened storefronts facing the empty streets. Every decoy reveler in town must have been in the ballroom, rather than out here where they could save my behind. The courthouse clock pealed the longest toll I'd ever heard in my life. Was it only nine o'clock?

"Ah! Here's the car, and here's Smollet!" she said as we approached the yellow Cadillac. His bald head gleaming beneath the streetlight, Smollet leaned over and opened the passenger-side door. "Hi! You comin' with us, Hollis?" he asked happily.

I was beginning to feel very sorry that I hadn't thought to drop a Glock into my evening bag instead of a handkerchief. "This is getting ridiculous!" I snapped.

"I don't know what to do with you now." Miz Fish frowned at me. "My dear, you media types are so inconvenient!"

"I'll take it from here, Caroline," someone said briskly, grasping my arm. Lenore appeared from nowhere. Her heavy parka was pulled over her teal gown, her sequined, high-heeled sandals glittered in the dim light from the streetlamps. I winced at the strength of her grip.

"Oh, that would be wonderful, Lenore dear," Miz Fish said as she buckled herself into her seat. "Smollet and I do have a plane to catch, you know."

Smollet, never too quick on the uptake, nodded. His hands were gripped tightly on the wheel. "We gotta go, Hollis, or we'll miss the plane." He grinned. "Whoo-eee! Lookit me drivin' a Caddy! And I didn't steal it, for once!"

"Smollet!" I gasped.

"Shut up, Hollis," Lenore said out of the side of her mouth, pulling at my arm. "Just let them go."

"Drive on, Smollet!" Miz Fish commanded crisply.

For a long second my eyes met Smollet's. He opened and closed his mouth, and a stunned, comprehending expression passed over his face.

"Do you want to go to Brazil or not, dear?" Miz Fish asked him. "I said, drive! We'll miss our plane!"

Smollet and I eyed each other.

Slowly he dropped his eyes.

He put the Cadillac in gear. Miz Fish pulled her door shut with a bang. She never looked back. The big yellow car hurtled down the street, disappearing around a corner.

"No good deed goes unpunished." I sighed.

"So true," Lenore agreed. "That's why I never perform a good deed!" She relaxed her grip on my arm, exhaling with relief. "God, that was close! I really think she was crazy enough to shoot you! Are you all right?" She hugged me, laughing with relief.

"You mean you're not in on this?" I asked incredulously.

"Not right now!" She grinned, then turned serious. "Look, Hollis, we've got to get out to Fish's house right away. I think I can prove who did kill Fin Fish, if I can just get into the pool house and look at the decoys." She gripped my hand. "You've got to help me, you know. I just saved your life, or at least saved you from being shot by a gun-crazed dowager."

"What about Miz Fish and Smollet?" I looked up the street. The Coupe de Ville had disappeared into the night.

"They'll never get out of Watertown. The police are setting up roadblocks on every street that leads to Route 50," Lenore explained tightly. "Your policeman friend got the Smollet–Caroline story out of Harry Truman! Good Lord, what a mess! Are you okay?"

"Miz Fish has been smuggling out the judge's decoys and replacing them with copies Harry Truman's been making," I exclaimed. "She's been selling them on the West Coast!"

"What?" Lenore demanded. "How did you find that out?"

"Harry Truman told me."

"Harry's been faking birds for Caroline?" Lenore rubbed her temples as if she was acquiring the headache from hell, which maybe she was. "Oh, my God. Hollis, it's all starting to make sense now! Come on, we've got to go to the Fishes'! I've got to get out there and look at those decoys!" She started to walk faster, and I had to run to keep up with her. "I think," she gasped, "that the clue to who killed Fish is in the pool house. I need to look at those birds before the cops get there!"

"Huh?" I said in my usual brilliant and incisive way.

Lenore unlocked the passenger door of the Rover for me. "Help me out here, Hollis, please. My whole career's at stake in this mess," she pleaded. "That state's attorney raked me over the coals. Now I know why!"

"Shouldn't we tell Friendly?" I asked, climbing into her truck. By this time, I was thoroughly confused. Well, you'd be too, if you'd just been through what I'd been through.

"Get real. We're both suspects. If the cops start tramping around the pool house, I'll never get to examine those fake decoys. And I think the fake decoys are the clue to the murderer. If I can see which ones have been replaced, I think I can figure out the rest from there."

"Who do you think did it?" I asked.

She swung herself, evening dress and all, into the driver's seat. "I don't know, but I intend to find out," she said tightly. She looked at me. "Hollis, I'll explain it all when we get there. Do you want this story or not? Because I can put you down right here."

"I want the story!"

"Trust me," Lenore said as she peeled into the street. "You'll get it tonight."

TWELVE

•

Our Goose Is Cooked

All the way to chez Fish, I lamented Smollet's betrayal. "I mean, I *trusted* that jerk," I whined, hunkering down in my seat and sulking. "I hid him out from the police. And when I was in trouble, he let me down!"

Lenore made sympathetic noises, but her mind was on other things. More precipitation had begun to fall, a light, wet snow that drifted slowly across the window and melted as it fell. It was a dead black night. Beyond the pitch of Lenore's head-lights, we could barely see the road.

As we drove out into the country, the snow began to fall faster and heavier, until Lenore finally turned on the wipers. The song they made as they stroked rhythmically back and forth across the glass was contrapuntal to my wailing and gnashing of teeth.

"I just don't get it. Maybe he didn't understand that I was in trouble!" I fretted.

"Maybe he just didn't *think* you were in any trouble, Hollis," Lenore finally said as we turned into the Fishes' lane and pulled up behind the darkened house. It was impossible to see anything more than the dim outlines of buildings in the darkness, but I thought I caught a glimpse of a car in the driveway.

"Someone's here," I said. "There's a car parked over there under the trees by the front door."

Lenore never even glanced at it as she pulled up beside the pool house. "That's the Fishes' second car," she said briskly. "Come on, let's get out of the weather!"

When I followed her out of the car and across the lawn to

172

the pool house, our thin-soled shoes crunched on the snow. I remember thinking that I couldn't remember a night as black as this, blindly following the sound of Lenore's footsteps through the snowy gloom. It was only when she put her key in the door to the pool house and flipped on the light that I had a sense of where I was.

The pool room, with its shelves and shelves of decoys and bird carvings seemed even more surreal in the dim glow cast from the underwater pool fixture. Thousands of unblinking, glassy eyes stared down at us, eerie and lifelike in the gloom. I shivered. With the shades drawn, the room seemed closed and airless, full of eau de pool chemical and mildew.

"Don't turn on more lights," Lenore commanded. "If the neighbors across the creek see anything strange, they might call the police."

"So what's the deal?" I asked, stomping cold, clinging ice from my frozen feet as I followed her into the pool room.

Her shimmering silk dress rustled beneath her parka as she briskly crossed the room, heading toward the shelves of birds on the far side of the pool. She seemed to be looking for something specific although I didn't have the faintest idea what that would be. You see one decoy, you've seen 'em all as far as I was concerned, and the past twenty-four hours had not changed my mind. I was tired, hungry and wanted a cigarette. I didn't want to look at all these stiff, fake birds. It was creepy in there. "The Jaycees could take over this place for a Halloween Haunted Duck House with no changes," I muttered uneasily.

"My entire professional reputation is at stake," Lenore lamented, ignoring my qualms. "I can't *believe* this has happened to me!" She ran a hand along a shelf of mergansers, the way one might search through a stack of library books.

"It's like 'The Purloined Letter,' " I said soothingly. "Something hidden in plain sight. If you weren't looking for anything specific, who'd know? By the way, what *are* you looking for?"

"Every carver has a distinctive style. Shape of the body, paint colors, type of bird he carves, materials, all of that. Since most of the collectible decoys have been made within the past ninety years, it's entirely possible for a skillful carver like Harry Truman to reproduce a particular style. A thing like this can pollute the entire industry! Suppose Caroline sold these fakes up as authentic decoys!" Lenore bit her lower lip. "Look, Hollis, do you see that flicker down there?" She pointed to a high shelf about four feet away. "The yellow-shafted flicker?"

"I wouldn't know a yellow-shafted flicker from a yellow submarine." I peered at the rows upon rows of still, wooden birds, frowning. "No, I don't see anything around here that looks like a woodpecker," I said uncertainly.

Behind me, Lenore was lifting one of the heavy mergansers off the shelf, grasping it by the ornate, crested head, which I always thought you weren't supposed to do.

"Just turn and look and see if you see it anywhere," she said. "It's very important."

I moved a few feet away, turning to stand on tiptoe as I peered over the highest of the shelves I could reach. I sensed, rather than saw Lenore moving closer behind me.

Then I heard a moan in the darkness. Spinning around, I saw a dim shape huddled by the deep end of the pool, leaning against the pool ladder. It looked like a pile of old blankets or towels.

"There's someone here!" I whispered. "Over there!" I pointed toward the far end of the room. Was it my imagination, or did that shape actually move?

"That's nothing, just some old towels or something," Lenore said, quickly stepping between me and the huddled shape, clutching the merganser by the neck with both hands. "We've got to hurry, Hollis!"

Another low sound escaped from the darkness.

"That sounds like someone in trouble," I said. "Stay here. I'm going to look. God knows what or who Miz Fish might have—"

I half turned to look back at Lenore, who was raising her arms over my head. I was just in time to see that big decoy gripped in her hands. Worse, I saw the look on her face. The phrase "murderous expression" drifted into my mind as I tried, too late, to move away from where she could bring that block of painted wood down on my skull.

When I felt my head explode, I knew it was too late.

I fell like a dead duck. I was dimly aware of Lenore swearing, and of being dragged across the tiles. They were cold. I wanted to protest that this was an expensive suit, but I was falling into a deep, black hole. Uh-oh, I thought.

The next thing I was aware of was a horrible headache, the kind of headache that comes from staying up all night drinking 400-proof Canadian navy rum alexanders and listening to seventies disco music, followed by a brunch of zombies and chili dogs.

Only worse, a thousand times worse . . . if there *is* anything worse, which I sort of doubt, at least when it comes to headaches. Believe me, I know from bitter experience.

Don't ask. Just take my word for it, my head was killing me.

I was dimly aware of a whimpering sound. It seemed to be coming from a great distance away.

When I tried to move, my wrist seemed to be caught up in something. I could move it up. I could move it down. I could even move my hand in a circle, but when I tried to move it or me from side to side, it just wasn't working. Each time I was brought up short by a restraint.

Uh-oh all over again.

I lay motionless, trying to gather my few remaining brain cells into some semblance of order. This probably took longer than I think it did, since my attempts to concentrate were periodically interrupted by whimpering, groans and thundering pain.

I finally began to figure out that the groans were mine, but that annoying whimpering seemed to be coming from nearby.

I tried to sit up.

Bad idea, very bad. Not only was something holding my wrist down, or back, or something, but I was dizzy and nauseated.

It seemed as if I were lying in a puddle of something warm

and wet. I tried to recall the last time I had gone to the bath-room, but somehow I didn't think that was it.

I tried to lift a hand to see what it was, but I was attached to something.

Slowly, I opened one eye.

I seemed to have a handcuff attached to my left hand.

The handcuff seemed to be slung around a metal pole.

Someone else seemed to be attached to the other handcuff.

Someone with a honey-colored, well-manicured hand that was shaking uncontrollably.

Someone who was whimpering.

I squinted. "Athena?" I asked.

After a moment, there was a moan. "B-b-birds. B-birds."

"I guess I'll take that as a yes." I tried to sit up, and as I did, I lifted my hand. When I lifted my hand, Athena's hand came up, too.

After I studied this for a moment, trying to put it all to-gether, it occurred to me that Athena Hardcastle and I were handcuffed together. Further study showed, and believe me, this wasn't easy given my throbbing, woozy head, that our handcuff chain was linked through one of the ladder railings at the deep end of the pool. It would seem that we were pris-oners of the pool house.

For some reason, this struck me as hilariously funny, but when I laughed, which sounded more like a strangled death rattle, it hurt.

"Athena, what are you doing here?" I asked. Oh, I was out of it, that's for sure.

She was curled into a fetal ball, her legs drawn up to her chest, her head between her knees, and she was shaking from head to toe. I couldn't see her face, but I could, from a long way away, sense her terror.

"She called, asked me to, to meet her here," she said. Athena's voice was tiny and muffled. She couldn't lift her head. "After I t-talked to y-you, she called. Said she had proof you did it. Got me o-out here and jumped me. I w-wrestled with her—she—she got my bag and my cuffs. Away from me. It was the b-birds. C-couldn't handle those damn b-birds!"

Like a thin trickle of water, enlightenment was seeping into my consciousness. "Aviaphobia!" I groaned. "You're afraid of birds!" I remembered that from that whole scene in chambers when Fin got his decoy.

Now the birds were all around us. Maybe not live ones, but real enough to trigger a massive, crippling anxiety attack.

"Th-this b-bird place!" Athena whispered. "I can't l-look."

Using my free hand, I checked the back of my head. My fingers came away streaked with red.

Blood.

Now I considered freaking out.

After all, I *was* bleeding; I figured I had a right to my own personal, massive hissy fit.

Some gingerly probing revealed the back of my head hurt like hell, but my skull seemed to be pretty much intact.

"For what it's worth, I seem to be pretty okay. The Balls are a notoriously hardheaded clan." I was talking out loud, real stream of consciousness raving, trying to pull myself together. "Someone tried to brain my uncle Albie with a baseball bat once, dispute over a stolen base when he was down in the minors, playin' for the Blue Crabs, but it didn't do any good. Albie went on to finish the game. He's my godfather, you know. I never could figure out why Perk and Doll chose Albie of all people to be my godfather, but I guess you just have to know Albie—"

Athena made a noise and my train of thought derailed.

"Are you laughing?" I asked suspiciously.

"Y-yes," Athena admitted. "You're funny, y-you know that? I just can't look up. If I s-see those b-birds staring at me, I know I'll get h-hysterical."

"Deep breaths," I said. "Take some deep breaths. You don't have to look up. Just take some deep, deep breaths. Like yoga."

I lay back down so I could rest my hand (and hers) on the cold cement. Something resembling my normal consciousness was returning, but my head still throbbed in big, shuddering waves of pain. In the light of the single dim fixture in the doorway, the birds cast long menacing shadows. I also began to notice that it was very cold in here. Miz Fish had no doubt turned the heat off before she fled the country. Were we supposed to freeze to death or starve to death? Nice choice. But compared to what Lenore had really planned, I would have taken either.

From somewhere, I heard the small sound of dripping water. I idly wondered if it was still snowing outside. Outside seemed like a place on another planet. Two feet away seemed like another country.

I remembered Lenore at the Decoy Jamboree, rushing up to me out of breath, complaining about having to go out to attend to some last-minute details . . . like luring Athena out to the Fishes' pool house. Try as I might, I was having a lot of trouble reconstructing happenings that had led up to this revolting development. I remembered hearing expert testimony that amnesia surrounding events immediately before and after a blow to the head wasn't uncommon. I wondered what my excuse was the rest of the time.

"Athena?" I said after a while.

"M-mmm?" She was still shaking, terrified. I could feel it through the handcuffs that chained us together.

"Lenore killed Fish."

"I know that now. I-I saw all those birds and I j-just collapsed. She had me then. I-I feel so d-damn s-stupid."

"If stupidity were a crime, I'd be in jail right now." I sighed, shifting around, trying to find a way to make my head stop pounding. I was amazed at how weak I felt. But my mouth never runs out of steam. "It's beginning to dawn on me that if I can keep you talking and thinking about anything other than birds, you might calm down enough to get a grip."

Athena gave a great, shuddering sigh. "Don't ask me to move," she pleaded. "All those birds. I kn-know they're not real, but it's—it's as if they are."

I bit my tongue before I could say that they were pretty creepy, and instead tried to pick up the shattered pieces of logic. "So. Lenore got you out here after I spoke to you. Why didn't you bring a cop with you?"

"I *was* a cop, I should have known better." She sighed.

"*You* were a cop? I didn't know that." My voice seemed to come from a great distance away from me, and the mouth was running with no brain attached. Lots of people would tell you that was business as usual for me.

Athena exhaled, a long slow breath. "I was a cop for twelve years. Friendly and I were partners."

Oh, yes, I thought. That's one of the reasons I don't like you. You were married to Friendly.

But I must have said it aloud, because Athena's end of the cuff bracelet jiggled.

"Ormy and I married? Get a grip, g-girl! W-w-whatever gave you that idea?"

"Up at the courthouse, you said, he said—"

Athena inhaled slowly and exhaled slowly. At least she was following my advice about that. "We were undercover together on a sting operation. A pack of Klan militia rats up in Cecil County burned an interracial c-couple's house down. We posed as a married couple as a part of the sting." The last word came out on a long, tired breath.

"Oh." Well, after you've said oh, what else is there to say?

"Why, does that upset you?"

"It did, but not for the reasons you think. You know, Athena, I wish I could get past the idea that you think I'm cheap racist Christmas trash from Beddoe's Island."

"It sh-shows, huh?" she asked with a spark of her old cold Hardass Hardcastle self.

"I'm not. I'm really not. And I'm sick and tired of people looking at me and thinking just because I'm from a waterman's town I'm a trailer-livin' cousin-marryin', hook-worm-carryin' bigot. Perk and Doll might have been poor, but Robbie and I weren't brought up to be ignorant nose pickers." I sucked in some air. It made me hurt all over. "Actually, if you saw some of my cousins, you'd know why I wouldn't marry any of 'em on a dare."

The thought of Sam drifted across my mind, and I found myself yearning for him. He could figure a way out of this mess. After all, somehow or another, it was his fault I'd gotten into it.

"Who's S-Sam?" Athena asked. She pulled her head up, looked around and went down again with a moan, paralyzed by fear.

Then I knew I was raving in and out of consciousness. "My late, dead husband," I heard myself telling her.

There was a long silence. Pain the size of an elephant tap-danced around the inside of my skull, and I had to concentrate on that for a while. Then it faded away, back into a high, steady whine.

"Athena, how are we gonna get out of this?"

"I-I don't know."

"Does anyone else know we're here? Did you tell anyone you were coming out here?"

"No." She sighed. "I thought I could handle this myself."

"So did I. So did I."

The elephant danced a waltz, a nice steady throbbing rhythm of p-a-i-n. I floated in it, none too happily.

I idly wondered if I was dying, and marveled that I wasn't really upset about it, because dying meant the elephant would sit out the next dance.

I was dimly aware of other sounds, but they faded in and out like a signal from a faraway radio station.

Then, after a blurred lapse of time, I heard the click of high-heeled footsteps across the tile. They echoed in the hollow silence.

I lifted my head so that I could see the teal swish of Lenore Currier's gown as she staggered across the floor beneath the weight of a heavy plastic container. She was wearing her parka; flakes of snow clung to the slick nylon, sparkling in her hair, fallen from its pins and hanging in lank blond strands around her face. The gown wasn't in great shape either; I was vaguely pleased to note that all this extracurricular activity had done some serious damage to milady's toilette.

Lenore's face was tight and pallid, a mask. As she pried the lid off the canister, she cursed under her breath, dragging it across the floor toward the nearest shelf of decoys. Lifting the plastic jug over her head, she spilled liquid across the birds.

The sharp, pungent smell of kerosene filled the air as she

ran down the side of the pool, pouring it across the shelves, saturating the birds with liquid.

The smell was getting thicker and thicker in the air. I feebly understood that Lenore was planning something nasty when she pulled out a pack of matches, and struck one.

"I'm almost sorry I have to do this," she said apologetically, not looking at us. "But I really can't have anyone ruining my career. I've worked much too hard to get where I am. You were just too close to the truth. I'm really not sorry about killing Fin. But I am rather sorry about having to do this."

She dropped the match into the pool of kerosene.

With a whoosh it caught fire, tongues moving in long, hungry strips, traveling across the shelves, igniting bird after bird. The dry, wooden decoys began to catch fire. I watched as flame spread from shelf to shelf, engulfing the south side of the room in tongues of hungry orange blaze. Great, billowing clouds of black smoke, fed by the oil-based paint, rolled out across the room.

Lenore watched it for a moment, a look of satisfaction on her face. Then, as a sudden flare leaped out at her, she turned and ran.

We heard the slam of the door and knew she was gone.

The fiery glass-eyed birds stared down from their shelves, watching us impassively.

Athena moaned, her phobia binding her more tightly than ropes. And I wasn't exactly in midseason form either. I started to cough; the fumes were getting into my lungs.

I felt as if I were inhaling fire. This was how Lenore Currier had left us to die.

Dense black smoke began to fill the enclosed room; I heard the crash of a shelf, and sensed, rather than saw, burning birds rolling into other shelves, spreading flame and smoke through the room. I'd never known fire could move that fast, but I was finding out now.

Then I started great gasping spasms. Every time I tried to catch my breath, my throat, nose and lungs seared. I felt myself asphyxiating and gagging all at once.

Athena was rolled into a tight ball, hacking and choking and definitely down for the count.

"Your time's not quite up yet!"

It sounded a lot like Sam.

I tried to open my eyes and get focused, but in that closed hell, that bitch's brew stung me blind. Through the pain and the tears, I caught a flash of Sam, hazy and dim, but Sam nonetheless. He was bent over the side of the pool, jerking at the ladder, as tightly focused into the material world as I'd ever seen him.

"Help!" I choked.

He shook his head, then held out his hands. "I can't get the screws undone! I don't have enough strength to make myself solid enough! You've got to stand up, Hollis. Come on, stand up!"

I shook my head. I didn't want to; I just wanted to lie on the floor and cough my lungs up.

Athena stirred, throwing her head back. The need to breathe was stronger than her phobia, the body's physical reactions automatically kicking in. Tears were streaming down her face in little rivulets of mascara.

Fire traveled across a wooden beam in the ceiling. Glass panes, cracking in the heat, began to pop and explode like gunshots.

"Tell her to close her eyes and keep them closed!" Sam yelled. I was aware of his ghostly shape, dancing around us helplessly.

"Athena! Keep your eyes closed!" I cried.

Sam knelt beside me. I was foggily aware of his spectral presence, a hand on my shoulder. "Holl, listen. Do what I tell you. You and Athena have to try to stand up. Try to do it together."

"Athena," I said, obediently as a child, "we have to try to stand up together."

She coughed, a horrible hacking sound, as if her lungs were coming up, but did not move.

"Tell her to keep her eyes closed. If she can't see the birds, they won't bother her!"

"We have to stand up together!" I called to her between spasms of coughing. The fumes were getting worse. Even with a few broken panes, there was no place for the smoke and fire to go; the burning paint was making it a thousand times worse.

"Come on. Keep your eyes closed, hold on to the rail and we'll get up together," I said, and it sounded as if I really knew what I was doing.

Sometimes I can even fool myself, but this wasn't one of them. I was so weak that it took all my strength to get a grip on the cold handrail.

I didn't think I could pull myself up.

I *knew* I couldn't pull myself up.

"I can't do it." I hacked.

Then I felt Athena's free hand lifting me up. She'd managed to get to her feet.

She grabbed my jacket and pulled with all her strength, until I was unsteadily on my feet, gripping the metal handrail.

Black clouds of smoke filled the room. Flames seemed to be shooting from every direction. I felt one lick at my ankles.

"Now!" Sam cried from a great distance away. "Both of you! Pull *up* on the ladder! Pull it up! Both hands! You and her!"

"Pull the ladder up!" I screamed, grasping it in both my hands. "Pull it up . . . !"

But I had no strength. My hands were weak and rubbery.

It was Athena who lifted that mass of tube out of its sockets in the floor, and Athena who dragged my arm free from the rail. We were still cuffed together, but without the ladder, we were at least free.

But where to go? I was dizzy and disoriented. Where was the door? In the black smoke and the darkness, we were blind.

"This way, Hollis, follow me," Sam yelled. I felt his hand, cold and dry, on my shoulder. "Get down on your knees! You've got to get below the smoke!"

The chill of his ghostly touch penetrated through my clothes. I went down, dragging Athena with me.

"Crawl! Crawl! Below the smoke!"

Athena coughed, but she was moving.

"Let's get out of here!" Sam yelled.

Tongues of flame licked at us as we struggled, blind inch by terrible inch, across the floor. As I groveled through the black, I trusted Sam, dragging Athena along behind me. I never looked back when a shelf crashed down behind us, scattering sharp shards of glass and burning birds across the place where we had been a second before. I'd never thought before about the roar, the engulfing sound a fire makes. It was almost deafening. The sound of fire feeding itself like a hungry god.

"Here's the door," Sam said in my ear, "but it's locked. You'll have to break it out."

Blindly, I put my hand on the knob and twisted it. It did not yield.

A cloud of dense sooty smoke rolled over us, and out of the corner of my eye, I saw tongues of fire licking, and they really do lick, just like people say they do, at the lintels.

"Stand away!" Athena cried, getting up on her knees with an effort. She had taken off a high-heeled shoe and now she smashed at the glass. Both of our hands, cuffed together, went flying through the opening. I felt the jagged ends slice at my flesh, but I didn't care.

It couldn't have been easy for Athena, with me manacled to her, but she pulled us both to our feet, pushed her own arm out the shattered window and undid the lock from the outside.

Together we fell out into the snowy night as a wall of fire, fed by the sudden influx of fresh air, rushed over our heads in a rampart of heat and flame.

"Roll!" Athena commanded, dropping and dragging me with her across the white crust of snow.

Me, I would have been happy just to lie there and breathe wonderful blessed fresh cold air. Athena, once liberated from her bird phobia, knew different.

"Get up! We've got to move!" she yelled, jerking on my handcuffed arm. "Get your white ass up!"

Well, reader, I got my white ass up, and staggered across the yard after Athena, because I really didn't have any choice in the matter. I was shackled to her, and where she went I was bound to go.

I must say that the flaming pool house illuminated the grounds of Stately Fish Manor nicely. And the sound of breaking, popping glass and omnivorous flame was like the Fourth of July, right under the fireworks.

But it was not as loud as Ms. Athena "Hardass" Hardcastle as she caught sight of Lenore Currier scurrying toward her Rover.

"Arrrrrrrrrrrrrrrghhhh!" Athena screamed, and it was not a sound I would care to hear again. It was pure rage.

Dragging me along with her as if I were nothing more than a cotton doll, Athena (and I) caught up with Lenore in the snowy gravel.

I really would not have wanted to be Ms. Currier at that moment. All of Athena's phobia-pumped adrenaline was flowing, and this is a woman who does not like to be made to look a fool.

Our state's attorney for Santimoke County lifted her elegant arm (the one with me attached) and brought the cuff chain down around Lenore's neck, jerking her backward and off her stiletto heels.

The three of us went down in a heap together.

"You look here, white bitch! I don't take this from anyone!" Athena screamed, holding Lenore's head in a hammerlock as the duck broker cursed, squirmed and tried to break loose.

I did the only thing I could think of doing. I rolled right over on Lenore, and lay there like a sack of dead potatoes, pinning her under me. For once in my life, I was glad that I hadn't lost that fifteen pounds.

I guess Lenore wasn't; she was gasping and cursing, writhing around like a big, angry eel. I just spread myself out on her and went limp, the way we used to do in student demonstrations. I'm good at lying down and doing nothing. Lenore couldn't move much, but she said some choice things. Since she couldn't hurt me, it didn't make much difference. I wasn't listening to her anyway.

But Athena also had a rather colorful vocabulary. What she was saying could have peeled paint twenty miles away.

"Who are you callin' a white bitch? Me or the white bitch?" I asked her, rather enjoying jumping up and down on Lenore's back.

Athena had grabbed the decoy broker by the hair with her free hand and was holding her head down. The state's attorney's headlock slowly tightened until our murderess started to choke and turn blue.

Frankly, I didn't care if Lenore Currier ever drew a breath again. I was ready to kill her myself.

Given these circumstances, I suppose it was a good thing that we both saw the headlights and heard the car, because I don't know what would have happened to the lovely Lenore Currier if something hadn't intervened.

Athena was as close to being out of control as it is possible to get and still be a lawyer, and I was just plain pissed and pained.

But when I looked up to see Smollet Bowley staring morosely down at me, his bald head shining by the light of the fire, I almost laughed.

"Are yew all right?" he asked, completely ignoring three women wrestling in the snow. "I'm sorry, Hollis," he whined, running a finger beneath his nose. "I just couldn't go through with it, not if I knew Miz Fish and her was gonna *hurt* you. I had to come back and give up to the cops." He swallowed. "I jes' hadda do the right thing, Brazil or no Brazil. I never mean no harm nohow, yew know that."

"Shut up, Smollet," I hissed. He just brought out the meanness in me, no matter what.

Behind him, I heard the voice of Ormand Friendly, and then, a wail of approaching sirens. The combined fire and rescue squads of five towns in Santimoke and Devanau Counties had turned out for this one. Must have been a slow night.

"Jesus H. Christ!" Ormand Friendly exploded, rushing up on the scene. "What the pluperfect hell are you two doing to that woman?"

"She killed Fish and then tried to kill us!" I said indignantly.

Athena just looked up and shook her head. "The cavalry arrived too late. The fair maidens have rescued themselves," she gasped.

"With a little help from their friends!"

Sam's voice hung in the air, then faded away, blurring into the wail of sirens and the roar of flames.

THIRTEEN

•

That's All There Is,
There Ain't No More

SMOLLET BOWLEY DEFENSE FUND said the jar beside the
cash register at Toby's Bar. PLEASE GIVE GENEROUSLY.
THANK YOU.

"Poor Smollet." Friendly dropped a five-dollar bill into it.
He had just come from district court, where Lenore, Miz Fish
and Smollet had been arraigned on a wide variety of charges,
and he was feeling pretty good. But then again, Lenore Currier
hadn't tried to do Ormand in with a decoy. That was something Athena and I immediately pointed out to him when he
walked in the door, since we'd been waiting all afternoon to
hear what had happened.

"Smollet's been pretty good about cooperating. Barry
Maxwell's got him cutting an Alford. He'll do a couple of
months for attempted escape and the original oyster truck
felony, but he really helped us chase down Lenore Currier and
Caroline Fish, so they're taking that into account, and he'll go
out on probation before judgment."

"Thus, he still escapes the wrath of Miss Bertha Denton, his
mama-in-law," I put in. "And when I went to see him, he said
he's through with a life of petty crime. He says he wants to
start all over again. As a carver. Harry Truman's agreed to
take him on as a pupil."

"There's a match, hon," Friendly put in, grinning at Athena
and me as he wiped up the last of his crabcake with the heel of
a french fry.

"Almost being done in with a decoy is just too humiliating a

188

way to go, after all the mean things I've said in my time about decoy collectors," I grumbled. "If Lenore goes up before a jury of them, for attempting to homicide *me*, she'll be a free woman. I'm almost glad she got you, too, Athena."

"Murdering an officer of the court and trying to murder a second officer of the court is pretty serious stuff," Athena pointed out as she reached for another one of Toby's famous crab balls.

"But you'll make sure the special prosecutor questions all prospective jurors about that on voir dire, won't you?" I asked anxiously. "I know you're as frustrated as I am that we have to be witnesses. Man, I really wanted to cover this trial in the worst way, and now I've been disqualified for conflict of interest! Rig his own self is covering it. Beware of garbled prose, gross inaccuracies and sloppy copy!"

"Witnesses are sequestered," Athena said. "Toby, these crab balls are great! I wish I'd known about your place long ago!"

Toby was looking at Athena like she was the first flower of spring. Of course, she was looking great, as always, today impeccably groomed and attired in olive green silk. "Can I get you anything else, Ms. Hardcastle?" he asked, hovering.

"No, this crab platter is wonderful, thank you. If I eat here often, you'll ruin my cholesterol level." She smiled at him and he floated away to attend the thinning lunch-hour crowd.

"Uh-oh," Sam said from the shadowy end of the bar where he sat with the silent shade of Scratch Wallace. Only Toby and I were aware of their presence, so I studiously ignored them. "I can see where this is headed. Does Athena want to be Mrs. Toby Number Four?"

My head still hurt, but it was more like a distant thump than a screaming-bat-out-of-hell pain. What hurt more was swallowing my pride. "Athena, I really owe you an apology. I thought you were a bigot who hated me because you thought I was Beddoe's Island white trash." It was hard to get it out, but I did, and in front of witnesses, too, which should tell you something about my humility.

She inclined her sleek head to one side, regarding me for a

moment. "You know," she said at last, choosing her words carefully, "I'd be lying to you if I said I didn't come over here from Baltimore with my own racial baggage about the Eastern Shore. We all have that problem, whether we want to or not. But in point of fact, I think you're a reporter. In my experience, it's always been wise for law enforcement to have a healthy mistrust of the media. Too many times I've been misquoted, or found reporters have their own agenda."

I nodded. "I can understand that," I said at last. "I've seen a lot of lawyers and cops who are the same way; some of them are worse than the criminals."

"You filed a good story," Athena conceded. "Before they took you off the case." Like me, she was irritated that she would be a witness rather than a participant in what promised to be the juiciest trial in Santimoke County this decade.

"You should have seen it before Riggle edited it!" I made a face, and Athena laughed.

She gave me a level look. "It was almost all the truth," she pronounced. That was when I realized that she did have a sense of humor. A dry sense of humor, but at least she had one. She reached across me and poked Friendly. "I've got to get back up the road. Court this afternoon. Thanks for taking me out to lunch. And thank you, Toby."

My cousin smiled a vast and stricken smile. "Anytime, anytime at all, Athena," he proclaimed. "For you, there's always something special on the menu at Toby's!"

"I'll remember that," Athena promised as she slid off her stool and gathered up her things. At the door, she paused and turned to look at me. "After the trial, Hollis, let's go out and do something like eat too much chocolate and shop too much and trade life stories."

"Absolutely," I agreed. "It's a plan."

I think she winked at me, but I'm not sure.

Toby flicked the remote, and the TV above the bar flickered into life. I'm glad I work because if I had to stay home all day and watch daytime tube, I think I would go mad.

"*Hapless Hearts,*" Ormand Friendly said, easing himself comfortably on his stool as he and Toby prepared to watch the watermen's favorite soap opera. I tried not to wince at his tie, which featured Mr. Natural rampant on a field of Flakey Foonts.

I'd spent several days waiting for him to tear into me for getting involved in a murder and almost getting myself and Athena Hardcastle killed. I thought maybe this would be the day the explosion came, but he merely stretched out his long legs and focused his attention on the soap.

Two could play that game. I concentrated on the agony between Jennifer and Stud now that Bambi had pressed charges against the evil Prince Oleg for holding her prisoner in his secret mountain cabin while he engineered a hostile take-over of Au Naturelle Cosmetics from Lulu and Gracie who didn't know they were mother and daughter because . . . well, I never watch those things. Almost never.

Oh, you get the idea. And so did Ormand Friendly, who laughed when I began to fidget in my seat.

He turned his gaze on me. "Look, Toby likes me, Athena likes me. Why don't *you* like me?" he asked me point-blank.

"I do like you, Friendly, but I don't know if I want to date a man who wears a drop-dead, sapphire, eyestrain blue tuxedo. Besides, in my experience cops are not great relationship material," I pointed out, trying to sound sensible. "And there's that conflict of interest thing, you being in law enforcement and me being a reporter. Pigs and the godless liberal media are oil and water."

Friendly nodded. We were both silent for a moment, while the other drama, the one on the television, droned on.

"I still don't get it. Why *did* Lenore kill Fish?" I asked at last.

"Irony 101," Friendly said wearily. "Fish thought the Scratch Wallace was a forgery. But, unknown to him, the Scratch Wallace goose was the only authentic decoy of any value Fish actually possessed. His wife had managed to switch every other expensive piece in his collection with a phony. The only real ones were junk. Given enough time, she would have been able to switch the Scratch Wallace, too. Your Miz Fish is something else entirely. She was smart enough to leave the second-rate birds alone. She only got Harry to copy the really good pieces that would go for high prices out West when Lenore took them to the auctions."

"What?" My jaw must have dropped. "You mean she and Miz Fish were in on it together?"

"Exact-o. Of course, Miz Fish says you could have knocked her over with a feather when she found out it was Lenore, not Smollet, who offed the judge! Ms. Currier was taking a large cut to broker the birds. But it was more of an ego thing for her; having a supply of great birds to release into the West Coast market enhanced her reputation as a decoy broker of note. She didn't know who Miz Fish was using to copy the decoys until you introduced her to Harry Truman. Miz Fish was holding back that information." Friendly poked a finger in my direction. "You had to go because you knew the missing link that could connect Lenore with Miz Fish and the fake birds. Missing link is not a bad description of Harry Truman, by the way."

"But why did she murder Fish?"

"She says she panicked, that she hit him in self-defense," Friendly mused. "Although that's gonna be hard for a lawyer to prove when Fish was hit from behind. But that's Lenore's logic. Apparently, after the verdict came in on Smollet, Fish went back to chambers to play with his new toy, and started having doubts. Fish was a man who instinctively distrusted others, maybe because he was so untrustworthy himself. Lenore had just left the building and headed back to the Decoy Jamboree, so Fish called Ms. Currier on her cell phone and expressed this problem about the authenticity of the Scratch Wallace snow goose in unpleasant and threatening terms."

"Ah," I said. "This is where the irony comes in?"

"Yes. Because the Scratch Wallace would have been the only real decoy of value left in the judge's plundered collection!"

"Then why kill him over an authentic bird?"

"Lenore was afraid the judge might decide to go back and take a second look at some of the other decoys she'd sold him, and see that they were fakes, so she panicked. If Caroline Fish told him that Lenore had been selling off the real ones behind his back, Lenore would be in deep, dark trouble. Reputation ruined, major lawsuits all around. Her future cushy job as a museum curator was on the line just as she was pulling out of shady duck deals and going legit. The way she saw it, one dead judge was a small price to pay."

"Ugh. That's cold. Even if the dead judge was Fin Fish."

"After she got the call from Fish," Friendly continued, "Lenore returned to the courthouse, then snuck back in by climbing the trellis, so no one would see her return."

"And she went into chambers through Edgar Allan Crow's open window and bashed Fin's head in with the Scratch Wallace?" I asked. "Thereby ruining the most authentic bird in the collection?"

Friendly grinned. "She's confessed to it. She tinkered with the main fuse box, killed Fish, then went flying out the side door, knocking you over in the darkness. She says on the way out she panicked and thrust the decoy into the trellis, hoping to come back and get it later. But of course, Smollet found it and it was pretty much over for the decoy. But everyone's prints were all over it. Hers, yours, Fish's, everyone's!"

"Then why did she try to kill Athena?" Toby asked.

Friendly picked up his beer and took a thoughtful swig. "Athena had been running a background check on Lenore, just as she had run one on you and Smollet and our Miz Fish. What Teeny was picking up was some rumors that the lovely Lenore's name had been connected with some shaky decoy shit before, with an auction house in New England, but no one had any proof. The decoy world is small and gossipy, so of course, some New England visitor at the Jamboree whispered to Lenore that the Santimoke County SA was asking questions about her previous duck dealings. Again, Lenore panicked. Knowing Teeny, who would imply that she knew more than she actually did about Lenore's past when she questioned her . . . you can imagine how the implications sent Lenore into a frenzy. So, she lured Teeny out to the pool house, knowing that the birds would throw Teeny into a panic state, then went back for you. She had decided the fake birds had to go in an 'accidental' fire. But we think she decided you two had to go with it when she guessed you both knew too much to wander around loose."

"I knew Smollet was innocent!" Sam crowed from his corner.

"Pay no attention to the man behind the curtain," I muttered, but Friendly was too caught up in the story to notice.

"The bad thing *you* did, hon," he observed, "was you introduced Lenore to Harry, as I said before. Then Lenore figured out where all those fabulous fakes were coming from; evidently Mrs. Fish had been keeping Harry a deep dark secret. You know that Harry thought Mrs. Fish tried to kill him, but that was Lenore, too. And now, he's mad enough to testify."

"But what did she say to Harry to convince him to come to the Jamboree? Harry hated that kind of stuff."

Ormand leaned over and whispered something into my ear. I felt the roots of my hair stand on end. "Awesome," I said admiringly.

"So it would seem." Friendly sighed.

"Wow. What a bloody mess." I shook my head. "She killed once and would have killed twice more just for her stupid job."

"Good career move." Sam chuckled.

"She'd never broker a decoy sale in this town again. She killed because another scandal would have ruined her stupid career."

"And murder doesn't?" Sam asked indignantly.

Beside him, Scratch Wallace chortled.

"Wow. Tough move. I hear Dr. Froston and Mr. Gareau are busy raising bail for her right now, and pressing for a speedy trial. They want that Scratch Wallace decoy back in circulation, where they can bid on it," Friendly observed. "It's one hell of a case, but with you and Athena as witnesses, we'll have a wrap on it."

"Collectors are so weird. Froston and Gareau are crazy!" I hissed in disgust.

Friendly shrugged. "Collectors *are* a strange bunch, hon. It's like an addiction." He glanced at his watch, then dug into his pocket. "Anyway, I've gotta go. Some hunters turned up a skeleton in a plastic barrel out on the other side of the county. We think the guy died naturally, but his girlfriend wanted to keep collecting his Social Security, so she just dumped him out in back of the barn. Toby, are we goin' out gunnin' Tuesday?"

While he and my cousin discussed their next big adventure, I studied Friendly's profile for a minute. I thought about that electric blue tuxedo, and I thought about how much more interesting my life had become lately.

"Ormand?" I asked as he stood up, pulling on his coat.

He turned to look at me, impatient to be on his way.

I took a deep breath. "If I told you that I was gun-shy, would you still want to, you know, like, go somewhere and do something sometime?"

He regarded me for a half second. "How about Saturday, hon?" he asked.

I nodded. "Sounds good to me."

"There's this estate sale over in Wallopsville. Somebody died and left a mess of decoys. I thought we might ride over and take a look at 'em?" He grinned.

I collapsed back onto the bar with a moan as Friendly ducked out the door, his laughter hanging in the air behind him.

Hapless Hearts rolled to a cliffhanger ending and the last of the lunch-hour crowd paid up and left. Toby gathered up dirty plates and headed into the kitchen.

Time spent in idle observation is anything but time wasted. I looked out the window at the cold afternoon. I watched as Harry Truman rode past Toby's on his brand-new John Deere rider mower, happily splashing through the puddles of melted snow, just another retired-bachelor-waterman-famous-decoy-carver enjoying the financial rewards of his newfound cult status. The doldrums of winter were creeping in upon us as the days grew shorter and nightfall came harder. It was that time of the day when the living and the dead gather down to Toby's Bar.

Toby himself put a Diet Pepsi and a Tobyburger platter down in front of me. "At least someone got something out of that whole decoy mess," he remarked. "Harry can go anywhere he wants on that rider mower without havin' to get a driver's license."

He disappeared into the kitchen again.

"So, you're really going out with cop boy, huh?" Sam asked after a moment.

I glanced over at him, but in the dim light I couldn't read his expression. "You don't like that, huh?" I asked.

He shrugged. "The Rules say I can't interfere. I just don't think he's good enough for you."

"Ah, like you were! That's why you have to haunt me, because you were so good to me when you were alive. Do I need to remind you that you deserted me on our honeymoon and sailed away for ten years?"

"Sometimes I wish I weren't dead," Sam said wistfully.

I put my hand over his; it was cool and dry and barely there.

"You know what? Sometimes I do, too."

But we both knew that F. Scott Fitzgerald was right. There are no second acts in American lives.

"Well, anyway, we rescued Smollet from a murder charge." Sam laughed.

"Which reminds me. Did you tell him to walk outta the jail?" I demanded.

"Well, maybe. But it all worked out, didn't it?" He nodded toward the Smollet Bowley Defense Fund jar on the bar.

Rather than start a fight and ruin the mood, I looked out the window.

"The other day," Sam said thoughtfully, inhaling a french fry, which is how he eats, in his ghostly way, "I was talking to Rheinhold Neibhur about how you can pray for something, but the Lord generally won't give it to you straight out. No, He, or She," he added quickly, seeing my look, "will deliver it to you in a way you didn't expect. You thought Lenore Currier was friend material, but she wasn't. You and Athena each thought the other was a jerk, and it turned out you two actually get along, and you have a date with Friendly, huh?"

"We'll see," I said cautiously. "Nothing's like set in stone or anything."

"You've gotta learn to start trusting people, Hollis." Scratch Wallace coughed from the far end of the bar.

I'd almost forgotten he was there, he'd been so quiet these past few days. Now that he'd finally heard the whole story out, he was ready to move on. His carpetbag was packed, sitting at the foot of his stool, ready for him to make the long journey back to Carver Heaven or wherever old hunters go in the next world. "It's been interestin'," he remarked. "But complicated. Too damn complicated. Glad I'm dead and beyond all this."

"Plus ça change, plus c'est la même chose." Sam sighed. He shook the old ghost's hand. "Scratch, we're gonna miss you."

The spirit shook his head. "Iffen I'da known what a mess I was walkin' into, I never woulda come back this year," he grunted.

"Well, it must be nice to know that after all these years, people still remember you and appreciate your work," I consoled him.

The old carver was fading fast. He grinned that skull-like grin and shook his hoary head. His laughter was the rustling of dry leaves on a cold wind. He was growing fainter and more shadowy.

"It *would* be all right," he said, "except for one thing."

"What's that?" Sam asked.

Just before he turned to mist, Scratch cackled, "I *never* carved no damn snow geese!"

*If you enjoyed DEAD DUCK, don't miss
the first Hollis Ball mystery:*

SLOW DANCING WITH
THE ANGEL OF DEATH

by Helen Chappell

Wealthy, charming Sam Wescott left Hollis
Ball on their honeymoon ten years ago, so
when he dies in a boating accident, Hollis
doesn't expect to mourn. But when Sam's
ghost appears, claiming that his death
was no accident and demanding that
Hollis find his murderer, Hollis agrees to
investigate. . . .

*Published by Fawcett Books.
Available at your local bookstore.*

LORA ROBERTS

brings you Liz Sullivan, freelance writer and amateur detective.

"A refreshing and offbeat take
on the female detective."
—*San Francisco Chronicle*

Published by Fawcett Books.
Available in your local bookstore.

Call toll free 1-800-793-BOOK (2665) to order by phone and use your major credit card. Or use this coupon to order by mail.

__MURDER IN A NICE NEIGHBORHOOD	449-14891-2	$4.99
__MURDER IN THE MARKETPLACE	449-14890-4	$5.50
__MURDER MILE HIGH	449-14947-1	$5.50
__MURDER BONE BY BONE	449-14946-3	$5.50

Name_____

Address_____

City_____State_____Zip_____

Please send me the FAWCETT BOOKS I have checked above.
I am enclosing $_____
  plus
Postage & handling* $_____
Sales tax (where applicable) $_____
Total amount enclosed $_____

*Add $4 for the first book and $1 for each additional book.

Send check or money order (no cash or CODs) to:
Fawcett Mail Sales, 400 Hahn Road, Westminster, MD 21157.

Prices and numbers subject to change without notice.
Valid in the U.S. only.
All orders subject to availability.   LROBERTS

MURDER ON THE INTERNET

Ballantine mysteries are on the Web!

Read about your favorite Ballantine authors and
upcoming books in our monthly electronic newsletter
MURDER ON THE INTERNET, at
www.randomhouse.com/BB/MOTI.

Including:
- What's new in the stores
- Previews of upcoming books for the next three months
- In-depth interviews with mystery authors and publishers
- Calendars of signings and readings for Ballantine
  mystery authors
- Bibliographies of mystery authors
- Excerpts from new mysteries

To subscribe to MURDER ON THE INTERNET,
send an E-mail to **srandol@randomhouse.com** asking to be added to the subscription list. You will
receive the next issue as soon as it's available.

Find out more about whodunit! For sample chapters
from current and upcoming Ballantine mysteries, visit
us at **www.randomhouse.com/BB/mystery**.